I0675184

Midnight Bloom

∞

Part 1

Lunar Eclipse Series

By Kristina Canady

Midnight Bloom: The Lunar Eclipse Series

Cataloging-in-Publication Date is on file at the Library of Congress

Book design by Kristina Canady
Cover design and layout by Sassy Queens of Design
Cover image/painting copyright 2013 by Kristina Canady
Editing Acknowledgments to: Karen Swank

Dedication: Thank you to my children who always inspire me to push my creativity to new levels and to my husband who is always there to love and support me. To my grandmother who inspired my love of books when I was young. To all my family and friends who are simply amazing.

Midnight Bloom: The Lunar Eclipse Series

Chapter 1

As I lie awake on yet another sleepless night, tossing and turning, I find my thoughts being sucked into a vortex of emotional hell. Stephan and I had another argument right about the time normal people should be sleeping. Funny how fourteen years together can make the love you feel for your husband wax and wane. My head is spinning, conflicted with so many competing emotions. In the end, they all lead to one constant, a lack of validation. For years, it has felt like we just don't quite fit anymore. A romantic at heart, I find myself longing for an epic kind of love. I feel guilty for doing so, and at times, a little angry for allowing my thoughts to stray down a disappointing and possibly dangerous path. Logic kicks in and tells me that I should be happy with what I have, that *I am* happy enough, and should just let go of childish longings. But, can complacency really last? Love has never been easy for me. I have always struggled to accept, express, and understand it.

For as long as I can remember, I have been perplexed by this notion of a deep-rooted connection, yet somehow continue to yearn for it. The only unwavering love I can get through my thick skull is the one I know for my children. My love for them is endless and patient; there is nothing they could do to weaken that feeling. As for the strength of the love I feel for my husband? It depends on which way the wind is blowing. I love him, of course, but loving someone and being in love are two different things. I know how that sounds, but it's the truth. Never have I known a deep, romantic love that was everlasting or strong enough to withstand the test of time.

That's not the only issue that has plagued me throughout the years, emptiness has as well. I feel as if there is a hole in the center of my heart, that there is something more within myself that I am not quite linked to. It is something that is right there- on the tip of my tongue, just out of my reach, pushing through the layers of my subconscious. Yet, I can't quite put my finger on it.

Here we go again, brain, I think to myself as my thoughts are plagued with this nonsense. Round and round we go with my short comings. It's a frequent intrapersonal monologue that takes me to a dark place, threatening my happiness. I refuse for now. Throwing the covers back so the cold can push my head back into reality, I pull my aching body up from the warmth of my husband and down comforter to go downstairs for some boob tube. Maybe the droning of some terrible but entertaining reality TV will calm my nerves and let me relax enough to sleep. The ridiculousness of reality TV has a time and place; like now, when you need a good train wreck to distract you from the spiral you may be flirting with.

A bowl of chocolate Cheerios and some "Real Housewives of Atlanta" later, I feel like I am connected again to the real world and the little voice in my head has shut up for now. Stupid brain, stupid emotions! So not going there again! It's already 3:00 AM, and I need to sleep since work, kids, and responsibilities don't care if I had another restless night. I really do not want to get sick again; it seems that I am always getting sick. As Guy Fieri embarks on another food adventure, tasting exquisite cuisines from hole in the wall joints, I finally feel sleep calling me... back to bed for another attempt.

I find myself walking barefoot down a starlit beach. Warm waves are creeping up the sand, lapping over my feet with each pass as I struggle to hold my long summer dress up from the water. I look around and realize that I am alone in the middle of nowhere; this must be another dream... The feeling of sand underneath my feet is glorious, and the smell of saltwater in the air is so real that I can taste it. I continue my journey down the sandy coast, picking my way along sea shells and other washed-up treasures. I am calm and submerged within my own thoughts. Looking up, there are a few twinkling lights off in the distance, giving me the sense that I have wandered far off from civilization. A gentle breeze picks up and carries on around me. It caresses my face and moves through the few loose tendrils of hair around my neck. The breeze suddenly shifts, bringing with it a strong scent of musk with hints of cedar and sweet tobacco. The smell reminds me of someone I once met, but I can't pinpoint who; it's wonderfully masculine and robust. I hear footsteps fall immediately behind me, so I turn around and find myself face to face with a beautiful, shirtless man with bronzed skin that looks like it was kissed by the sun. His long, wavy, dark hair is dancing around the tops of his broad shoulders. I can't breathe... he is dazzling with his soul-piercing blue eyes, chiseled jaw, chiseled... everything, like he was carved from marble. It's as if every muscle was defined to perfection by the hands of master craftsmen. We know each other. Somehow, this is familiar; my body responds without my permission. Dropping the lengths of my dress, I step forward into his arms, into his warmth. He feels like home, and the hole in the center of my heart swells closed in his presence. His hands come up and around me, forcibly bringing me in closer, claiming me like I am his. The embrace is powerful, as if we have not seen each other in years, and we are finally reuniting after a very long time apart. His lips brush my cheek and quickly move to meet mine. His hungry kiss devours my senses; his touch sends electric pulses throughout my body, stirring me to life. As his hands travel, a need awakens in me that quickly becomes all-consuming. I need more of him- more of his touch, more of his kiss, more of his embrace. Urgency builds between us, and I begin to ache for him to be closer. He reaches up and runs one hand through my hair, cups my behind with the other, and starts tracing the contour of my neck with tortuous kisses. As he reaches the base of my neck, he stops suddenly and buries his face into my neck in agony. He starts to cry my name in a deep, sorrowful voice. He's still holding me, yet frantically calling my name like he's looking for me... as if I am suddenly lost once more.

"Sasha!"

What the hell is going on; this makes no sense... hello, I'm right here... in your arms!

"Sasha!!"

No, this isn't happening! No...no... no, I sob as the realm of my dreams slips away and I come crashing back into reality.

"Sasha!" Stephan is yelling up to me from the downstairs office. "You need to get up and get the boys from school; it's time for my meeting and I need to leave!" Damn it, Damn it, Damn it! One of the wonderful conveniences of having a husband who works primarily from home... there is never a minute of privacy! The clock is glaring 2:00 PM; I guess it's time for me to start my day. I do believe a cold shower is in order first. I drag my butt to the bathroom and do the quick tits, pits, and ass (TPA) soap-up. I don't know what's worse- scintillating dreams like that...or rudely being yanked from one when you're deep in. What the heck was that about? Why do I feel guilty? It was just a dream. IT WAS JUST A DREAM! It was just a really good dream that felt... familiar. If it was just a dream, then why does my heart ache with longing all of a sudden? It's as if I am back to missing out on something that is meant to be. I guess that's what late night snacking and reality TV will do to a girl's head.

After quickly dressing in some jeans and a warm, cream V-neck sweater, I throw my wet hair up in a bun, add a couple swipes of mascara, and I am out the door. As a night-shift nurse, my days and nights are a bit "bass-ackwards" in relation to the larger percentage of society. When it comes to my days off, I find it hard to keep a "normal" schedule; late night TV surfing and sleeping past noon have become my normal. My husband is able to work from home most days and usually picks up the kids so I can sleep, but occasionally, he has meetings he has to attend. I pull up to the school just in time to line up with the rest of the parents for pick-up.

Looking up, I see my twin boys barreling past the teachers who are lecturing them to slow down, but it is too late to get them to listen to anyone. They saw me the minute they emerged from the door and high-tailed it toward the car like two bats out of hell. What else do the teachers expect from nine-year old boys who have been cooped up in school all day? "Guys, slow it down please!" I yell after them just to appease the staff as I know it must be difficult to be a teacher. I respect their dedication and hard work. Lord knows that I do not have the patience to spend all day trying to teach grade-school kids who can barely sit still in their seats and pay attention. Plus, I am a bit too sympathetic with kids who don't want to be told what to do; I can't stand that either. Teachers are amazing.

"Mom! Ethan took my seat!" Aiden exclaims.

"Yeah, and you hit me earlier on the playground, so I'm gonna sit where I want!" Ethan yells back.

And it begins. I wish I would have grabbed that last cup of coffee in the pot on my way out the door.

"Guys, please stop; everyone in your own seats, or I will not stop by Subway on the way home to get you a snack." Bribes. I've come to love bribes as a parent.

"Okay, we'll be good, but can I get a soda?" Ethan, my little negotiator, asks.

"What do you think the answer is to that?" I say.

"No," I hear in unison.

I try to make them eat well; I know there are going to be plenty of times in the future that they will make bad food decisions, so while under my rule, I am not as forgiving. Plus, a sugar rush after school makes getting them to focus on completing homework something that makes me want to stick a fork in my eye.

∞

Bellies satisfied, all three of us are parked at the kitchen table ready to tackle some third-grade homework. This shouldn't be too bad. My boys are very smart, and it helps that they are the oldest in their classes due to missing the October cut-off for birthdays. I just have to keep them focused long enough to finish. That reminds me, I should start planning their birthday party that's coming up early next month; school will be letting out soon for Christmas break, so I need to have the invitations out to their friends before school ends.

"Mommmmm, are you paying attention? I need help with my math homework!" Aiden whines impatiently.

"Yes, Aiden, let's start from the beginning." Who am I kidding, I am the one who needs to focus.

An hour later, they are engrossed in their allotted, and much coveted, video-game time as I hurry to throw together dinner before I have to get out the door to work. I guess it's leftovers and a salad tonight. I love to cook, just not while I am in the middle of my shifts at the hospital. I try to have meals pre-made and ready, but it doesn't always work out that way. Thank God that I tend to make enough to feed an army when I do get the energy. Three males in the house will make a woman prepare food in excess, for you never can fully predict the amount three men can consume in one sitting.

"Daddy's home!" I hear being called out, followed by the stampede of little feet headed for a daddy wrestle session. Stephan is great with the boys; he always has the energy to play with the kids no matter what his day was like. He also has unprecedented patience. I have learned over the years to develop some form of patience, but it is still a struggle for me at times. While putting the finishing touches on dinner, Stephan walks in looking like a tornado hit him. His hair now loosely resembles a mohawk, and his clothes are mussed and wrinkled. I can't help but smile. Even in this sloppy state, he is still handsome; his mother's Latin genes dominate his features, and he has a smile that lights up a room. He bends and plants a kiss on my cheek.

"You get enough sleep?" He asks, hesitantly.

I really never know how to answer this question as it is mostly a "no," but I try not to sound so negative all the time.

"It was okay, it took forever to fall asleep as usual. How was your meeting?" I say, trying to change the pointless subject.

"It was good; I think we closed on a big account that we've been working on for a while. What's for dinner? Oh, and did you remember that I have a dinner meeting tomorrow night?"

Ah yes, my corporate finance manager who is forced to swoon clients by night as well. "I work, remember? I couldn't get anyone to trade with me? You will have to call the sitter," my voice edges. He never can remember my schedule since he got promoted into this new position- nor does he seem to try, even when I write it down on the big calendar in the kitchen.

"I will call my mom instead; she has been asking when would be a good time to come over and spend an evening with the boys."

Good, he solved a problem all on his own. "Sounds good. I need to go get ready. Dinner is on the table, and please clean up after!" I smile and head for the bedroom.

"Si, mi amour," he calls after me.

When we have been fighting, my ability to deal with his male brain is even thinner than normal. It is good to hear that his mom will be with the boys tomorrow night; I really love his mother. She is an eccentric, fiery, Columbian woman who loves old French movies, food, and the many volunteer causes she immerses herself in. She is a force who moves a room the minute she walks in. She is intelligent, witty, and has an infectious laugh. The boys adore her also. She is usually too busy with her volunteer work to visit, so I am glad that she will be spending the night here with the family. Mrs. Green moved out here from San Francisco to be close to us after Stephan's father passed last year. He was a strong military man whose heart couldn't handle all the career stress. It's a shame that he was lost before his time. Stephan was named after his father and looked up to him greatly. He hasn't been the same since the loss of Mr. Green.

Rummaging through my closet, I can't find my scrubs. Crap. I run to the dryer to search for good news. A flood of relief takes over when I realize that I did think far enough ahead to wash my work clothes. Scrubs aren't very flattering, but they are comfy and I don't cry when someone throws up on them. Looking in the mirror, I catch a glimpse of the damage control I must do to look presentable... time to break out the blow-dryer and touch up the makeup. With my lunch packed, coffee in hand, kisses and hugs dispersed, I am on my way.

Chapter 2

I hope we have a decent night tonight. Work is usually so stressful. I like what I do, love the crew that I work with, but get burnt out fast on the three-ring circus sometimes. St. Mary's Community Hospital is the place I have the pleasure of calling my work home, right on our medical surgical floor or as we call it- "med-surg." Being situated in the heart of a big city, our hospital takes care of a plethora of different human varieties. We are the crapshoot-catch-all for the hospital. Do you need a psych medication adjustment? Need to withdrawal from drugs or alcohol? Broke a leg? Asthma exacerbation? Heart or lungs backing up with fluid? Had a quick surgery and just need to stay one night for observation before going home? You've come to the right place, and we've got room for more! At least I can say that my job is never boring, and always keeps me on my toes.

"Hey Sasha, have a good few days off?" Nico calls down the locker room. He's a good nurse, very popular with our lady patients.

"Sure did. I was just beginning to feel relaxed, then I walked in; it looks like we have some really sick people with us tonight," I say, superstitiously treading lightly, not wanting to jinx us.

"Yup, we sure do," he replies quietly, getting my drift.

I just hope that no one cores tonight, meaning that their heart stops, and we attempt to bring them back from the dead. With this many acutely sick people on one floor, stuff like that tends to happen. Grabbing my stethoscope, I head down the hall to the nurses' station to get report. Checking over my assignment, a smirk plays on my lips as I see that I have my favorite patient back tonight. Yes! Mr. Rosen, who is a 70-year old version of Buddy Holly, has become a fast friend. He is dressed to the nines at all times (as he refuses the typical hospital gown), has manners that all men could learn from, and a smile on his face whenever anyone walks into his room. He is always so cheerful and pleasant.

He's been here for weeks with heart failure and is just too sick to go home. Anytime he tries to get out, he ends up right back here. I tease him each time he returns, telling him that he's purposely faking being sick because he misses us. Truth is, he will die soon from his condition. He knows it, yet makes the most out of everyday despite being locked in by four walls.

Whenever I have a few extra minutes, I like to take him for a ride in his wheelchair to explore the different units and offer a change of scenery. When the weather permits, he prefers to go for a ride around the perimeter of the hospital and through the little community garden just off of the parking lot. Even at night, the garden seems to bring him peace. Sometimes, we even sneak him down the back elevator to the newborn unit to see the babies. He enjoys looking at the babies and making up life stories for each one. It's as if he is writing an autobiography for each precious new life just as their story is beginning. He loves our little trips. We chat about movies, books, and art. He's more of a British-classic fan when it comes to literature, and while I prefer more modern text, I can still keep up with him. Well, maybe tonight won't be so bad.

"Code blue! Room 20! Code blue! Room 20!" The intercom sounds off just as I begin to get report from one of the day nurses. *Shit. I spoke too soon,* I think as I go running down the hall. Grabbing the crash cart, I steer it toward room 20. I don't know this patient so I hope the day nurse gets there fast to give us the low-down. Passing Mr. Rosen's room on my way to the code, I catch the scent of a man's cologne: sweet, yet musky. Huh, that's not the usual cologne that he bathes himself in every morning. Why do I know that smell? No time to let my mind wander. Rolling up to Room 20 to park the crash cart in place, the charge nurse comes over to the cart and temporarily leads the code. A few of us line up to help with compressions as the charge nurse starts to run things until the doc arrives. The room is filling up with staff. Codes are always congested with necessary and unnecessary staff, and while we usually don't mind having onlookers, it gets hard to move around when you all are knocking elbows. "If you are not here to jump in with compressions or bag the patient, I need you to get out and make room for the docs when they get here!" My charge nurse, Lisa, yells. God, I love her- a very practical, no-nonsense lady. My turn. I jump on the stool, position my hands over the sternum, and begin to compress the chest with all of my strength. The patient is an older gentleman and looks frail despite his girth. I fall into a rhythm counting to 30. The body does a lifeless, doll-like flop along with the compressions; it's always disturbing when that happens. *Shit, there goes a rib*, I think as the chest wall reverberates with a little crack, followed by the slight release of bone under my hand. Breaking ribs is just part of what happens as we have to push hard to compress the chest deep enough to get the blood pumping. It's still not as disturbing as the lifeless body flopping. Damn, still no heartbeat. The next staff member is up, and it's time for me to take a break, so I jump off of the stool as the next person quickly gets into position. My arms hurt, and I am out of breath. *No biggy*, I say to myself as I shake them out, trying to release the cramping. The doc runs in, and she starts calling off orders as we all fall into line, working as a well-oiled machine, doing all that we can to bring back this poor man. After about 30 minutes of compressions, forcing his airway open, and slamming in medications, we finally get a heartbeat, yes! "Let's get him to the unit!" the doc calls out. "We got it," two of the dayshift nurses respond and start getting everything ready to move him to the ICU. This means that even though this poor man will be bruised to hell, have a lot of pain from the broken ribs, a possible anoxic hit to the brain and could crash again at any time as he is medically unstable, he will live for now. Hopefully, he will be conscious soon and get to see his loved ones.

I need to start rounds and get busy in order to take my mind off of this core. It is always rough on a person's psych to try and bring someone back from the dead, never knowing if they will survive it for long. It also reminds us how short life really is, and how fast it can slip away. Quickly rushing off to finish report and to start rounds, I steel myself for the fact that all of my patients will now be late in receiving their evening medications. Ugh. At least we brought that one back for now, and I have a good assignment for the rest of the night. Only starting with four patients means that I am open for an admit; I will save Mr. Rosen for last as he loves to talk and is the most understanding when we are running late.

∞

All caught up, I gather Mr. Rosen's medications and head to his room. There is that smell of an odd, yet familiar, cologne again, crazy. Opening the door to rush in and greet my Buddy Holly incarnate, I am greeted by his warm smile and big, black-framed glasses. The smell from the hall is stronger inside the room, permeating every corner. I notice a very large, dark figure looming over the window while talking on a cell phone with his back toward me. Instantly, I am drawn to him. He is speaking low in a language that I have never heard before; I can't put my finger on what part of the world it possibly comes from. It sounds like it could be Turkish or Hungarian, but I am not sure.

"Well, there is my favorite young nurse!" Mr. Rosen chirps at me, bringing my focus back.

"Hello, Mr. Rosen, how are you this evening?" I ask, trying to shake off the effect that this faceless man has already had on me.

"Please, dear, call me Ed; you should know that by now!" he says playfully.

"Okay, okay, I give in. Ed, I have your evening medications for you," I chuckle. What can I say? His enthusiasm always brings it out in me.

"Have you picked up 'Jane Eyre' yet?" he asks quizzically. Here comes the third degree.

"Now, Ed, are we going to go there again? You know I like a little more imagination, mysticism, and bite to my books. And by bite I mean all things paranormal. "How about I go and rent the movie; will that count?" I respond, knowing what he will say.

"No dear, it's simply not the same; how can you fully capture the portrait of the characters then? And the depth? No, you must read it! " he says with so much seriousness that I am surprised it doesn't lead into another long lecture on the importance of British classics and how they should be the foundation of all English classes, starting way early in grade school.

"Okay, Ed, I will add it to my list; does it count that I have read 'Oliver Twist'? 'Pride and Prejudice' was next on the list, but I guess I can move it down for 'Jane Eyre'." Which is the truth; he has been successful in getting me to broaden my library.

"I guess that Dickens will do… for now, but yes, you should move 'Jane Eyre' up on your to-do list."

I laugh as I continue to scan in his medications and pop them out of their wrappers into his pill cup. I am still laughing to myself as I begin to turn toward Ed, but quickly stop as I realize that the conversation that was taking place over in the corner has ended. Now, a very well-built figure is sitting comfortably in the recliner next to Ed, watching me intently. My cheeks heat up under the pressure as I walk forward to hand the pill cup over to Ed, trying to ignore the stranger's gaze that is unnerving. He hasn't even said a single word to me, yet my heart is racing like a school girl's. Looking up once more, against my better judgment, I gasp as I lock eyes with the stranger, and realization sets in. The dream. The man in this room and the man from my dream, they are the same. I am so confused. I have never seen this man before in my life, yet I know him. I have dreamt about him in the most intimate way.

The pill cup starts to slip from my hand as my brain struggles to register the connection it is making. Ed clears his throat. The sound brings my gaze down to see

Ed holding the cup with an expression resembling that of a well-weathered wise man. I am pretty sure I turned ten shades of red right here on the spot. Surely, he can't know about the dream I had last night that included this man whom I have never met before! Ed clears his throat again, his dark eyes now dancing with excitement.

"I believe that I am being rude as introductions are in order. I was having so much fun harassing you about literature that I forgot my manners; Sasha, this is Etienne, my young nephew from France. Etienne, this is my favorite nurse, Sasha, who I have been telling you about."

Just like that, this impeccably dressed man with golden brown skin, which provides the perfect backdrop to highlight his electric blue eyes stands and holds out his hand to shake mine.

"It's a pleasure to meet you," he says with a thick, deep accent that makes my legs tremble slightly.

Oh my, he wants me to shake his hand. Simple enough, right? Wrong! Okay brain, you can do this; pull yourself together and stop being rude! Sucking in a gulp of air, I reach forward to meet his greeting. As my hand travels the short distance between us, it begins to feel as if someone has suddenly suspended me in slow motion. It is like trying to move my arm up through quicksand. What in the world? Am I about to pass out? Is that why my arm is so heavy? The air starts to change somehow, becoming charged and palpable. I am soon surrounded by thick humidity, and time continues on like molasses as the scent of his cologne gets stronger. It fills my head and smothers all other senses. The combination has me caring less and less about the likelihood of what I am experiencing being real at all. The moment our skin touches, upon our hands' embrace, an electric shock slams through me, as if I have just stuck my finger in a light socket. He, in an instant, has become a burst of light, igniting my soul, awakening a lost part of me that I have never known to exist.

After what seems like hours of standing here in amazement with my hand glued to this complete stranger (with what is probably a very unflattering expression on my face), I quickly retract my limb. The memory of his touch is still lingering on my skin. He looks shocked also as he wrings his hands together, his brow furrowed deep in thought. It seems that he can't believe what has just happened either. I thought I was the only one who felt it. Glancing at Ed, knowledge and understanding fill his eyes once again. Well, isn't that great; everyone knows what in the world is going on but me. I still am not sure if any of this is even real.

"It can't be, how?" Etienne says, looking to Ed with questioning and wonder in his eyes.

"Because you too, my friend, are worth a great love; the essence never lies," Ed replies in awe.

"No, it can't be. This is impossible! I did not ask for this!" Etienne says in a shocked, pissed and inconvenienced tone.

WHAT THE FUCK IS GOING ON? I need to get out of here. Fear of the unknown is starting to wash over me, making my feet very antsy. A complete unwillingness to even begin to decipher "you too, my friend, are worth a great love" takes over and turns my panic button up a notch. Wait, did Ed just call him friend? I thought he said that Etienne was his nephew? Great love? Surely he doesn't mean me; I belong to someone else. Okay, feet, this is way too weird and awkward, even for me; it's time to get to stepping. I can't do this.

"Ed, Etienne, it has been a pleasure, but I really must get going," I say quickly, while I realize that I am shaking. A man has never, in my life, unnerved me this much.

"Sasha, please, do wait a minute, dear; I know you must be confused, but I must explain," Ed says urgently.

"Ed, I can't; I need to get to work, and I can't even begin to wrap my brain around what any of this is about," I say, backing toward the door.

"Sasha, there is so much that you don't know, yet need to know as soon as possible. Etienne and myself are the only ones, at this time, who are knowledgeable about what's on the horizon for you and are able to give you the explanations you deserve. I had my suspicions, but one never wants to jump to conclusions." Ed moves like he is trying to get up out of bed to come toward me.

"Ed, let me stop you there; I can't do this, whatever this is, right now," I say, waving my arm in their direction. I had inched about a foot from the door when *his* deep, rhythmic voice spoke, stopping me cold in my tracks. His words float around me like a gentle wave, caressing my fear, trying to soothe it.

"Sasha, please, do not be afraid; do not run, we must speak. It is a matter of your wellbeing; you are in danger." He rushes on, trying to fill the space between us with as much information as he can before I bolt. "You have, what we call in our... culture...," he trails off in thought as he continues to pick his words carefully, "an essence. It's part of your genetic make-up. This essence can be dangerous if not... handled correctly; you will need our help very soon." He takes a few steps slowly toward me.

"You're kidding me, right? Ed, when you spoke of me to this man, did you also inform him that I am a perfectly healthy, and very married, mother of two?" I say in desperation, refusing to accept what I am hearing.

"Well, not quite, my dear, but you must understand that this situation is not affected or influenced, shall we say, by any life choices that you have already made; it happens in its own time whether we want it to or not."

Okay, I am done with a capital "D."

"Gentlemen, if you will excuse me, I have a job to do.

Ed, I will be back later to check on you; please call me if you have any *medical* needs this evening." I reach over to the counter, grab my stethoscope, and turn to the door without looking back; I cannot bear to look at them right now.

Chapter 3

I must be dreaming. Surely, only a dream would be this ridiculous, this intrusive. I think that it's time to take a 15-minute break from the floor. A quick glance at my watch shows that it's 10:30 PM. I was only in there for 20 minutes? All of "that" took place in 20 minutes? It must have been a crazy dream, right? Yet, it was a "dream-like" experience that gave me the feeling that my peaceful little bubble that I call life is about to pop. I have got to take a walk!

"Lisa, everyone is taken care of at the moment and caught up on meds. I am going to grab a break; can you watch my patients?" I ask, slightly pleading.

"Sure can. Give me your phone too, so it's an uninterrupted break; you may not get another chance tonight to have a minute of solitude," my charge nurse says in a half-serious tone.

True enough, though, we are lucky to be able to snag five minutes to ourselves, which has us breaking the no food or drink rule at the nurses' station frequently. Most nights are very busy, so if we want to have even the smallest chance of staving off hunger or thirst, we better have it ready at hand. We run non-stop, shoveling in food and drink between calls from patients for medication, requests for help to the bathroom, and reports of changes in patients' symptoms that could send us in a whole new direction, pending their stability. That's not including the other 101 things that can come up in the blink of an eye. To be a good nurse, you must be able to think on a dime, re-prioritize constantly, and be okay with change after change being thrown in your direction. Good thing I love a challenge, at work that is.

Another positive to working nights is that there are not as many people humming about the hospital, which makes it more peaceful to go for a stroll through the halls to clear your head. I decide to mosey down to the vending machines and see what form of chocolate therapy they possess. Pulling out my cell-phone along the way, I shoot my best friend- Ang, a text message to see if she is still awake. Knowing her, she is on a cleaning rampage at this hour. "You still up?" I round the corner to the vending machines and see that I am in luck: Zingers, M&Ms, and Snickers. Hhhmmmm, the choices, what shall it be? Snickers it is, since it does have nuts, and nuts are healthy. My brain feels fuzzy; I can't even begin to put one thought into the forefront of my brain to process. I am on total auto-pilot. The phone vibrates in my pocket. Reaching for it, I see Ang is, in fact, still up. "Yeah, just getting some cleaning done while everyone's asleep." Angelique Montoya, do I know you or what?

I text-message her back. "Having a rough night, I really need to talk. You free for lunch before the kids get out of school tomorrow? Maybe we can go for a walk?"

She answers immediately, "Sure thing, 1:00 pm, let's go for a walk at our usual spot."

That means just a few hours of sleep after work, but I can make it happen. Worst-case scenario, I can always squeeze in a quick nap before work if Stephan is home. Plus, a dose of sunshine might do me good. "Okay, it's a date," I reply.

Angelique, or "Ang" as I call her, was my soul-sister from the first time we met at a "mommy and me" class. We hit it off, making fun of how cliquey the moms were in the group, how they acted like we were back in high-school, and we didn't quite fit their group standards. We were both in our early 20s at the time with toddler twins, trying to break the monotony of staying at home all day. I have twin boys: Ethan and Aiden; she has twin girls: Elizabeth and Alyssa. We each married our high-school sweethearts and, surprisingly, found ourselves knocked up way earlier in life than we had planned. Our lives are so parallel at times that it's kind of creepy. We speak each other's language, we finish each other's sentences, and we talk one another down from the edge when life is rough. Needless to say, I am so glad to have her. Tomorrow, I will have to fill her in on all of this; maybe she can spread some of her light on the situation and confirm that I am crazy and need to be committed. In the real world, people don't shock other people just by touching them.

Time to head back up to the floor to round on my patients and make sure everyone is okay. With a heavy sigh, I head back down the hall toward my unit.

By 12:00 AM, I find myself hovering by Ed's door. I need to remember that I have a job to do, and part of that job is routinely checking on my patients to make sure that their needs are met and they are safe. Taking a deep breath, I slowly reach for the door handle and say a little prayer that I won't be bombarded with nonsense. Hesitantly opening the door, I peak in to find him sleeping soundly. Fortunately, there are no visitors with ridiculously good-smelling cologne hanging out in the room. I close the door and exhale a deep sigh of relief before heading back to the desk to finish charting. Charting (a nurse's paperwork) is a looming task that is mandatory and doesn't really care if you are having a rough shift.

"Sasha, we haven't had any new patients admitted to the floor tonight, we're overstaffed, and you haven't been cancelled in a while, so I am going to go ahead and have you leave early. Divide up your patients to the others however you see fit, plan on leaving at 1:00 AM." Lisa calls over to me at the desk while I am in the middle of paperwork hell.

No! I need to work and keep my mind busy right now! "Okay, Lisa, I'll just finish up some charting until then; I understand."

I really do understand; during the holidays, we don't usually have as many patients as we normally do, so we all have to take turns losing hours in some fashion. Good reason to always leave a few PTO (paid time off) hours in your bank. I guess I can always lie on my couch and contemplate my apparent "you're in danger" situation that is probably a made-up hoax by Ed to give me one last good zing while he still can. That doesn't explain everything that happened. Who am I kidding; this is probably for the best. My brain is on the verge of frizzing out.

∞

Leaving work in the middle of the night can be tricky business, especially downtown. As hospital staff, we are constantly being reminded about safety when going to and from our cars. Security guards are always available to walk us out when needed. The smart thing to do, at this hour, would be to call them and have them walk me out. Of course, I don't have enough patience to wait considering that it's three degrees outside. There isn't anyone mulling about suspiciously, and all I want to do is get home at this point. Trekking down the icy pathway to the parking lot, I spy a shadowy figure leaning against the side of the building off a little ways into the distance. I dismiss the figure and continue on my trek to the promised seat-warmers waiting for me. The air is so cold that the little hairs inside my nose are frozen solid and my lungs burn with each breath. Halfway to my car, I start having regrets about not calling a security guard to walk me out as I see the figure in my peripheral vision begin to walk in my direction. His head is down, and his hands are buried in a huge, dark winter coat. He is trying a little too hard to look inconspicuous, while also keeping up with my pace. Shit, I hope this is just my imagination! The closer I get to my car, the louder the sound becomes- the once-distant, heavy boots crunching the salted path along the icy ground. It's too close for comfort as he continues to follow me through the parking lot. *Maybe, he's not really following me. No need to overreact so soon. What are you going to do now, Sasha, if he is following you? How will you get yourself out of this one?* the little voice in my head asks while I look around to see if there are any bystanders in the area at all. Nope, I am still totally alone; there's not even a security vehicle driving the perimeter.

Now, only a few yards from my car, I start thinking that my best option would be to book it as fast as I can, then lock myself in; it is closer than turning back to the hospital at this point. I pick up my pace, remove the glove from my right hand, and position my keys between my knuckles as a defensive measure. If this guy really is following me and tries anything, I am going for the eyes. I do a good job of keeping a clear head in most emergency situations; reflexes, don't fail me now! I'm trying not to be too obvious as I get ready to execute my plan. Shit, I guess it was obvious; the stranger just picked up his speed as well. He really is following me; this really is happening. Using my other hand to push the unlock button on my key fob, I never let the keys loosen in my grip. Almost there... almost there... I reach forward to open the door to jump in, but it's too late.

The stranger grabs my hair, snapping my head backward, using my ponytail to dictate the position of my head- like a puppet-master pulling strings. The straps from my tote bag slip, sending my belongings to the ground with a loud thud, scattering its contents. The keys, however, are still within my grasp.

"Where the fuck do you think you're going?" he asks harshly.

The stranger has my head back so far that it's hard to breathe, let alone answer this motherfucker. God, my neck hurts. He tightens his grip on my hair, then quickly slams me face-first into the side of the car, pinning my head to the biting, cold metal. Pain explodes through my skull, and I feel the release of my glasses as they break; the pieces fall to the ground with a barely-audible clink. Pain starts to disable my ability to think clearly and, the metallic taste of blood becomes evident as a stream trickles down the side of my face. I feel his weight shift as he leans in so close to me that his stench violates my nose.

"Now, what is a pretty lady like you doing out here on a cold night like this? Guess I need to heat things up for you."

And, I, *guess* this isn't a robbery! Instead of fighting him, I hold my keys close to my stomach so he can't see them. I need this guy to relax his grip just a bit so I can turn and stab him, kick him, run, anything! Maybe he'll do something stupid that will give me the opening I need. He leans back just enough for me to pull in a little fresh air, briefly chasing away the smell of cigarette butts drowning in Olde English with a touch of rancid milk.

"No response? Guess you're not much of a talker, but that's cool; I don't need that shit anyway. Now, if you scream, I WILL knock you the fuck out, so be a good little girl and stay quiet; this won't take long," he says as he thrusts his hand up under my coat, feeling his way up to my breasts, making my skin crawl in repulsion the entire way. I think I am going to vomit. After what seems like a lifetime passes of unsolicited, disgusting groping, the piece of shit quickly removes his hand and goes for his fly. Wrong move, dude. I am so pissed off at this point. My mortification, disgust, and fear that this won't end well for me, all serves to fuel my anger. His hand, which is pinning my head to the car, loosens up for a split second; this is the opening I need.

Planning on taking full advantage of his mistake, I quickly inhale as much air as my lungs can take. Pushing my face further into the car so I can brace myself against it, I turn my body to the right-just enough to reverse round-house kick this piece of shit in the jewels. He screams a high-pitched bloody squeal, followed by a string of cuss words as he stumbles backwards. His head snaps forward from the impact, and I quickly turn to lunge for his eyes with the keys that have become permanently glued to my bare hand. I miss, more or less, depending on how you look at it, and end up giving him a key knuckle-sandwich to the nose. The impact of my hand to his face causes my keys to tear away from my hand and clatter onto the ground, just out of my reach.

He looks up at me with scarlet streams pouring from his nose and a mocking grin. "You fucking cunt. Guess you ain't so quiet as it seemed, and you're going to make me work for it. S'ok, I like the feisty ones-makes it more fun," he slurs out as he spits out a mouthful of blood onto the cement. His eyes are black and brimming with excitement, a predator stalking his prey. Slowly, he takes another step toward me, watching me, planning his next attack. Booze and adrenaline fueling him with all that he needs to continue on.

Shit. Where are all the security guards; where is anyone? I find myself crouching slightly in defense, ready to fight until the bitter end. The cold air bearing down on me is causing my breathing to become more labored and making my joints scream, while freezing the blood in place that was trickling down from my left eye.

He sees my protective stance and laughs out loud. "Oh yeah, this will be fun." Advancing forward, he stops about a foot in front of me, squints his beady little soulless eyes, and moves slightly as if he's getting ready to attack again. Bracing myself, I get ready to fight back. I'll be damned if I am just going to sit tight and let him do whatever he wants and pray that it ends soon. He may be stronger than me, but that won't stop me from trying to defend myself. Just as he moves to lunge forward, a low, animal-like growl echoes from off in the distance. A split-second later, a blur of black comes out of the darkness from my left with impossible and inhuman speed, knocking my attacker off into the shadows behind my car. The sound of my attacker's scream pierces the bitter night. Quickly, the scream becomes garbled. Then, another deep, animal-like growl sounds out, followed by the sickening snap of bone. Finally, there is silence.

Dropping immediately to the ground on all fours, I start looking for my keys; adrenaline is flowing freely at this point. My "fight or flight" reflex is telling me to find any way possible to get the hell out of here. I can barely see with only one lens of my glasses still in place; why didn't I wear contacts tonight? Squinting through the lonely piece of compressed plastic, I grope the icy ground, searching for anything that resembles keys. My instincts are driving me to move faster than my body will allow. Hands numb, fingers fumbling, I find I am frozen to the bone. My hands are now more like stumps that I am propping myself up on. Willing my one gloved stump to move again, it reaches out to something that looks shiny next to my tire. I command the frozen body part to grab it and bring it up closer; crap, it's a can. Why couldn't I see that coming? It dawns on me that I can't see at all out of my left eye; it seems to be crusted in blood. Instinctively, I reach up to my battered eye for assurance, but that quickly becomes a moot point as my fingertips are too frozen to give me any feedback. For whatever reason, this makes me more upset; the fact that I can't assess my own injuries makes me want to stab something. The overwhelming need to cry out in frustration is unexpectedly cut short by the jingle of keys close to my right ear. I don't want to look; I want to run away.

Slowly, turning in pure fear toward the sound, I see from my right eye that a set of car keys is being held out by a large, gloved hand. I didn't even hear this stranger approach; what the hell does that say about me? Stupid me, letting my guard down. Now, with nothing to say, not to mention in shock, I stare dumbfounded at my keys instead. My lack of response slowly brings forward another hand, motioning an offer to help me up. Sluggishly, I suck in air to fight back the sobs that have been threatening me since this dark figure fought off my attacker. I guess that it would be okay to take his hand; if he really wanted to hurt me, he would have done so already when I was a fumbling mess looking for my keys, unaware of my surroundings. Reaching forward with a frozen limb, I find myself grabbing for this strange hand like it is a lifeline. This person helped me by keeping my attacker from raping me, or beating me, or whatever was to come. I shouldn't be afraid to take his hand, right? There is no strength left to draw from; I can't pull myself up, and my legs are frozen stiff. Slow tears start to pool in my eyes as I struggle to stand; he takes this as a cue and finishes the job that I cannot, pulling me up as if I am as light as a feather. I still can't see worth a damn. With my one, semi- good eye, I make out a well-tailored trench coat coming my way as he pulls me close to his chest, holding me tight. The warm, soft, cashmere-wool blend feels good against my cold cheek and offers me comfort. His chest is rising and falling in a calm, even rhythm, as if nothing has even happened. Being held this close to a strange man doesn't feel as awkward as it should. A few heartbeats pass before his scent begins to invade my frozen nose; it is a Moorish musk with hints of cedar and sweet tobacco, punctuated by the briskness of the surrounding air. Etienne. Quickly, I look up into his face; I can barely make out his outline. Squinting to focus, I pick up on a worried pair of baby blues staring back at me, accompanied by a frighteningly fierce expression on his beautiful face.

"Are you hurt; are you okay?" he asks in his accent, and the sound of his voice renders me stupid for a moment.

"I'm o-o-ok, c-c-c-cold, only eye hur-r-r-rt," is all I can forcefully chatter out.

He holds me away from his chest slightly, opens his soft coat, then, pulls me back to him, closing the lapels around me. His body heat is like a furnace; I didn't think that it was possible for anyone to be this warm. He begins to speak in a gruff voice, in that strange foreign language of his, before ending in English- "bring the car around to the back parking lot." He must be on his cell-phone. He has a driver?

A minute later, I hear a dense set of tires pull up. Stuck in place, I can't bear to look up; I don't want to see who it is, nor do I want to be questioned by security, or cops for that matter. I also am not in a hurry to see if there is a body behind my car. Plus, leaving my secure location at this moment in time is not high on my priority list.

"Take care of that." I hear Etienne order someone. I have no clue who he's talking to and am not concerned enough to look. A set of heavy footsteps echoes throughout the parking lot as someone eases out of a protesting car and walks toward us. Instead of stopping, they continue on just past where we are standing to where, I am guessing, the body of my attacker lies. A cool breeze brushes against my cheek as Etienne pulls back one of the lapels. With a long finger, he lifts my chin to meet his gaze.

"Ma chérie, if you would, please get into my vehicle so that I may take you to get cleaned up, fed, and warmed." He wants me to get into a car with a stranger? Nice.

"I-I-I-I can't; I need to get home. I-I-I am okay, I can take care of myself." Is that the best I can come up with? Yup… judging by my denial, I just might be in shock.

"No doubt in my mind, ma chérie. I did, in fact, catch a glimpse of you defending yourself as I was trying to get to your side to assist. I am afraid it would be difficult for you to see out of those glasses well enough to drive."

The man has a point now, doesn't he? Part of me thinks that even if I try to get into my car to drive off, he won't let me. Well, I have come this far; I might as well. Something deep within is telling me to go with him, it went against my better judgment, but the unnamed force compelled me. I nod up at him and attempt to leave the comfort of his jacket by taking a step in the direction of the car, but my legs refuse the request and give out from under me. Just before my ass meets the frigid, snow-laden pavement, he catches me with one arm around my shoulders and one behind my legs, lifts me up, and carries me to, what I can see as being, an SUV.

"It is okay to ask for help, as well as receive it, you know," he says with a full-watt smile, perfect white teeth and all. God, what a smile! Even through my broken glasses, his smile is like watching the sun rise over an ocean bay, sending glittering reflections dancing across the water. I smile back, just a little, before quickly wincing at the sharp pain that shoots through the left side of my mouth. My sign of pain quickly shuts down his smile and returns the outlines of his face into something frightening. He sets me carefully into the spacious passenger-side backseat, walks around to the other side, and gets in next to me. My one good eye is still locked on him, trying to take all of him in. I can't seem to turn away.

"Nous prendre à la maison," I hear him say in a language I recognize. All I know is "maison" is probably "house" in French, so I guess he is telling the driver to take us to a house of some sort. OH NO?! I hope it is not *his* house! We can't go there; I really hope he said my house!

As if sensing my unease, he turns to me. "Do not fret; I will have my assistant bring your car to my home. Once I am certain that you are okay to drive, you may leave at any time. No harm will ever come to you as long as I am near," he states so intently that I actually believe him. Thinking about his words for a second, my shoulders relax a little on their own instinct.

"Okay, I trust you," I surprisingly hear myself say. At that, he smiles again, like I had made his day.

Did I just tell this man, who looks and acts like he's in the mob, that I trust him? The stranger part is that I know I really do. As the SUV begins to roll forward, I can't bring myself to look out the window at what might be happening to the body of the man lying behind my car. One thing is for sure; this glorious man next to me is a force of his own, makes his own rules, and must be affluent to some degree judging by his ability to bark out orders to staff who quickly respond without any question. Maybe he is in the mob! Hhhmm, I had better stop there. My mind will run away with me if I let it.

As the SUV leaves the parking lot and hits the smooth asphalt of the road, I allow myself to lift my eyes and look about. The driver is stiff and very professional, never letting his eyes wander to the rearview mirror. He appears to be just as well-dressed as Etienne, but I cannot be certain. The driver doesn't say a word the entire drive.

Chapter 4

Fifteen minutes later, the SUV heads north off of 6th Avenue for a few blocks before pulling up a short driveway that leads to the front of a large, newly restored, old brick home. From what I can tell, it's one of those glorious craftsman style mini-mansions, tucked away somewhere near the Congress Park/Hale neighborhood. The car stops, Etienne gets out, and comes around to my door to open it for me. He offers his hand to help me out, and I gladly take it; I don't really want to do a face-plant getting out of his vehicle. To my surprise, I find that my joints have thawed, and everything is working again. He doesn't let go of my hand; instead, he takes it and tucks it under his arm, then leads me to the front door. He remains quiet, just like the ride over here. I am guessing that he is deep in thought, or he is just afraid to say anything that might make me run screaming into the night. All of which could easily happen at this point, I am not going to lie. We walk up to the large, wooden front door, and it opens on its own from within. Stepping over the threshold, I am able to see a figure, resembling a slightly older woman, closing the door behind us; her eyes are turned away in respect. Why is everyone acting like this is the 1800s? Will no one look at me because they are afraid of offending me by staring at the gash on the side of my face? I mean, I know that I look bad, but it can't be that horrible. I am starting to feel like I just walked through a door that really leads us into the twilight zone. Shaking away any crazy thoughts, I follow Etienne into the belly of the house. The entry leads us into the foyer where beautiful craftsman wooden beams line the ceilings. The floors are all stained in an elegant, dark finish. I think it is safe to say that they are real hardwood floors and not those snap-together composite floors. There are some scattered works of art and decorative knick knacks, and from what I can see, it all seems very clean and simple. Etienne, who is still silent, leads me upstairs to a master suite.

"On the bed, you will find clean clothes that should be your size, while the bathroom counter contains towels and other amenities that ought to suit your needs.

I will be downstairs in my study should you need me. Take all the time that you need. We will dine together when you are ready."

At that, he turns and closes the heavy, ornate, white door behind me and leaves. He is pretty damn bossy. "We will dine together," rather than, "will you stay for dinner?" I really do not like being told what to do.

Standing for a while in the same spot that he left me in, I let my one good eye wander around the room; it is luxurious. A large four-poster bed dominates most of the room, and its linens are done in creams with hints of some sort of reflective material. The walls are dark burgundy with white trim, and heavy-looking drapes pour out over the windows. There is a fireplace that is lit, the room is clean, and it smells fresh like gardenia and lavender. I can't see the rest of the room's detail very well, and as much as I long to walk around to explore, I have to get cleaned up so I can quickly get out of here. The fact that I trust Ed and this guy is somehow related to him is probably the only reason why I've allowed him to lead me this far. Off to my right, I spy a soft glow coming from what looks like a bathroom. Walking in that direction, I can see the clothes on the bed that he spoke of. Grabbing the items that I need, I head into the bathroom before closing and locking the door behind me.

The bathroom is cozy with creamy travertine tile lining the floor, while warm limestone creeps up the walls partway and outlines the shower too. Sure enough, the counter is lined with amenities just as he had said. Soaps, shampoo, and makeup containers, all still in their package, are laid carefully along the counter top. What the hell? This is odd. Who has all this kind of stuff just ready and available? Approaching the counter to see the goodies on display, I catch my reflection in the mirror; it is of a woman whose face has been bloodied, with hair that has been ripped out of its ponytail. I reach up and remove my broken glasses so that I can examine them closely. The left lens is missing, and that side of the frame is bent to hell; there is also a crack in the bridge. Great. I guess that I won't be driving myself home. I can't bear to look at my face close-up in the mirror, so I opt for bathing first. The thought of sitting in a steaming hot shower for about a day straight, until my skin is as withered as a prune, puts a little spring in my step. At this moment in time, I feel so gross. I can still feel where that horrible man touched me; my neck aches from the whiplash, and my face and hand, where I held the keys, are throbbing. Turning on the shower to full blast, "HOT," I begin to slowly undress. My joints are stiff, but they are not as bad as they were. My scrub pants are ripped in the knees, and my white winter jacket has red flecks of blood spattered all over it. Without thinking, I throw all of my clothes into the corner by the bathroom door. I stop, give it a second thought, however, and consider picking them up and taking them out into the bedroom to throw them into the fireplace instead. I decide against it as the steam wafting out of the stall is beckoning. What the hell are Stephan and the boys going to say when they see me? It's not like I have any evidence to back up my story! There were no police involved with this assault, just a powerful mob-like man who apparently knows the right people. Stepping into the hot water, I secretly wish it to wash away the night like it never happened. Instead, I find myself reflecting on the night's events, replaying everything from the dream I had last night up until this very moment, here in the shower. Nothing seemed to add up.

I take my time and gingerly wash my face around the tender spots, then move to the rest of my body. The shower is so humid that I can't see through the glass door to the rest of the bathroom, bringing the feeling of being wrapped in a warm stone cocoon. The blazing water never seems to end; it continues to wrap around me, warming my bones. I stand there, staring into space and finally allow myself to weep silent tears for what seems like an eternity. The evenings stress, fear, and tension flow forward with the water and circle the drain before exiting the stone cavern.

Getting out of the shower to towel off, I let my brain turn back on. I feel better; the steamy "therapy session" proved to be helpful and much needed. I still want to know how he got clothes and makeup here so fast! Does he just keep this kind of stuff around for lady visitors? Slow down, Sasha; you don't want to go there. I grope the counter in search of my broken glasses; I need to be able to, at least partially, see my way down the stairs so I don't fall. I find them, pick them up, and realize they have been repaired. Okay, how did that happen?! Who the hell came in through the locked door while I was showering?! My heart-rate picks up as I quickly glance over to see that the lock on the door is still in place. My blood pressure starts to rise as I hold them up close and look them over. Aside from the slightly scratched lenses and a crack in the bridge, they look good. Wait, both lenses?! I thought I lost one of them in the parking lot. I am beginning to feel a little freaked out. Too many things have happened in the last few hours that I cannot explain, and *that* does not sit well with me.

Glancing into the mirror once again, I assess the damage control that needs to be done. Wet, matted-down hair and green eyes stare warily back at me. The left eye is working much better now that all the dried blood has been washed out. I actually look pretty good considering what has happened. The gash at the corner of my left eye is about an inch long, but superficial, so it won't need stitches. On the counter is a first-aid kit; of course he thought of everything. Using some Neosporin and a Band-Aid, I do a quick patch-up. It shouldn't need more than that. Next, using the hair dryer, I attempt to remedy the situation that has become my hair; I can't go out and face him looking like a drowned cat. Last, I look over the makeup. There is a pretty good selection here. Maybe he has an operation that robs Target trucks and has a garage full of contraband.

Skipping the foundation and eye makeup, I opt for just a little cover-up instead. Aside from the gash and a little bruise on my cheekbone, I am okay. With the addition of a little lip gloss and blush, I am already looking better. My long auburn hair is now dry and hanging in waves down my back. *Hey, Sasha! Welcome back!* I think to myself. I clean up pretty good, if I do say so myself. The blue jeans and cashmere sweater fit well too, which is weird, again. I guess it's time to face him. I have a lot of questions, and he has the answers I need.

Leaving the false safety of the bathroom, I head downstairs to find the study. From the kitchen, delectable smells of wonderful food being prepared hangs in the air. I really hope that he doesn't have his staff going to town on my accord; they have done so much for me already. The study is situated off to the side of the staircase. It is easy enough to find, and given the fact that someone broke into the bathroom with me naked inside, I head in without politely knocking. He looks up and smiles at me. This time, it is not that full-beam with teeth; it's more of a guarded, half-smile.

"You look more relaxed now and finally have a little color back into your cheeks; are you hungry?"

My stomach answers him with a growl before I can. "Uh, yeah; food sounds like a good idea. Plus, it smells amazing," I find myself saying timidly. Why does he make me nervous? Duh, Sasha, because he is a complete stranger.

"Good, it's settled then; let us dine, ma chérie."

He gets up from behind his desk and walks forward to meet me in the archway that divides his office from the hall. He has changed into a pair of jeans and a loose-fitting, silk, button-down shirt. Even through the shirt, it is possible to see how muscular he is. His pecs are well-defined, and his washboard abs are slightly visible through the fabric. He continues past me and stops in the hall before motioning me to join him. I follow his lead with great reward, as the view from behind is almost better than the front. I bet I could bounce a quarter off of his ass. Oh my, that backside is pretty damn perfect. Get it together, girlfriend; he is no different than any other man… they all have their flaws!

We walk into the dining room to a king's feast laid out on the table. The spread before me is probably the only thing at this very moment that could possibly break my concentration from the view I was fixated on. The elegant dining room is large, but feels cozy like the rest of the house. Heavy, satin curtains frame one end of the room, and a large, vibrant Persian rug sits at the base of a heavy rectangular dining table that seats eight. Etienne pulls out one of the high-back, leather dining chairs for me to sit in before taking the head of the table at my side. A man that pulls out a lady's chair… and I thought chivalry was dead. The food looks amazing: rosemary chicken, rice pilaf, warm spinach salad, prime rib, mashed potatoes, and more. A bottle of wine sitting at the head of the table catches my attention. Now, that sounds like the best idea of the night! He pours me a glass of wine without asking if I would like any, then motions to the food laid out before us. Did I step into an enchanted castle of sorts? Perhaps, my head was slammed into my car harder than I thought.

"Please, eat with me," he urges.

"First, Etienne, I have so many questions-starting with earlier when we first met, up to how my glasses were fixed while I was in the shower!" I feel my cheeks flush as I mention the shower in his presence.

"I am aware. We will discuss all that we need to; first, eat with me. I do not wish to see you go into shock, and I am sure that you are hungry," he persists, curtailing my attempt to get any more information.

"Etienne, please don't brush off my questions! How did my glasses get fixed while they were in the locked bathroom with me?" My blood starts to boil slightly, while my voice sounds out about two octaves higher than normal. I am determined to get some answers.

"No door is ever, truly, locked in my presence, and Molly, who runs my household, can fix just about anything! Now, please eat, and we can discuss more after your appetite has been satisfied," he says curtly, dismissing my attempt, again but with a darker edge this time.

Yes sir! Good God, he is demanding. I guess that will have to do for now. Judging by his expression, it would be best if I didn't push him. Even still, I really want to scold him for picking the locked door while I was buck-ass naked in there!

∞

I am pretty sure this was one of the best meals I have ever had; even the wine is spectacular.

"Room for pastries?" he asks as I push away from the table.

"No, I couldn't possibly. But, I would take some coffee if you have any," I say, not wanting to be rude.

"Are you sure that I cannot interest you in dessert? You really didn't eat much."

What is he talking about? I ate plenty! "I am fine, thank you; I truly am as stuffed as a turkey," I say, emphasizing the "fine." Why is he so insistent on me eating? There is no way for me to go into shock at this point, and I am far from anorexic. I am quite curvy for a white girl with plenty of junk in the trunk, but, by no means, am I fat either. I prefer "curvy and athletic" when describing my physique.

"Alright, Sasha, I will not pressure you further on the matter. Shall we retire to the living room for some coffee, then?" he says, enjoying himself by bantering me. I bet he likes making me flustered; my short temper amuses him somehow.

"Sure," I reply, eyeing him with scrutiny. He may be used to pushing people around on a daily basis, but I will not be one of those people, even if this is some sort of parallel fantasy world.

The living room is just on the other side of the hall from the dining room. The ceilings are tall for a house of this era, at least 10-12 feet high. Two plush chairs and a chaise are centered around a long coffee table, which seems to be perfectly aligned with the roaring fireplace. A large armoire, which, I suspect, holds a TV, stands close to the entrance. Someone, I am guessing Molly- the woman who had opened the door earlier, has laid out tea and coffee on the table, along with some petit four cakes.

"I see you couldn't help yourself on the dessert matter," I grumble.

"I swear, Sasha, that was Molly's doing, not at my request," he insists with a crooked, half-smile with lips once again cautiously covering his teeth.

We sit across from each other; he is on one of the plush chairs, and I have taken residence on the chaise. Both of us symbolically taking a stance on the conversation soon to come. I make myself some tea instead of coffee. I really do prefer tea; coffee is a necessary evil that I have come to depend on ever since I started working nights a few years ago. Hhmmm… rooibos chai, that looks to be a good one.

"I thought you wanted coffee?" he says; eyes alight with humor, taking in my every move as if he is intently following an amusing movie. It's more like a documentary from hell.

"I did, but that is more of a nasty habit I have developed over the years; I have always preferred good tea." I quickly avert my eyes back down to my task of pouring hot liquid, making sure I don't spill it.

"Petit four?" He banters.

I scowl at him; someone is feeling cheeky.

"Alright, I will take that as a 'no'," he continues on, still enjoying himself. "So, my dear Sasha, we have had an interesting evening, haven't we? And, you have stated that you have questions. I am guessing that this also means that you will allow me to tell you the truth about what happened upon our first encounter with one another," he says with fading humor.

"I am ready to talk about all of it. At the time, it was all too much for me; it still is. But, I find myself in a position where I don't think I can ignore any of it anymore." My words are more prudent than I intended.

"True, you can't deny it, and neither can I. If you don't mind, I would rather start where we left off in Edward's room instead of the more current turn of events. It is everything I can do to, at this time, maintain my composure after such a situation that made me want to do more than just snap that disgusting gutter rat's back. However, you were present, and I did not want you to bear witness to anything more gruesome."

Fear licks my belly at his confession. Wow! I mean, I know I heard that sickening snap, but I hadn't let myself think in-depth about the details. How the hell did this man have the strength to do that? In addition to that, how did he come out of nowhere like he did? Is he even human? Now, isn't that a good question. He looks human, he is warm-blooded... maybe a little too warm, if I recall correctly. Taking all of this into consideration, it would be smart of me to question what he is. Somehow, it doesn't seem to bother me that there may be more to this mystery man than meets the eye. It is at this point that a person with a greater sense of self-preservation would excuse herself and leave, but I find myself drawn in and need to know every ounce of truth. Perhaps, my recent binge reading of Anne Rice has permanently altered my logical brain. I don't even know myself at this very moment.

"You first have to promise that you will keep an open mind and you will hear me out completely. No running off if the conversation gets, shall we say, uncomfortable," he says thoughtfully.

"Promise. I already told you that I trust you, and that is not something to take lightly. People usually have to earn my trust over extended periods of time; though, you seem to have bypassed that rule of mine quickly." That brings another half-smile from him, and his eyes are now dancing with intrigue.

"You are wise to be cautious of where you place your trust, and I did not forget what you entrusted to me.

I do believe that we should start at the beginning. Forgive me if I add questions along the way, but, it is necessary so that we may understand all that has taken place." He leans forward in his chair and picks up a small, frosting-coated cake while glancing up at me with raised eyebrows. He really does enjoy getting under my skin, doesn't he?

"I guess that's okay," I say, ignoring his smug gesture.

"Sasha, tell me about your parents and where they come from," he continues on, plopping the cake in his mouth.

What? Questions already? What does this have to do with zapping me earlier? I guess that I will play along, considering all that has happened, for now, that is.

"I was raised by my mother and stepfather; I never knew my birth-father, and I know very little about him. My mother's family is from Russia, and as far as I know, my birth-father was a good-looking Irish man whose hobby was women. My mother fell in love with him, but once he found out that she was pregnant with me, she never heard from him again. That about covers the picture."

I really don't see how any of this has anything to do with the pressing question at hand... How am I in danger? Wait, why did my mouth just run away from me like that? I never would normally open up so easily.

"So, you never knew your biological father? Did you grow up here, in Denver?"

Really, Etienne? "Are you more interested in getting to know me or focusing on the problem at hand?" I sass back, irritated by this whole situation that made me uncomfortable yet equally entranced me to continue on with his charades.

His immediate, threatening glare answers my question instantly. He really isn't going to tell me anything unless I play nicely. Ugh!

"Fine! She met and married my stepfather when I was three; he has raised me as his own. Good ol' dad never showed his face again. I was born and raised in San Francisco, then moved here a few years ago when my husband had a job offer to relocate." Etienne seems to stiffen at the mention of my husband. "I have been here ever since. What else would you like to know before you actually answer any of my questions?" I feel my temper rising; I take a deep breath and count to ten in my head. This man really does get under my skin. His incredible good looks, self-righteous mannerisms, and brutal edge prove that appearances are only skin deep.

"You never knew your birth-father or his background? Interesting...," he says, while running his hand through his wavy brown hair that falls just below his jawline, disappearing deep into thought for a moment. "Do you have a good relationship with your mother?"

"Yes," I reply, dryly.

"It seems to me that it is your birth-father who is the missing puzzle piece to this picture, as your mother would have begun to groom you long ago...," he trails off like a detective trying to solve a mystery.

"What does that even mean? What puzzle? I really wish you would just get to the point. I have had a horrible night, and my patience is hanging on by a thread," I snap. He glares back at me as disgust fills his words. "The puzzle of how you were birthed into the role of being a half-breed who is apparently my chosen mate," he retorts back.

As the last word leaves his mouth, I am sure you could hear a pin drop in the room. My jaw drops and my brain, once again, fuzzes out.

The right words escape my reach. How the hell do you reply to that? Mate? That's a title that I don't want to begin to even try to touch with a ten-foot pole. Half-breed? What the hell is that? I mean, I know I am Heinz 57 like most Americans, but damn. Does he have something against Russians and the Irish?

"Half breed?" I question him, as that is all I can formulate at this time.

He lets out a long sigh, and his expression softens as he eases back into his chair. "Yes, Sasha, you are half-human and half..., well..." He seems like he doesn't know the best way to finish that sentence.

"Well, what?" I urge on, hypnotized by the oddity of it all.

"You are half-vampire," he says matter-of-factly.

Well, that's that, people; step right up to see Sasha go crazy. Yes, that's right: flat-out, padded-room crazy. Anyone have a Posey vest that they can put on me right here and now, before escorting me to a psychiatric hospital? Who would have thought that just hours ago, I was minding my own business, living my life, and now, I have lost my ever-loving mind. Maybe that douchebag did knock a few screws loose in my head back in the parking lot. Before you know it, I will start to see cartoon birds circle about. I start to laugh. I full on burst out in a side-splitting, pee-in-your-pants laugh, and I can't stop. I look up at him through blurry eyes, half expecting him to say "gotcha!" But no, he is just starting to look pissed off again. I try to control myself, but can't; it's all too ridiculous.

"This is no laughing matter; I hardly see the humor. I just told you that vampires exist- a very important and, far from minor, detail, and you are laughing!" he says sternly as a vein starts to bulge on the side of his neck from his rising anger and he purposely opens his mouth and curls back his lip.

"Oh, Etienne, I am sorry," I snort. Take a deep breath and get it together, Sasha; he is really serious. Shit! He has fangs! HE IS SERIOUS! I straighten up and lean back into the couch a little more. "I don't understand. You are warm-blooded, you eat human-food, and we ate a crap-load of garlic at dinner. I don't really see the vampire part very fitting," I say, suppressing the urge to keep laughing while subconsciously talking myself out of what I had just seen.

"Sasha, do not confuse my kind with the tall-tales that humans have constructed in an attempt to understand and rationalize the fear they have experienced on a few chance meetings with those of my species. There is much that you do not know, and we have little time as it is nearing 4:00 AM; you will probably need to be home soon," he continues on firmly, as if hoping to force the reality of it all onto me. "We are living, breathing, and very much alive. Yes, we may eat food and have some other similarities as humans, but we are very much our own species."

Gulp. Double gulp! I can't think of anything to say; wait, did he say "we"? "Are you a vampire?" I ask, not really wanting to know the answer, even though I already knew.

"Yes," he replies with trepidation.

Shit. That explains the not-so-quite-human qualities of this man. That also means those really were fangs.

"How old are you?" I blurt out as I steady myself on the armrest, the room slightly spinning. Apparently, my filter is broken by the absurdity of all of this.

"Old enough."

He doesn't want to answer me! "Don't do that! Don't start indirectly answering my questions after dropping a bombshell on me!" He looks at me smugly while contemplating my demand.

"Very well, 110."

Wow, Grandpa, you look awfully good in your old age! That's it; good ol' humor, cope me through this Q&A. I hurry on in fear that he will stop talking, not really knowing if I am even going to retain any of this.

"Are you immortal?" I ask hurriedly. Damn that broken filter.

"No, we just have a long lifespan in comparison to humans; we die eventually," he responds.

"Blood?" I can't seem to help myself.

"Yes, we need blood, but it is not as you think. We thrive best on the blood of our own species. It sustains us longer and lends us more strength. Human blood is a dangerous, slippery-slope for vampires. It is a quick high that wears off fast and does not contribute to our survival. Hence, the gruesome fairy tales humans have constructed. Like any drug, vampires are susceptible to addiction: human blood being the main one," he sighs.

Gulp. Again, how am I mixed up in any of this? There are things in life that are better when left to the unknown; life is complicated enough by itself. This is one of those things! Why couldn't I have just gone into Ed's room later on… skipping the part where I met this crazy man?

My head is still spinning. Grilling him with all of these questions is just a way of coping with it all, but I am not prepared for the answers. All of this must be wrong; how does he know I am half vampire?

"Because I can smell it in your veins, and our little handshake back in Edward's room cemented it," he says bitterly, as if he doesn't like this anymore than I do.

How does he keep popping off answers to the questions rolling around in my head?

"Are you reading my mind?" I ask.

"No, but I can sense your emotions and read them just as easily."

Well, talk about being an open book. God, I am so tired; the adrenaline has left the building. This conversation of vampires existing, with special powers mind you, has officially overloaded my sockets. One should really not be surprised about anything at this point. Shit, maybe the sky really isn't blue either! I let out a big sigh and sit back into the chaise, and I realize that I have been sitting on the edge of it, white-knuckled, ready to fall off.

I just have to know…"How am I in danger?" This question elicits another sigh from him, and his 110 years show through his 30-year-old complexion.

"Your vampire essence was triggered at our introduction. You will turn soon, and it could cost you your life."

"Die? I don't understand; you can die from being half vampire?" My last little twinge of adrenaline surges again.

"This is why we urgently needed to speak about all of this. One doesn't die from being a vampire, but they can when turning into one. Vampires are creatures that have evolved, just as man did. We start off very human, with a few exceptions, then somewhere in our early to mid-20s, our vampire essence is triggered forth from our DNA to turn us into fully-functioning vampires. It is very dangerous, especially for half-breeds that do not have the right support. This is why Edward and I were trying to discuss this with you. If you turn, you could die without the right resources."

Well, there is the cherry on top of my Sunday from hell; I could die.

"I'm about to be 30, and I haven't turned yet. What makes you think I even will?" I challenge.

"Because I can smell it, and I can sense it; it's been on the brink for you for a while. Unfortunately, I believe our handshake triggered it," he refutes.

"Triggered it? Brink? I feel fine." Maybe, he's the one who is crazy; yes, that's it. Maybe, he is ex-military and lost it after seeing too much.

"Tell me, Sasha; do you find yourself sick a lot? Avoiding the sun? Having a lot of body aches?"

His words hit home, not allowing me to take cover in my denial. How could he know any of that? "Well, I don't see the relevance in that. I am sick a lot, but I have kids and work in a hospital, which are two important roles that leave me always exposed to bugs. The sun is fine, and I appreciate it from a distance; I don't spend a lot of time in it as it gives me headaches. My body most likely aches from the long hours I spend on my feet taking care of others," I implore, not wanting him to be right.

"Those are all rationalizations for your mind to avoid accepting the truth. Vampires can turn in their 30s, though it is rare. It is usually elicited later in life by meeting a chosen mate, which is what I suspect, happened with us," he says warily with a hint of distain.

"Mate? I cannot be your mate; I belong to someone else!" I say angrily. My heart is now beating so loud that it is reverberating in my eardrums.

"Yes, you have made that point many times, but in truth, he is only human and time will claim him soon enough. You will need me, Sasha, for I am the only one who can get you through the transition when your body decides to turn. A mate's blood is the strongest and gives the best chance for a half-breed to survive such a traumatic awakening," he says with certainty.

"How dare you speak of Stephan as if he is nothing more than a pesky fly that will be swatted away soon; he has a full life ahead of him, and I took an oath before God to be his wife, to be by his side," I say in defense of my husband.

"Just so you are aware, this situation is less than ideal for me as well. Keep in mind, he is but a human, and when you turn, you will out-live him by many lifetimes. It is what it is; it cannot be what it is not," he says with a defeated sigh. He looks as exhausted as I feel.

It's now nearing 5:00 AM, and I need to get to bed. Silence drifts between us for a while as neither of us want to continue on this path. But, that's just it; once you're in, you're in. And, I am in too deep as it is.

All I can think about is my family and how I can't bear to die and leave them. My children are still so young.

"How...," I attempt, but my voice gets lost, trapped behind the ball of emotion stuck in my throat. "How will I know... if I am turning?" I whisper.

"You will begin to feel weak and achy, like you have a bad case of the flu. After that begins, your headaches will become intolerably painful. When it starts, you must come to me immediately."

Then, with ridiculously impossible speed, he is suddenly kneeling before me, grasping my hand. The warmth stemming from him creeps into me, consoling my conflictions and fear. My blood pressure starts to lower with his touch.

"I am sorry that this situation is not ideal; it was never my intent to cause you pain. Please, you must promise me that you will return to me when the symptoms start," he pleads, as his eyes bore into mine.

I can feel the truth of his words to my core; the truth in everything. He is really scared that I will not return in time, if at all. My heart begins to ache at the thought of disappointing him. He, in this moment of time, is showing a quick clip of vulnerability, something I didn't think possible for someone like him.

"Okay, I promise; I will do whatever I have to do to come back to you *if* it happens."

He squeezes my hand in response. Turning over my hand, I find a small piece of thick parchment paper inscribed with his phone number and address in perfect cursive.

The grandfather clock in the corner rings out that it is five o'clock, so I decide that it's time to head home. He walks me to the door with neither of us speaking, both too tired to try. At the door, he hands me my clothes that were sitting neatly on the console next to the entryway. They appear to have been laundered, and are most likely repaired, knowing Molly. I put on my winter coat, slip the piece of paper into my pocket, and head to the car. With nothing left to say, I turn and offer a weak smile; he nods in response. Time for sleep, then I have to figure out how, or what, to tell Stephan.

Chapter 5

Pulling up to my house, I see that all is still dark. Good, everyone is asleep. There is no strength left within me to try and explain what's going on with my face. I will have to make something up later because I can't tell Stephan the truth about the attack; he will insist that we report it. What the hell would I tell the police? "Ya, hi officer; some dickhead tried to rape me in the parking lot after I was too stupid to get a guard to walk me out. But, it's okay 'cause a vampire saved my life and killed the guy, so we're good here, right?" That would go over well. Tip-toeing into the house, I head straight for my bed and fall face-first onto it. For the first time in months, I fall fast asleep like a stone being thrown into a lake, sinking fast into the realm of dreams.

"Buzz…buzz…buzz…,"over and over; what is that horrible sound? Why won't it stop? Why must it wake me up? "Buzz…buzz…buzz." That's it; I'm going to break it, whatever it is. I open my eyes to find the offending noise and realize that it's my cellphone. I grab it and hit "answer."

"Hola chica! You standing me up for our date?" Ang's voice sings out.

Shit. I totally forgot to set my alarm.

"What time is it?" I yawn.

"It's 1:00 PM, but since I am usually the late one and you are always punctual, I figured you overslept."

"I'll be there in ten."

I hit "END" before jumping up, then realize that I'm still dressed in the clothes Etienne gave me. Well, that's convenient. I give my hair a quick comb-through and rush downstairs. Stephan is nowhere in sight; he must have had a meeting or something. Good, that means I get to dodge the bullet about my eye for now.

Ten minutes later, I pull up to the park by the kids' school and see Ang waiting for me. In her hand, I spy a Starbuck's cup and what looks like one of her burritos rolled up in foil. Have I told her how much I love her lately?

"OMG, thank you; how did you know?" I say gratefully, reaching for the goodies.

"I've learned over time." She smiles back. Her smile quickly turns into a frown as I push up my sunglasses without thinking. She must have seen my eye.

"You gonna tell me what happened, or do I have to nag it out of you?"

Ugh, I don't want to talk about any of it. But, she won't stop until I do. She might also be able to help me figure out what to tell Stephan.

"You want the whole story or the 'Reader's Digest' version?" I ask, looking for an out.

"Do you really need to ask me that?"

No dice, time to fess up.

"Fine," I sigh. "First, the eye; then, the real reason I text-messaged you last night. Some douche-bag attacked me in the parking lot in the middle of the night when I was leaving work. I got sent home early; we were over-staffed. He tried to rape me, but I fought back. It ended quickly when my patient's nephew appeared out of nowhere and...rescued me."

She gasps, and for the first time in her life, she doesn't have anything to say. After a minute, she finally finds her voice. "Are you okay? I mean, he didn't actually, you know...," she squeaks out.

"No, Etienne got there first and probably saved my life," I say, trying to ease her fear.

"Etienne?" She asks, confused.

"Yeah, the guy who saved me- my patient's nephew," I reply, as she grabs me and hugs me quickly with tears in her eyes. "Ang, I'm fine; look at me, I'm okay." I don't want her to worry like this!

"Okay, okay; I know! I just can't imagine what you were probably feeling. I'm so glad that you are okay," she responds, and finally lets go of me; she knows that I am not a big hugger.

"Me, too. I was mostly feeling pissed off and scared." This was the truth.

"What did the police say?"

Uh-oh, here we go. "Well, that's the thing; I didn't report it," I confess.

"What? Are you crazy? Why not? What if he tries to do it again? That was stupid not to report it!" She's fuming at this point.

"Ummm, Etienne took care of the situation in a way that I can't report it. The guy won't ever get a chance to be a repeat offender, if you know what I mean." She stops and gapes at me.

"Oh no, that's bad news. I mean, it's good about scum-ball, I guess, but what did you get yourself into?" Her suspicions are heightening as fear pins her eyes into a horrified look.

"It's not what I got myself into, necessarily, but what I fell into... with no choice." I am going to have to tell her the truth. Even though I'm not sure it would be smart to bring her into all of this, I am not fully convinced any of it is real.

"I don't get it," she says.

I take a minute and sip some of my chai and dig into the burrito; I need to buy myself some time to figure out what to say. Do I tell my "bff" all that went down? Will she still be there for me if she knows the truth? I trust her; she is the type that will keep a secret even if you torture her, and this is one she will have to keep.

"Helloooooo!" she nags on.

I clear my throat and start from the top; I tell her every detail: from the dirty dream to the hand zap, then, about the piece of paper that he slipped into my hand. For the second time in her life, she has nothing to say.

I finish with the details, as well as the burrito and chai, and she is still staring at me with her jaw on the ground.

"Okay, Ang, say something, you're freaking me out. Are you going to run away screaming?"

She blinks a few times, then looks away to the duck pond. "Sasha, I am your best friend; I'm not going to run off screaming into the night like in a horror movie," she says quietly, but with conviction, like she is trying to convince herself. "You sure that you don't need to get your head checked out?" She pleads, not wanting to believe me.

"I am completely fine," I sigh.

"I gotta admit that it's a lot to take in. And, can I say, holy shit, girlfriend? That sucks. All of it!"

I grunt in response and turn to gaze out at the duck pond too.

"Are you sure, Sasha, about all of this? I mean, I believe you, but, do you believe it?"

Good question, I have no idea what to believe anymore. "I don't know, Ang; part of me, or should I say most of me, is still in denial. You know how I am! I don't want to believe any of it, but I have a nagging suspicion it's true."

"Yeah, I know how you are. Miss 'resilient'. You're laid back about most things and have more fortitude than anyone I have ever met. But, I would think this would rattle even you to the core." She scoots in closer and puts her head on my shoulder. "Sasha, I have to also say, if it ends up being true and you come out of this okay, you would be pretty badass," she says with a little twinge of excitement.

I laugh; only she would be able to find the silver lining in all of this and take the unbelievable this well. But, she also believed to her core in things I never have, like angles, demons and ghosts. God help the soul that might attempt to get in her way of one of those ghost shows she loves. "Yeah, or something like that," I say with another heavy sigh.

We sit there for a while and stare off into the distance, trying to figure out what it all means.

"You really believe me? Or believe that I am crazy?"

"Sash, you know I still believe in things that most adults abandon. It is farfetched, I am not going to lie, but you would never make something like this up. And even if you hit your head, the fact that you saw his fangs says a lot. Neither of you seem to want to be going into this at all. What motives would he have? From what you said, he only seemed to be helping out of obligation of some sort." He did seem disgusted by the situation at times.

"What do I tell Stephan?" I ask her.

"You have to tell him the truth. I would leave out the attack, though; you can't tell him about that. Tell him something instead, like, 'oh, you know how clumsy I am; I slipped in pee at work and hit my face.' The vampire stuff is enough for anyone to handle. I am still trying to grasp it, and I am the one who goes on ghost hunts."

She is right; Stephan is one of the most patient and understanding men that I have ever met, but even he has his limits. I can get past the attack part, but he couldn't. He would hold onto it: be afraid to touch me, to hold me, or to let me go out in public by myself. We will have enough problems with the vampire part; I don't need to add to his stress. He always worries too much about me as it is.

"Oh Ang, what if he takes the boys and runs off, thinking that I am too dangerous or something?" I ask her, hoping she has all the answers.

"Will you be?" She returns.

I really don't know the answer to that, but I have to go on faith for that one. "I don't think so. Etienne said vampires have been living side-by-side with humans from the beginning, so I will learn to control it." I only hope I am right.

"I sure hope so; I think you need to figure that one out for sure before you tell Stephan. You should probably talk to the knight-in-shining-armor and get more details first. Hey, does this mean that we can't go for our afternoon walks anymore? You know, the sunshine and all?" She asks, half joking.

"Shit, I don't know. He said there are a lot of tall-tales out there about vampires that aren't true; let's hope that's one of them. Though, I wouldn't mind moving our walks to the evening time; the heat gives me headaches," I say, finally admitting that I hate meeting this time of day.

"See, it all makes sense; it's not 'cause you're the weirdo I always thought you were, it's 'cause you're not normal," she says with a smile.

Normal. There's a funny word; what the hell does that mean anymore?

Chapter 6

Sitting at the kitchen table, staring off into space, I contemplate the questions that Ang had brought up. Will I be safe to be around my family? Will I be able to control myself? I have no real clue, but I do know someone who does. Should I call him? No, not right now; I need space and time to process. However, since Stephan called and said that he is picking up the boys today so I can sleep longer, there is a little time. Maybe, I should call him. Stephan and I need to talk about all of this soon, and I need to have as many answers as I possibly can for him. Pulling the piece of paper from my jacket pocket, I start to trace the writing with my fingertip. What a trip, all of this. Why am I so afraid to call him? It is probably because, whenever I am near him, I get the sense that he plays by his own set of rules. Also, the fact that, every time he looks at me, despite his mood swings, it feels like he is debating whether or not he should throw me over his shoulder and run off with me caveman style… no matter if I am willing or not.

Phone in hand, I decide to call. Wait, it's almost 3:00 PM; is he sleeping? Do vampires even sleep? There is so much that I don't know. I hardly think my small library of supernatural fiction is a fitting comparison in this situation; though, a handbook would be nice right about now. Yes, call him, I tell myself. Worst case scenario is that he doesn't answer, and I am right back at square one. Or, is it the worst case that he answers and adds more complications to my life? With shaking fingers, I dial his number. As it begins to ring, my finger moves to hover over the "END" button to hang up; this is probably a bad idea.

"Oui?" rings out over the receiver before I end the call. His deep, silky voice stops me from hanging up. Crap, why did he have to answer?

"Did I wake you?" I question, all other words evading me.

"No, Sasha, you did not; I am glad you decided to call. I hope that you slept well." He sounds like he means it, although, maybe he is just a suave playboy who is good like that.

"Do vampires sleep?" I blurt out, trying not to let the effect his voice has on me show, while resisting the urge to just hang up.

"Is that why you called? To ask if we sleep?" Is he laughing? He is!

"No, not the main reason, but, do you?"

"Yes, we do. Now, why don't you tell me the real reason for your call," his voice is teasing me once more. He sure does find me amusing.

"I am scared I won't be able to control myself after I turn and that I won't be safe around my kids. Then, there is what to tell Stephan..." I trail off as my voice cracks- a sob sneaking up on me from nowhere.

"My darling Sasha, don't worry. Tell your husband what you must; you will be different, and he deserves to be prepared. You said that you trust me, right?" His words are full of compassion.

Oh, he's good. "Yes, I do."

"If you decide to tell him, he must understand that if he betrays your trust with this sensitive information, he will endanger himself. While I wish you would reconsider bringing humans into this, I understand if you must. This is a secret that he will have to keep indefinitely." He sounds as if he doubts Stephan's ability to keep a secret.

"I am not worried about that; I trust him with my life," I say, defending my husband's good name once more to this man.

"Good. Moving forward, you will become safe, although, at first, you will not be. I will have to teach you. In the beginning, it is best that you be removed from the human world for a period of time until we are confident that you have your urges under control."

I have to leave my family? I guess it makes sense; I would do anything at this point to keep them safe if that is what it comes down to.

"How long will I need to be...er..removed?" I question.

"It depends on the vampire; turning, itself, takes about two days. After that, training promptly begins, which can span up to two weeks, on average, for most vampires."

Great. How do I arrange a "two-week vacation" for one? Juggling responsibilities, along with life-changing events, all while making it seem effortless, is proving to be taxing.

"Sasha, are you still there?" he asks.

"Yes, Etienne, and I understand. This is just so hard," I sigh.

"I know; I am here, and you may call upon me at any hour if need be."

I hear the garage door go up and a car pull in. "Etienne, I have to go."

"Oui, ma chérie; until next time."

"Until next time," I say as I hit the end button, just in time for the boys to rush in. Either this man truly is a crazy stalker who made up this grand story and just master-manipulated me into disappearing with him for two weeks, or he really is trying to help me through this impending doom that is looming. Either way, it is going to end badly for me.

"MOM! What happened to your face?" Aiden questions me.

"Yeah, did you get in a fight?" Ethan adds.

I chuckle. "No, I didn't get into a fight; I slipped at work and hit my head on the side of a table. Mommy is okay." Stephan, thankfully, walks in right as I am talking to the boys; no further description is needed.

"You sure you're okay, mi amor?" he probes.

"I'm good; it is nothing a little time won't take care of, but you and I do need to talk, Stephan. It's really important." I urge, wanting to get this over with.

"I know, I hate when we argue. Things have been rough with my hours increasing at work. But, we will get through it, we always do," he says, assuming what I have to say is related to our last conversation.

The last time we were in the same room together longer than five minutes, we were arguing about the lack of time we spend together. It seems like years have passed since then, but in fact, it has barely been two days. Won't he be surprised when he finds out the real reason we need to talk.

"I know we will, Stephan, but there are some other pressing matters we need to discuss."

He raises his eyebrows with a questioning look. "Okay," he says.

"Boys, you can start your video-game time now, but remember I'm timing you; it ends the minute Daddy and I come back downstairs!" I call out to them.

"Yes! Okay, mom," Ethan says.

"Ha, I get first player!" Aiden yells.

"No way, it's who gets there first!" Ethan hollers back, and then they are off down the hall.

Stephan and I prefer to disappear to our room to talk as it has the most privacy in the house. An open hallway divides our room from the rest of the upstairs, so it is like our own little wing. He sits quietly on the bed and appears to be going back over the events of the last few days in his head. I bet he is trying to figure out what else we possibly need to discuss. I pace while we both take a minute; I can't sit down to tell him this. I decided earlier that Ang is right, and I have to tell him the truth.

"Stephan, you know how I never met my biological father and no one knows much about him?" I ask, urging his memory- figuring this is the best place to start.

"Si," he says, still not knowing where this is going but looks relieved that it is not something related to our relationship.

"Well, I found out last night who, more like *what,* he is and how it affects me." I don't want to do this! Telling him this could potentially tear apart his world. He doesn't deserve this and neither do the kids.

Why couldn't this have happened years ago- before I got knocked up and we had a shotgun wedding at his mother's request?

"What he is?" he replies softly, unsure if he wants me to continue.

God, this is a hard conversation to have; maybe, I should just disappear into the night, never to return.

"You know how sometimes things happen in life that we can't explain? You say all the time that there is so much that we don't understand about the world and all the wonders it holds." Hopefully, I can appeal to his mystic side, which is receptive to the unexplainable. He is always telling me how humans are way too self-absorbed in their thinking, and that out of all the different galaxies that exist, it is selfish to think that we are the only life forms... or populated planet out there.

"Yes, scientists are always uncovering discoveries, why?" He looks like he really wants me to get to the point.

"Well, apparently, I am half of one of those things that are hard to explain as science hasn't caught on yet." How to say this...

"I don't understand, Sasha."

Pacing, more pacing. "Stephan, my biological dad was a vampire; I am half vampire."

He starts to laugh and looks at me bizarrely; it's funny how much alike we are in some manners. It's been so long since I have heard him laugh, and it is a sound that I have missed. Too bad that I had to hear it under these circumstances; he probably thinks I'm crazy.

"Stephan, I am not joking," I say, with tears of frustration starting to line the rims of my eyes. The magnitude of the possibility of this all being true is hard enough to handle.

"Sasha, okay! It's okay," he says, as he walks over to me and pulls me in for a hug. He is not used to seeing me cry as it is a rare phenomenon. He bends and kisses my forehead. Still laughing, he continues, "Sasha, okay, I will try to believe you. It's hard and far-fetched, even for me. Are you certain you didn't hit your head too hard?"

"Yes! I am sure!" I exasperatedly cry. I may be many things, but crazy isn't one of them.

"We have always been truthful with each other, but this is a bit much. What does this mean exactly? You seem the same to me."

I look into his chocolate brown eyes; oh, how I used to love staring into their depths when we were teenagers- fantasizing about nothing and everything. I hold him close and begin to tell him about the essence in my DNA, turning, and the possible two weeks of vacation from reality that I will need to take. I add a very clean, simple version about Edward and Etienne with many details withheld, of course. He walks us over the bed so we can sit.

"I hate to say this but first, I think you've gone and read too many books. Second, I am going to need proof, and lastly, my answer to you disappearing with some guy for two weeks is 'hell no'." His anger is more than obvious.

"You think I wanted any of this? You think that I would make this up just to have some excuse to run away with another man?" I stare at him disbelievingly, hurt that he thinks I would do such a thing and frustrated that he thinks I am crazy. "Forget it, forget I said anything. I'll go get my head checked tomorrow," I pull away; stomp off to the bathroom and slam the door.

"Sasha, don't act like this, you can't blame me for being skeptical!" His voice thunders from the other side of the door.

Ignoring him, I grab my phone from my pocket, and absently send Etienne a smartass text while drawing myself a bath.

"Ha! It went so well that I now have to have my head examined and he thinks I've lost it completely. Guess I suffered a head injury. So whoever this really is, thank you for your help but I will no longer be needing your assistance."

Well, it was a fun fantasy ride while it lasted. Maybe Stephan is right. Stripping down and slowly climbing in, I hear Stephan in the bedroom fumbling around as well as the doorbell in the faint distance.

"I'll grab it," his voice muffles before his heavy footsteps trail off.

After a while, he trudges back and knocks on the door before the sigh of fabric brushes along the frame as he leans into it.

"Sasha, I know you wouldn't intentionally make something like this up. I know that you are telling the truth. I am sorry for not believing you. We will do whatever we have to do to make it work; I can't lose you." His voice is now full of sorrow.

I get out, wrap up in a towel and open the door.

"Why the sudden change?" I curiously ask.

"I believe you," he smiles sorrowfully as if the reality is finally catching up to him. What an odd sudden change.

"Who was at the door, Stephan?" I probe, my suspicions getting the better of me.

His handsome face glazes over as he tries to remember. "A salesmen," he seems to settle on after a few seconds of uncertainty.

Is he finally seeing that this is more than a theoretical "what if" scenario? Or is there more to this one-eighty he's done. Not wanting to question it too much, I move on.

"You believe me and what we may need to do to get through it all?"

"Whatever it takes, mi amour. Whatever it takes to keep you safe."

"Stephan, it's also about keeping you and the boys safe."

"You would never hurt us, no matter what you turn into; I know that above all else."

I hope that is true. "You also have to swear on your grandmother's and your father's graves that you will never tell anyone the truth about me; it would endanger everyone we love if they found out," I say solemnly.

He has to understand the weight all of this carries. Vampires have hidden their existence this long; something tells me that they go to great lengths to keep it that way.

"It's that serious? Okay, I swear," he says hesitantly. I suspect the gravity of it all hasn't entirely caught up to him because he seems to still be grappling with a bit of denial. "We will get through this, Sasha; I know we will."

Heck, we've been together since we were 15 years old. We have survived financial hardships, having twins way before we were ready- right smack in the middle of college, job losses, and moving across the country with two babies. We can get through this.

We continue to talk through all of the details: how to make this change work and what to tell people. Stephan deserves a round of applause; he ended up taking it better than I thought he would. He is handling it all in stride, not pressuring me for more and more answers to things I have no clue about. I almost think he finally believes all of this is really happening. But, I know that he is probably holding out hope that I will yell out "April Fools!" or something. We head back downstairs to order pizza as there is no time to cook before I have to go to work. Yay. Going to work for a twelve-hour night-shift on five hours of terrible sleep sounds like so much fun, not to mention being stressed out beyond belief?

"Why don't you call in sick tonight?" he asks, not wanting me to leave him right now.

"It's too late for me to call in, and I can't leave the floor short like that." This is partially true; the other part of the truth being that I need to keep busy, and work is a good way to try and do that.

"Okay, I just thought that I would mention it. We've still got a lot to process through. Plus, we need to talk about the boys' birthday plans and how they may be affected."

He is right; how do we keep life as normal as possible for the boys? "Let's make some time tomorrow; I'm off."

Pleased with the compromise, he smiles. "Deal." Positive, he is always so positive, and I am the negative-Nancy.

Christmas is also coming up in a couple of days. There are so many family things planned over the next few weeks that could easily be disrupted by this crap. Why couldn't this have started during a boring month-like February? No holidays in that month that are dependent on families all being together for happy festivities and stuff like that. Thankfully, I am a planner, and everything has been purchased and wrapped for Christmas, as well as the boys' birthday, for weeks. Shortly after New Year's Day, there is the big birthday celebration that we do every year for the boys with our family and close friends. I just have to get through the next few weeks. Come on essence, or whatever you are, just a few more weeks; you are not allowed to do anything until after the boys' birthday. Give me that much at least!

∞

Work is weirdly slow tonight; although, that is about the normal right before a major holiday. It just feels odd since we rarely ever get a break like this. Ed usually keeps me entertained when I have free time, but he went down for an MRI right as I came on tonight, so we haven't had a chance to talk. I was hoping for a night that would keep me too busy to think, even though I should be happy for this rare slow time. My work phone rings loudly from my pocket, interrupting my daydream.

"This is Sasha," I answer.

"Mr. Rosen just got back," says Steph- a fellow nurse.

"Okay, I'll be there in a minute." Time to talk to my friend. The cat's not only out of the bag, it has gone and torn up my house too. I head down to his room.

"Ed! Glad to see you came back and didn't try to sneak out for a night on the town!" I joke. He gives me a weak smile in return. Uh-oh, he's not feeling too hot, is he? "Ed, you okay?" I ask, searching his eyes. My nurse assessment skills detect that he is way off his normal.

"I am alright, dear, just tired. They have had me up all day for all of these tests; what else do they think that they are going to find? I am already dying," he says with weighted words.

"I know, Ed; they just want to make sure they are doing everything they can," I reply. His words hit a chord of sadness in my heart.

"Well, my dear, that ship has sailed. I finally signed a DNR form today. But you probably already saw that. By the way, Etienne called me and told me that he finally talked to you. Or, is it that you finally listened?" He chirps back, a little sparkle back in his eyes as he glosses over the elephant in the room.

"We did, and Ed, I would be lying if I said that I am not scared."

He sighs deeply and leans back onto his bed. "I know, dear, it's okay to be; your world was just turned inside out, and it gets worse before it gets better." He motions for me to come and sit at his side.

"Great, that sounds comforting," I say as I comply with his simple yet weighted request.

"It's the truth, which you deserve at the very least. Can I also tell you that I have known him almost all of my life, and I have never seen someone rattle him the way you do? It's quite amusing, if I do say so myself. I must also add that he has never taken a mate in all of these years," he says, as he reaches for my hand. I don't want to broach the topic of mate; it's too much.

"All of your life, Ed; I thought he was your nephew?" But, I knew that wasn't the truth.

"A ruse, my dear; he is actually my best friend from childhood. A bit of the vampire essence rubbed off on me over the years and lengthened my life a tad; it gave me an extra few years or so. But, my human body is giving out." I squeeze his hand. Well, that makes more sense, sort of. "Don't fight it, dear; he will take good care of you, and he will make it possible for you to survive the change. You know, come to think of it, I do believe you will be the first he has ever turned. All these years, he's only overseen the transition of others and helped them perfect the craft," he says, as he relaxes back into his pillow.

"Perfect the craft?" I question.

"Yes. He has disciplined young vampires and taught them self-control; he could very well write a book on the matter."

Huh, that explains a lot. "Well, that explains his bossiness," I say with conviction.

Ed chuckles. "Yes, it does; it has also never changed. More likely, it's gotten a bit worse over the years."

I smile, but it is soon replaced with worry. "Ed, can you tell how long I have until I turn? I am so afraid I won't make it through the holidays and the boys' birthday," I ask with false hope.

"No one can be certain, Sasha; there is no written rule. All we can be certain on is that it will be soon." He squeezes my hand back.

"Okay, Ed, I will take that for now. Get some rest, and you can lecture me on 'Jane Eyre' in the morning before I leave." He smiles back and closes his eyes. Little did either of us know that would be our last conversation.

The next morning, I head over to check on Ed one last time before I leave for the day. He slept soundly all night and seemed as stable as Ed could be. Peeking my head into his room, I see him lying on his back, which is something he only does when he is in pain. "Ed, are you okay? Can I get you some pain medicine?" I ask, walking forward, trying to see if his chest is rising and falling. He doesn't respond. Running over to get a closer look, I see that he is not breathing. I quickly move my fingers to his carotid artery- no pulse. My body collapses on the side of his bed, and I subconsciously grab his hand in disbelief. Tears start to fall from my face and patter onto the sheets. My friend has finally passed and escaped his pain, along with the constant feeling of subtle suffocation from the fluid that was perpetually chastising his heart and lungs. I should be happy for him; he was waiting for this, and he was tired of it all. Instead, my heart selfishly aches for the loss of him, and loneliness shadows the room.

After a few minutes of sitting there with Ed, I decide it's time to start getting him ready. As much as I would like to sit here and hold his hand all day... and cry... that is not what is best right now. What is wrong with me, I never cry. I grab my cellphone with the other hand, never letting go of Ed, and call his "nephew" to give him the news. Ed had no other family contacts listed, so it will have to be Etienne to arrange everything. He answers after the first ring.

"Two calls in 24 hours? To what do I owe this pleasure?"

How do I tell him this? "Etienne, it's Ed; he…," I can't finish the sentence.

"He passed?"

"Yes, I am so sorry."

"Are you with him now?"

"Yes, it must have just happened because he was fine 15 minutes ago when they took his vital signs. I will stay late and start the paperwork. Do you, or anyone else, want to come and say, 'goodbye?' We can leave him in the room as long as you want."

"No, the facility he chose is already listed in his chart. They will pick him up shortly, and we will begin our grieving process once the body has been prepared, per our tradition." His friendly tone is now stern and strictly professional.

"Etienne, can I do anything for you?" I feel the need to reach out and comfort him in some way. I can't imagine how he must be feeling right now. To be 110 years old and to lose the one person who you've been the closest to for most of that time is heart-wrenching.

"No, I appreciate your concern; have a nice day, Sasha." Click. Did he just hang up on me?

Well, everyone deals with grief differently, but damn. Ed said he has never taken a mate; maybe, it's more like a mate has never wanted to put up with him.

The body before me looks so relaxed and almost happy. Ed's peaceful expression eases my grief. Knowing that his kind soul is no longer trapped in a dying body allows me to let go and be at peace. Only his empty body remains here; his love, laughter, and joyous wit will forever stay with all of those who he has touched.

Chapter 7

Christmas has come and gone in one big blur; was it really just yesterday? The winter festivities began too quickly after Ed's passing. I found myself going through the holiday motions purely for the kids and family; my mind won't stop drifting off into the other details surrounding my very existence. It has been hard to live in the moment with the weight of all that has happened bearing down on me. It is as if I am present in body only; my brain is too busy gearing up for what is to come. Will I ever really be ready?

It's the day after Christmas, and I received a short and oh-so-cold, business-like voicemail from Etienne earlier this morning, inviting me to Ed's funeral tomorrow. It is so inviting that I don't bother returning his call to let him know that I am actually going. Ed is the only reason why I am going to go; it definitely has nothing to do with his extremely moody "nephew." Swinging back and forth from genuine, caring guy to cold and distant asshole just irritates the hell out of me. I wonder if pharmaceuticals work on vampires; he needs something.

Not knowing if this is a human, vampire, or mix of both type of funeral, I asked Ang to be my wingman. She said, "Yes," of course; purely out of morbid curiosity. Plus, the countdown is on for me, and we are using any excuse we can to get away from our daily responsibilities in order to spend time together. Our occasional walks and weekly fitness class of choice just aren't enough when you know that your person is going off the grid for an extended amount of time. Stephan is being more attentive too, trying to schedule me into his day. Who knew that all you have to do is tell your husband that you are turning into a vampire and will be going on a two-week vacation to learn how not to eat your family to get some time alone with him? All in all, the vibe over the last few days has been dialed in on "weird." It is everything I can do to keep it together and act as normal as possible for my family and friends.

Turning off of Quebec Avenue into the north side of Park Hill, I head toward Ang's house to pick her up for the funeral. Funny how Etienne's house is situated smack in the middle between my house and Ang's. It would be so easy to make a pit stop at any time if I really wanted to torture myself. Why the sudden urge to stop off at his house? It's probably the masochist in me. Some deep-down, demented part of my brain is drawn to that dangerous and inhuman male. As much as I try, I can't shake it.

Pulling into Ang's driveway, I send her a text message, letting her know I am outside. While sitting in the car, I find my irrational, girly side coming out as I start to fuss over my reflection in the rearview mirror and add another layer of lip gloss. What is with me? I never care about my makeup! Maybe it is because I haven't seen Etienne in about a week, so I want to make sure that I look halfway decent, considering that the last time we saw each other I was battered and covered in blood. Or, it could be the simple fact that this random savior of mine is ridiculously attractive that has me acting out of character. It shouldn't matter, though; yet, I still can't help myself. Today, I wore contacts, more makeup, and a very nice dress. Ed would approve of the dress; he always said how he wished more women would wear dresses these days. He thought that feminine women, who tastefully show a little leg, are, by far, sexier than those who leave nothing to the imagination. Finally, here comes Ang. It seems like she got the "Ed liked women to wear dresses" memo too.

"Ready?" I ask.

She looks at me like I'm crazy as she climbs in. "As ready as anyone can be for a funeral," she says in a huff.

Ha, good point. She isn't thrilled about the funeral part, but her natural born inquisitiveness has overrun her dislike for viewing dead people in pine boxes. It also helps that we both are still having a hard time believing any of this is real, and we are secretly hoping for some hardcore proof to manifest while we are there. It's early evening, and the church isn't far. I don't think that I have been to an evening funeral before; this ought to be creepy.

"You think any zombies will be attending?" I poke fun at her discomfort.

"Ah man, come on Sasha! But with you, anything is possible I guess." Hahaha, isn't that the truth. "Judging by your dress, you must think that we are going to a black-tie cocktail party!" She chastises me.

"It's the only black dress I own. The jacket is keeping it modest. Hey, you're one to talk, missy!"

"What? This old thing? You don't want me to walk into a room full of beautiful vampires looking like I just rolled out of bed, do you?" she asks, innocently.

This, coming from the same woman who puts on makeup to go to the gym. She is wearing a snug fitting, black and white, bold-print, A-line, knee-length floral dress. The bodice is black with sleek cap-sleeves and shows a lot of cleavage. It is impossible for her not to show cleavage in anything she wears, unless she dons a trash bag, but even then, they would probably pop through. She is very happily married, but loves having fun and breaking hearts everywhere she goes. She swears she doesn't even notice, but I think she secretly gets a kick out of torturing men.

Over the years, she has rubbed off on me a little- not in the men department, but by getting me to try to put more effort into my appearance. Aside from consistently working out and keeping fit, caring about my appearance was a little lost on me. Ang has taken over my closet and trained me on the best makeup. Her time and energy have paid off. Who would have known what a transformation the right clothes can make. I have never been ashamed of my curvy figure; I just never knew how to dress right until Ang came into my life, or closet, I should say. I must admit that it has made a difference, and I like it.

We arrive to the church, and there is hardly any parking. It is packed. All of these people must have just had a hospital phobia because Ed rarely had visitors.

"Look at this crowd; are you really taking me to a surprise concert and not a funeral?" Ang asks jokingly.

"Yeah, a Christian cover band for The Eagles; you know, 'cause hell apparently already done froze over," I reply.

"You're horrible," she laughs out.

I finally spy a space I can squeeze into. "I know; let's do this!" I say, as we get out and head into the crowded, little stone church that looks on the ancient side. There is barely a place to sit.

We should have gotten here earlier if we wanted better seats. It is my fault for assuming this would be a small and quaint event.

For being in the dead of winter, it is dreadfully hot inside; I start to sweat immediately as we inch forward into the crowd to look for a seat. Ang and I find room in one of the back pews and cram ourselves in next to an elderly couple. I make Ang go first so I can sit at the end; the heat, along with all of these people, is making me claustrophobic.

"You think I might find my future ex-husband here? This place is full of beautiful men; Lord Jesus, help me," Ang whispers in my ear as I peel off my little evening jacket.

I can't help but chuckle, she is right. We are surrounded by attractive people, including the elderly couple next to us. If I had to guess, the few random, average-looking faces scattered about are human; the rest are probably not. Many of the men start to turn their heads in our direction the minute we sit down. It must be the double set of voluptuous twins we are sporting in these dresses. Or, is it because I am sweating bullets?

"Here, take some tissues and pat your face; you look like shit."

"Thanks, love you too," I reply, as I quickly snatch them from her.

The longer we sit here, waiting for the service to begin, the closer I come to darting back outside to where it is nice and cold. Did someone leave the heat on in here? I dab my brow with one of Ang's tissues as another hot flash sweeps over me. And what is wrong with these men? The younger ones are the worst, constantly staring back at us, unapologetically. At first, I think that they just happen to be looking at something in this direction, but then, I keep getting direct eye contact and receive a few grins in return. Am I really sweating that bad?

The couple next to us starts to whisper to each other while casting sideways glances. What is wrong with these people? That's it; we should leave. Before I can nudge Ang to tell her that we should go, an elderly man in a ceremonial black and silver robe with strange, unique markings down the front of it starts the service by singing out in a low, attention-grabbing hymn. The language resembles the one Etienne was speaking at the hospital, the one I couldn't place. The doors behind us promptly close as two figures in matching silver and dark purple robes come down the aisle. The low thud of closing doors sends beads of sweat running down my back. It must have something to do with all of these people crammed in here- well, some of them are probably people. There goes my chance of an escape.

I wonder if Ang has a beach towel in that purse. Oh no, Ang! What if I just put Ang in danger by bringing her into a church full of hungry vampires? Ha, that's funny- church full of vampires... I chuckle to myself for a little too long on the irony of that last thought. I am starting to feel silly-drunk and not in the good way. I knew I should have eaten something before I left the house! It feels like someone has started to spin the insides of my head like a top. *Du-du-dududto... Afro circus, afro circus,* I think, as I start singing the "Madagascar 3" movie theme-song over and over in my head.

Ang is locked in on the service, and it seems that I am only picking up bits and pieces as my concentration keeps wavering back to thoughts of circuses-uses-es. Periodically, I sneak a quick glance at Ang, just to make sure that something hasn't happened to her. Why did I bring her here? The robed figure continues on, and the young men have remembered their manners; they have finally stopped craning their necks. The loss of the added attention allows me to relax a little. It really is a beautiful service; it isn't religious, but very spiritual.

Come to think of it, I don't really know what religion this is; the ceremonial outfits and flow of the service are like nothing I have ever seen. The robed figure speaks in English and that other language I don't know. The wording and mention of things like Mother Earth brings a Native American tone to the tribute. Everyone around us is hanging on to the poetic flow, lost in their memories of Ed. I knew he was special, but in this moment, I am able to see just how loved he really was.

The robed figure finishes and introduces Etienne as the next speaker. Crap. I hope he doesn't see me back here; maybe, I should trade places with Ang so I can hide better. As he walks to the podium, I elbow Ang and mouth, "that's him." She nods in approval, mouths back a long, "niiicccee," and adds an eyebrow waggle. I elbow her again; I know exactly what she is thinking. Aren't we just a couple of dirty birds in a pew. Etienne approaches the microphone, but before he gets ready to speak, he spots me and glares: the kind of piercing stare that makes you sink lower in your seat while feigning innocence, even if you did nothing wrong. What did I do now? He abruptly looks away, leans into the microphone, and begins an eloquent, heartfelt speech. Released from his horrible scowl, I am able to sit up and take in the homage. His sorrow reaches out through his words, leaving an imprint on all of our hearts. This dark, intimidating, bordering-cruel man is truly devastated by the loss of Ed.

At the end of the service, someone announces overhead that the wake will be in the room next door. We all rise and respectfully file through the adjoining doorway to mingle and have a drink. It feels good to stand and walk around. After we squeeze through all of the ridiculously beautiful and good-smelling people, we find a high-top table close to the exit and take up residence.

"That service was amazing! I have never heard anything like it; I just may need to attend this church once in a while!"Ang says.

"I only caught a few pieces; I like how spiritual it was." I should have been paying better attention.

"Only a few pieces…, are you feeling okay?"

"Yeah, it was just so hot in there... it was hard to think straight." The wake area feels cooler for the moment and allows me to clear my head.

"I think you need a drink; I'll go get us one."Ang gets up to head to the bar.

The thought of Ang disappearing in this crowd is too much; I would rather have her stay by the exit. "No, I'll go; you wait here," I say, and take off before she can say no.

While waiting for my turn at the bar, I start to get uncomfortable as the stares from the men are starting to pick up again. Good God, what is wrong? Did I sweat my eye makeup off into a horror mask?

"Good evening, what can I get for you?" The bartender asks with a heart-stopping smile. I better order a few drinks as I don't want to have to come back up here.

"Four vodka and cranberries, please." He smiles again and gets to work. I notice the two men on the other side of the bar who were paying way to much attention to me when I first walked up are starting to make their way toward me. Ugh, I hope this guy finishes my drinks fast!

"Hello, are you a friend of Edward's?" The taller of the two asks. They are attractive, but not like Etienne, and thankfully, they don't make me stumble on my words.

"Yes, I am," I say quickly, looking back toward my drinks being made... almost done.

"I haven't seen you before; are you from here?" he asks me.

What a pick-up line. Finally, the bartender hands over a little tray with all of my drinks and I drop a tip in his cup. "No, I am not from here. Have a good evening, gentleman," I say, dismissing them and take off. Whew.

I get back to the table to find that Ang is still in one piece. Thank goodness!

"Holy cow; thirsty, Sasha?"

"Yes, and I don't want to have to go back up to the bar and get hit on again, so I thought I would plan ahead," I say gruffly.

"You got hit on? Told you that dress was a bit too sexy for a funeral." She chastises me.

"Have you noticed all of the stares, too?" I thought I was the only one who noticed.

"Yeah, I guess- wasn't really paying close attention," she responds wide eyed as I down my first drink.

Another man approaches- this one with beautiful mahogany skin and perfect white teeth.

"May I get you another drink?" he asks me seductively.

"No, but thank you for the offer," I say with a smile and pick up my second glass. He nods and politely walks away, taking the hint.

"You weren't lying, were you; I have never seen someone come up and offer to get you a drink!" Ang sings out in amazement. I think she is a little disappointed that she isn't getting all of the attention for once.

"Do I look horrible or something, or look like people should feel sorry for me? I mean, I know I'm sweaty and all, but what the hell is wrong with me?"

Ang looks at me surprised. "No, you look stunning; you're glowing, actually."

Great, just as she solidifies the reason why I am getting all of this attention, the hot flashes begin again.

A few more vodka and cranberries later, and too many baby-faced men trying to hit on us, I grab Ang and bolt for the door. I need cold air, ice-cold air. I was melting in there. Plus, I don't know what to do with all of the added attention. Never have I had so many men hit on me in my life, let alone all in the same night! The breeze outside is glorious; I can't get enough. For good measure, I start to pat down my face with a tissue as Etienne suddenly appears at my side from out of nowhere.

"You promised that you would come to me the minute you started to show symptoms!" he hisses low into my ear, his rage palpable.

"What are you talking about? I have no headache or flu-like symptoms; I am fine, thank you for your concern. I am just sweating, that's it; it was really hot in there!" I yell back, pissed off at his audacity. Crap, I should quiet it down.

People, or whatever they are, are starting to look in our direction. A few observe in shock, like they can't believe that I just yelled at him. Yeah, well, I'll yell at him anytime I damn well please if he deserves it.

"It's at the very beginning; this is the start," his words quietly bite back into my ear, anger still simmering below the surface, sending shivers down my spine.

He can be really scary when he wants to be, can't he? Ang sucks in air fast, trying to mask her reaction as she catches, what I'm assuming, is a very scary glimpse of his face. Seeing Ang's face makes me realize that I haven't introduced her yet. I know she is dying to meet him, so I ignore him.

"Oh, Angelique, you haven't met Etienne yet. Etienne, this is my best-friend, Angelique."

He looks up and gives her a friendly, dazzling smile that makes her blush. "It's a pleasure to meet you. Pardon my manners, but would you mind terribly if I borrowed Sasha for a moment?" he asks with such elegance that one would never know he is boiling over, but I do; I can feel it.

"Not at all, just bring her back; she *is* my ride home," she says with a weak smile, not knowing what to make of this man.

Etienne takes me by the elbow and leads me off to the side, just out of earshot. "It's time. You must come with me," he says with such force that I am surprised he doesn't pick me up and throw me over his shoulder to carry me off right here and now.

"No, I will not. There are no headaches or body-aches. I was overheating, and that is that. I have to make it a few more days for my boys' birthday party. I promised them. I WILL be there." I refuse to accept what he is saying.

"Your essence cares not about a party you have to go to or promises you have made. Your scent is so strong that it is like waving a red flag over your head, which is not the best idea considering the company we keep at this time! There are many male vampires who would love to take advantage of a newborn on the brink!" he says, while trying to restrain himself.

Well, that explains all of the baby-faced men. "Ah-ha!" I say, and rudely point my finger in his face. Well, that was brave of me. "I knew it! I knew there were mostly vampires in there. You know something, you are pretty damn bossy, and that doesn't fly well with me, mister; you would get a lot further with me if you minded your Ps and Qs." What the hell just came out of my mouth? I must be drunk. Without his permission or another word, I walk back toward Ang and hand her the keys. "Ang, someone must have slipped me a mickey or something; you need to drive us home now, please." I give her the "rescue-me" look. Etienne shakes his head at me and walks back into the church, muttering something in French to himself.

"What was that about?" she whispers.

"Someone is grumpy because he thinks I'm turning and wants me to go with him now. I told him he's wrong." He has to be wrong. Anyway, I still haven't decided if any of this is real or not.

"You sure that's a good idea? He knows a little more than you do on the subject," she says, as she looks after Etienne, probably contemplating whether or not to run after him and have him haul me away.

"Ang, I have to make it a few more days; the boys' birthday is just around the corner. I am going to be ripped away from them for weeks; I can't miss their 10th birthday! It was just hot in there; why won't everyone give me a break?" I start to yell again.

"Okay, okay; give me the keys, and I'll drive," she says in defeat.

We head back to her house in a fog of senseless chatter. After dropping her off and getting a minute alone, I feel much better. Something about being in a room full of vampires got my essence all excited. Note to self: when attempting to prolong an impending doom, stay away from a shit-load of vampires.

Stephan is still up watching TV when I get home, and the kids are already asleep.

"Hhhmm, don't you look good; you sure you are supposed to go to a funeral looking like that?" he asks out of nowhere with that slow, devilish smile that got me pregnant in the first place.

I can't remember the last time he looked at me like that. *I've missed this side of him,* I think, as a small thrill runs through me. It's been almost a month since the last time we even made love. The tension-filled night, mixed with booze, makes my need to be close to him crank into overdrive. He is all I have ever known when it comes to sex. From what I can tell on movies and the few pornos that I've run across, we've got it down okay. It's not the most exciting love-life- usually pretty quick and to the point, but it has worked this long.

He's very vanilla, not adventurous at all. I have learned over the years that it is no use to try and experiment or "spice things up," shall we say. No matter how many trips to Fascinations or Victoria's Secret I made, he never could leave his comfort zone. My hormones are raging now, something deep within me needs its thirst quenched. Not knowing what to do with all of these strange sensations flowing through my body, I take his hand, pull him off the couch, and lead him upstairs to our bedroom. I need a whole lot of predictable and comfortable right now. A girl with all of this pent-up frustration is just going to have to take what she can get.

Chapter 8

Etienne

It has been days since I last saw Sasha at the funeral; she hasn't called either. *Maybe she began to turn after our last meeting and decided death was a better option.* As soon as the thought passes, my heart, for some strange reason, begins to ache. Nonsense, she is a practical woman; she wouldn't take that road.

"Sir, what time do you want supper to be served?" Molly's voice rings out over the car's intercom.

"Entre chien et loup, s'il vous plait, Molly," I respond.

"Very well, sir; see you at dusk."

Afternoon meetings are not my favorite. It is a good thing that today is an overcast day. The sun is extremely uncomfortable and gives us headaches, among other deficits. Posing as human, and interacting within their world, requires certain sacrifices. The human government has called a meeting, requiring foreign dignitaries with military involvement to attend. As a "member" of the French foreign legion, it would have been rude of me not to show. I am glad all the huffing and puffing is over. I am not a fan of the human world, but it is necessary for me to have a few façades going that allow me to keep tabs on the humans from the inside. Because of this, I can help facilitate a more peaceful existence for both species.

"Boss, Emile called a few times while you were inside; seems there is a situation that needs your personal touch," Erik says from the driver's seat.

Well, well, I guess I get to have a little stress relief after all. I have been in a foul mood ever since my last run-in with Sasha.

"Lâche alors," I order. Erik smiles back with a cruel grin; the boy loves watching me work. Last I spoke to Emile, he was overseeing the transition of a wealthy and very influential vampire's son. It's usually the well-off ones that demand we send a high-up officer of The Guard to handle a newborn's training, along with breaches in the vampire code, should that arise. The affluent vampires do not like to be embarrassed, nor do they care to have their newly-transitioned children attracting unwanted attention. Hence, the calls that lead to one of my top "taxiarchos."

Emile would only call me if something was going wrong. Erik takes the highway just south of downtown Denver and gets off on Belleview, heading into one of Denver's wealthier neighborhoods. Sure enough, Erik pulls into a long driveway that leads to an ostentatious residence. Of course vampires live here. The more in your face and "over the top" it is, the more likely it is a vampire. Some feel that the best way to hide is in plain sight. Erik opens my door, and I step out to assess the situation. The scent of the newly-turned male within the house is strong, along with a few mature vampires- one being Emile. I can feel the different emotions flowing from the individuals present; it's as easy as reaching out and running my hand over the blades of grass present under my feet. Anger and fear are the most prominent. This is a skill-set that has helped me greatly in multiple lines of work. Knowing what individuals are feeling gives me access to the most efficient ways to manipulate them. Erik leads the way to the front door; it's not locked, not that that would matter, and we grant ourselves permission to enter.

A tall, slender man meets us in the entryway. He is well-groomed with black hair slicked back and murky eyes that miss nothing. This must be Robert; he has a reputation in the art world and likes to have his hands in multiple transactions at any one time- all benefiting his bank account, of course.

"Sir, I don't see why it is necessary for you to be here; we really have everything under control. All is quite well." He tries to convince me as well as himself.

I ignore him; I do not have time to hear his nonsense. Emile is in the basement, so I bypass the pretentious weasel and head straight for the door that leads below.

"Sir, please, take the time to hear my plea; he's a good boy, and we will get it under control. Please!" His voice is already too high pitched as it is, but it has now just hit a particularly high note that does nothing to calm my temper.

He is also following too close for my comfort. Looks like he needs a friendly reminder regarding who he is speaking to. I turn, put my face inches above his, and allow my nasty side to creep through.

"Do not follow me, do not speak to me; if you cannot do these two things, I will not waste my time trying to assist in this situation. Instead, your lovely wife will ascend to find you hanging from your overpriced chandelier with one of your solid silver candelabras shoved so far up your ass that no one will be able to remove it for your open-casket viewing!" As my anger rises, I am able to project it upon my intending recipient so they truly feel just how serious I am. Robert turns ghostly white, bows his head, and slumps back to whatever rock he crawled out from under.

Walking into the basement, I find who I am looking for- Emile and his top lieutenant, Antoine. They are circled around a pitiful, blood-soaked newborn; I think Eric said his name is Lane. The blood that he is covered in is most definitely human. Cowering off to the side is a female, and judging by her horrified emotions and internal struggle, she must be the mother.

"Sir, glad you could join us," Antoine says.

"Fill me in, Antoine, and be quick," I demand, reading further into all of the emotions in the room.

"Yes, sir. Lane thought he could bypass his training in bloodlust and decided last night was a good time to visit a sorority house fresh after turning." Antoine remembered that I prefer the quick versions. Good.

"Interesting, Antoine; please remove the mother while Emile and I discuss the truth behind your words with this young gentleman. You may stand guard within the room, along with Erik, if you like." He responds with a sly grin; what is it with these young men and their love of violence? Maybe time has just softened me.

"Now, Lane, please tell me exactly what happened, and, may I remind you, I will know if you deviate from the truth."

This newly-turned boy, who was standing proud upon my entrance, hangs his head and begins to tremble as I walk closer. He keeps looking in the direction that Antoine took his mother, yearning for her protection, but gives up the nearer I come. Nothing will save him now. I stop within a foot of him. He begins to speak and tells me the same story that Antoine did, but includes all of the gory details. What a mess! It takes so much to clean up one of these situations. I nod in understanding, turn, and remove my coat. From inside its breast pocket, I remove a small, black case. Erik appears quickly to take my coat, then, returns to his post.

"When a hard-headed newborn breaches the code like you have done, you put the entire race's safety at risk, and that is something that I cannot have. It would be best just to kill you and get it over with. Instead, you will walk away alive, but just barely. You would be wise to have your mother call your blood partner once we have departed," I impart on this pitiful soul.

Speed is another one of my talents. Now, all vampires move with speed that seems to defy natural limits, but I happen to be ranked with some of the fastest of my species. Within a few beats of his heart, I have him bound at the wrists with my personal supply of cable wire and suspended by the rafters of the basement, hanging like a piñata. I also take the time to gag him because I don't care what he has to say. And so the torture begins.

I prefer slow methods that drag on, igniting more nerve endings along the way. Vampires have more nerve endings than humans, so they tend to feel things on a heightened level. The difference is, most vampires are very hard-headed and have an extreme learning curve- much more so than humans. In many cases, brutality must be met with brutality. I open the small, black case to reveal a few thick, long needles, which are typically used for acupuncture, a few blades of shredded bamboo, and a pair of pliers. Inflicting pain and torture is an art. Knowing exactly the right place to insert your needle for maximum effect is important.

Taking one of the longer needles, I begin to test his pain centers. By the third pressure point, he is already weeping like a baby.

"Please stop," he whines through the gag. I ignore him and choose to leave the current needle I am working with lodged into one of the more excruciating pain centers near the back of his neck.

"It saddens me to think that someone of your affluence would think that you would be immune to the repercussions that come when one does not follow the rules. I thought someone of your breeding would be smarter than that." I know damn well he was not smart enough; many of the affluent think they are above the law. Reaching into his cortex with my gift, I can see that he still feels no remorse for his actions. The flow of his emotions seem excited, as if he is reliving the massacre and enjoying the memories.

"You just won't learn, will you?" I ask out loud, more so to myself. He does have a hint of fear hidden behind all the sinister feelings of pleasure that are coursing through him. I ignite a match under the flicker of fear within his mind, making it burn brighter, until his heart beat picks up speed and his eyes widen in horror. I, then, take one of the bamboo slivers and begin to inflict hundreds of tiny cuts, scattering them around his torso and back. I save the last few for between his fingers and toes. He continues to whimper like a baby as snot and tears distort his face, but he no longer bothers with any other sound. The initial gagged screams didn't do him any good, forcing him to give up on those. His emotional grid is now lit up with fear and dread now, but still, no remorse. It's amazing how a little emotional manipulation, mixed with pure pain, can break down even the strongest of wills.

Time to remove the gag and begin some behavioral modification. He is so weak that I am able to break his will in a matter of minutes. This soft little pastry bag will not last long enough for a full session. I signal Emile for the bag of human blood; it's very efficient for teaching young vamps new behaviors. I tear the top off of the bag, open it, and the smell explodes throughout the room. So inviting for a newly-turned vampire, yet a slippery slope. His fangs begin to elongate as soon as the smell hits him. I, in response, use the pair of pliers and slowly peel back one his toenails. He lets out a bloody scream, signaling that we have reached a new level in our little game. I move the bag closer to his nose, and his fangs just can't behave themselves, which costs him another toenail. I continue using my other gift to reach into his mind and manipulate his emotions. I pull his fear and anticipation forward, while expanding it, causing him to feel more pain than there really is, intensifying his experience. We continue on this path for some time; each time his fangs betray him, I hand out his punishment. His screams and pleas do nothing to sway me; I've heard it all before, and seen it all, as well.

Void now of ten fingernails and ten toenails with an added knife gash that starts from his inner ankle and extends up at a snail's pace to within a hairs-width of his ball sack, I sense that I have finally pushed him to the brink, and remorse finally starts to fill his grid. I take my finger, dip it in the blood, and smear it across his lip. He doesn't take the bait; his fangs stay retracted in place. I reach into his mind and search for any longing or desire for the human blood. I find a twinge left. Taking that little piece and bringing it to the front of his mind, I try to expand it, enhancing his need for the drop of blood sitting within his reach. He pushes back to the point where he douses the need and is consumed by repentance. He still doesn't take the bait; his will has been permanently bent without him knowing it. The merciless beast within is slain, for now. Extreme blood loss, pain, and emotional exhaustion have dictated his acceptance. Good boy.

"Antoine, you may release him." Antoine nods in agreement and pulls the main slip-knot free. The pastry bag lands with a thud in a pool of his own blood and doesn't move.

"Newborn, know that this was a light session; if we shall ever meet again under these circumstances, I won't go so easy on you, and it will end in death."

As Erik and I leave, we do not look at the parents nor do we speak to them. I just want to get to the car. Despite what my crew thinks, I am not a sadist, just one who is willing to do what is necessary. Over the years, my methods have proven to be the most effective, while past methods have always ended in the senseless death of vampires or vampires shedding more human blood- all of it happening unnecessarily.

Curious if I have any missed calls, I reach for my phone after getting settled into the back of my Infiniti. I hope Sasha has called, or Molly, to tell me that Sasha is there. Still nothing. Damn, time is running out for her. Why the hell do I care? If she refuses me, it is her death wish.

Chapter 9

The sound of a gut-splitting scream wakes me up in a panic. I sit straight up and look around before I realize that the scream didn't really happen. Dreams of horrible pain and torture plagued my slumber, causing me to toss and turn all night. What the hell is with the dreams? The clock says it's 6:00 AM, and I am drenched; there is no way I can go back to sleep like this. I might as well start the day now; there is so much that needs to be done. The boys' party is this afternoon, and there is a lot to do before the whole family comes over. I feel so stiff and sore- probably from sleeping wrong; maybe, a hot shower will help. As the water runs over me, I realize how achy I really am. No, not yet! Please! Let me get through the day. I get out, towel off, and head for the medicine cabinet in search of something for my aching joints. If this is really happening, I WILL drug this thing into submission for just a few more hours.

Tons of water later, some Tylenol, and a happy-birthday breakfast for my boys, I feel like I am going to make it. I take advantage of my second wind and continue cooking like I have never cooked before. I have to have everything done in time. Guests start to arrive and the house smells amazing from all of the food preparation, not to mention that the boys are well distracted from my distraught state as they play with Ang's girls while waiting for the rest of the guests to arrive. Ang and Stephan keep looking at me like I have a third eye. Crap. It must be obvious that I am not feeling well. Keep fighting it, Sasha; you can do this.

Stephan tries to give me space, but he keeps popping his head into the kitchen every five minutes. Ang won't leave my side. I don't speak to anyone, and Ang knows I am doing everything I can to hold on and does the speaking for both of us. I trudge forward-continuing to cook and set everything up. At least Ang and Stephan know well enough to allow me to disappear into my zone without any questions or pressure. This is how I cope with stress and illness- by diving into something I enjoy to take my mind off what really is bothering me. Once I go into this funk, it's best just to leave me there until I resurface.

Four o'clock in the afternoon rolls around, and the party begins. I am happy that I made it this far! My body-aches are still there, but they are tolerable. I am so glad I have a high pain tolerance. Everyone is having a wonderful time; the boys devoured the cake, and now they want to do presents. I am even able to manage a few words here and there to our friends and family. The boys get so spoiled this soon after Christmas that we've had to tell the family to pick one- Christmas or their Birthday, to go crazy on and slow down on the other. Ethan and Aiden are chomping at the bit; they want to open presents, so I tell them to go ahead, might as well. As the paper starts to fly, a pounding begins in the base of my skull. It started as a dull ache at cake time, but now, it is throbbing. I guess that I really am not being swept up in some crazy guy's fantasy world where the unexplainable exists; this is really happening. Shit.

I say a little prayer, sneak into the hurricane of paper, and kiss my boys. They smile and continue on the rampage, none the wiser. I nod to Ang, and she heads upstairs to grab my suitcase as I head over to tell my mother-in-law that it's time for Stephan to run me to the airport for a work-related symposium that I couldn't reschedule. We had constructed this fib soon after Stephan learned the truth. We called on Ang to be the standby babysitter since she is in on our secret and wouldn't prod for more details like Mrs. Green might. It was the only story we could think of that would explain a long absence, as well as missing the boys' birthday if that is what it came down to. We thought of saying that I had a family emergency back in California, but Mrs. Green is close with my parents, so that wouldn't work. If it was related to my job somehow, it would be more believable. Occasionally, I have been known to sign up for random stuff in the past, like when I went down south to get my FEMA disaster training just for the hell of it, so the family would believe this.

Stephan is across the room watching me for a signal; I mouth "it's time." He gets up to grab the keys, as Ang emerges from the garage. She has tears in her eyes, which sways me slightly from the stance of resolve I had taken early this morning. Giving her a big hug, I whisper, "I love you, friend; take care of my boys, please, and yourself too." She lets me go, and we are off.

The migraine/ headache, whatever it is, will not let up; it is starting to cause my neck to tense under the pressure. Stephan sees me struggling to get to the passenger door under the weight of the pain, and he doubles back to help me into the car. I can barely see straight at this point. Once the seatbelt is clicked, I hand him a little piece of paper with an address on it, written in perfect cursive.

In no time at all, my husband pulls up in front of the old brick home. The action going on upstairs has me so foggy that my perception of time is blurred. I think it is evening time. Funny, the last time I was here, I couldn't see the front of the house well then either. I try to squint out the window to see if anyone is home. The headache soon puts a quick stop to my efforts, as it is now pounding down on me to the point where I think my head just might pop.

Stephan comes around to my door and opens it to find me in the fetal position on the reclined seat. There is no way I can move; he picks me up and carries me to the door. I don't know if Etienne is even home; I didn't call first, maybe I should have. As we reach the threshold, the door swings open in a hurry. There, before us, is Etienne, filling the entire door frame in all his magnificence.

"She told me I needed to bring her here," Stephan says cautiously, taking a step back at the sight before him. Maybe, I should have prepared him a little better on the whole "Etienne" subject. It's too late now.

"I will do all that I can to make sure she makes it through this in one piece, but you must go now; it is not safe to stay," Etienne eloquently responds.

Stephan pulls me in closer and takes another step back. "Stephan, it's okay. It's going to be okay," I squeak out as my body starts to violently shake. He wearily nods in agreement, kisses my cheek, and hands me over to Etienne. Etienne receives my weight easily, reciprocates Stephan's nod, and quickly closes the door. The minute the door is closed, it is all I can do to keep from screaming out bloody murder as the throbbing in my head turns to scorching pain.

Chapter 10

With eyes clamped shut, I feel us descend as Etienne carries me down a flight of stairs to a cool, damp room. Basement, we must be in the basement. Another wave of searing pain hits as if someone has just laid my entire body on top of a roaring fire-pit and I am being burned alive. I can't hold back this time; I scream like I have never screamed before, causing my face to swell, my temples to throb, and my throat to go raw from the pressure. The pain is ripping me apart from the inside out. "This is normal, my darling; I will get you through it," Etienne whispers as he holds me tighter. The tortuous waves keep coming- pulsating from the base of my skull, down the length of my spine, then branching out, wrapping itself around every inch of my body, blanketing me in pure misery. "Molly, bring fresh water and towels now!" I hear him yell out. Where am I? I try to open my eyes, but can't; the pain is too much. He lays me down on what feels like a soft bed, then he is gone.

Where is Etienne, did he leave me here like this? Oh God, I hope he didn't. Panic starts to rise into my throat. "Shhhh, don't worry, Sasha, I am right here; I am not leaving your side," he says, as I feel his weight settle next to me. He pulls me close to him so my back is to his chest and holds me. The pain is relentless. After the first scream, I gave up on that; it does no good and was a waste of energy. There is no escape. The demon that was once confined within my genetic makeup has broken free with extreme intent to consume me. Etienne begins to wipe me down with cool cloths as I sweat and sweat and sweat. I am crawling out of my skin, there is no end in sight. My hands are pulling at my clothes, trying to rip them away; my nails are digging into my skin, wanting to rip it off too. The rhythmic waves of torture, as well as the searing of a white-hot poker, work in harmony up and down my body, tearing every cell of my physical existence apart. I am stuck in hell; truly, this must be hell.

After what feels like an eternity, a new pain begins-one that feels like someone is breaking my bones without the snap or crunch. It's as if something deep within the marrow is clawing its way out, leaving scattered hairline fractures in the wake of its long talons. Another scream arises from the depths of my soul, so long and hard that it tears my throat apart, while popping all of the blood vessels in my face. I half expect to start spitting up blood as it ceases. This new pain falls into rhythm with the others. What I don't understand is why I am not blacking out. I see patients come in with excruciating pain at the hospital. When the pain level soars to an unprecedented point, the nervous system goes into overload and tries to protect the body and mind; most people black out in response. Instead, my blood pressure just sores; I can hear my heart beat at an unnatural rate, pounding away in my ears. I can still feel everything; this demon has no limits, and it continues to push me beyond the brink. As this new pain continues on, I hear a gentle voice drift in through the madness.

"Sasha, it's time. You need to drink from me. Come, ma chérie," he says, as he rolls me over to lie on his chest. He sits us up a little and positions my head to his neck.

"I need water, I need morphine, I NEED SOMETHING!" I croak out through a throat that feels like I have just attempted to swallow a handful of cotton, still attached to its brittle, thorn-like capsule from which it sprouted. Why am I laying on top of him? That's not very appropriate. Drink from him? What does that even mean? Ugh! This is miserable. I'm too weak to care at this point; I let him reposition me without a fight. As I lie there, I feel him reach up to his neck quickly, and then his arms fall back around me, holding me, as the pain marches on.

Wrapped around him, I find more comfort, as if our bodies were created to fit together- two pieces to a puzzle. My breath falls in line with his as an intoxicating scent begins to call to me, promising to drug my brain into a much-needed fog. Warm liquid trickles down and tickles my nose; Lord Almighty, what is this divine aroma? It smells like heaven. Another trickle drips down his chest and hits my lips. Instinctively, I lick my lips and am instantly rewarded with an explosion of flavor in my mouth; the liquid is like velvet across my tongue. More, I need more. I am so thirsty. The pain still has my eyes pinned shut, so my tongue takes over on its own accord and traces a path upward to the source of the heavenly liquid. It's like nothing that I have ever tasted.

It reminds me of a floral red wine with hints of chocolate, but that doesn't even do it justice.

Slowly, I continue to search for the source. Etienne's body has become stiff and motionless beneath me as I absent-mindedly complete my task. *Oh well, more for me...,* I think, as I reach the source that seems to be coming from his neck. Huh, that's strange, why would it be coming from his neck? Reaching the mother-load, I find my teeth taking charge by biting down, all on their own, to draw out more of the liquid; I need more. Whatever it is, it has begun to calm the beast that has been tearing my body apart from the inside, quenching its thirst. The combination of the liquid's taste and the soothing of the pain, encourages me to sink my teeth in deeper and drink feverishly. I hear a deep groan come from Etienne. His arms tighten around me and shift me over so I am more on his side; his quick movement breaks my concentration for a second. That's when I realize that I am drinking blood from his neck. Instead of being revolted, a strange, primordial thrill runs through me, and I bite again to draw more. Etienne bucks below me, then quickly stills, trying not to disturb me.

I take more of him in; the waves of searing, white-hot pain, as well as the breaking sensation in my bones, begin to slow; it is there, but it is more tolerable. His blood continues to coat my throat and ease the burning lump that has been sitting there. After a few minutes, I find myself unable to continue on as a heavy, weighted sensation has started to pull me down. Withdrawing my teeth from his neck, I slightly crack my lids open as I lick his neck to get the last little trickle, and then watch in amazement as the wounds close on their own. Fascinating. Too tired to question any of it, I fall asleep in his arms; the pain still rages through me, infiltrating every fiber of my being, but somehow, I don't care nearly as much as I did in the beginning. A dreamless sleep quickly claims me.

Chapter 11

Etienne

God, the sound of her screams is threatening to tear my heart from my chest. I have seen so many turn, but it has never bothered me this much. In fact, it has never bothered me at all. This little half-breed has been spinning my world inside-out from the moment Edward introduced us. That sly devil, he knew all along; he knew exactly what he was doing. He purposely arranged the "chance" meeting with Sasha, making sure I came to visit him on a night he knew she was working.

For as long as I can remember, Edward had been insistent that I embrace all that life has to offer, including love. When we were children, he would incessantly nag me to come out of my shell and play in the countryside- to do what most young boys ought to do, explore. As we got older, he came to know the real me, and true to his romantic self, he fell willingly into my world, wanting to learn all there was about my species. He never judged me, instead, the truth made us closer. Edward was always a touch stone, keeping me grounded, handing out reality checks when needed. My world became his- a much needed distraction on his behalf considering the filth and neglect he was born from. He became fixated on all aspects of my culture, especially the phenomenon that a few vampires get to experience- having our essence lead us to our soul-mate. When the two destined vampires meet for the first time and have some form of physical contact, their essences begin to bond to one another. While Edward was certain I would be one of those lucky vampires, I truly believed that it would never happen to me.

I never wanted to feel any of this and had no desire to bond to anyone. I take my work very seriously and have allowed it to consume me. There is no time for this nonsense. This hot-tempered little woman surely doesn't want anything to do with me if she can help it. Yet, here we are- two stars racing across the night's sky, in opposite directions, along a determined path, who find a way to collide. *Half-breed*, I think to myself as I pass cool cloths over her naked body. She is so beautiful, lying here against me in all of her splendor. She ripped the clothes from her body the minute the essence took full charge. All newborns have their unique ways of coping with the pain; hers is so raw- less refined, less controlled than others. Most whimper in the fetal position until it stops. She allows it to take over, then immerses herself in the throes of it, giving it all access. She is glorious.

Her pulse is starting to speed up, and her blood is starting to smell ripe. It's time; the transformation portion has started. She heaves her chest and screams to the point that images of my own turning flash before me, and her pain becomes my own for a moment in time. It is so loud, so long, that it breaks my heart in two. I wish I could take the pain away from her. All I can do is calm it by feeding the essence as it spreads and renovates her; it needs male vampire blood. "Sasha, it's time. You need to drink from me. Come, ma chérie." I gingerly take her naked body and reposition it over my chest so she can easily feed. It is all I can do to control myself. Sex is an easy way to distract one from the pain of turning. Many use it as it can be some of the most animalistic and carnal sex that one can have. It is hard not to give in to its calling. This is exactly why I was so pissed off at

Edward's funeral. Those vultures were circling her like she was fresh meat, ready for the picking. Male vampires are true to their nature, especially when it comes to sex. The last thing she needed was someone taking advantage of her. Plus, the thought of anyone else being with her on that level makes me want to rip their throats out.

"I need water, I need morphine, I NEED SOMETHING!" She forces out. *Morphine won't help you now, and water will make you vomit,* I think to myself. She is so clueless about this whole situation, or in denial; it's one of the two. If she doesn't feed soon, it will be too late. She needs to have blood hit her system now to calm the essence, or it will kill her instead of transform her. She needs a little push. I reach up with the knife I always carry and slice an inch-long incision along the base of my neck. The blood begins to flow forward, and a drop hits her lips. She instantly responds and turns her mouth to the trail of blood. That's it; drink, my love. Did I just call her "my love?" I know what our essence wants, and it will come to a point where I can't deny it; for now, I must remember that she is not mine.

I feel her warm, wet tongue start to trace the contours of my body, following the trail of blood I left.

Oh God, she feels so good. I start to get hard; no-no-no, hold still Etienne, don't give in to it. Calling on self-control, I focus my breathing and try to block out the sensation of her body moving against mine. As she stops at my neck and hungrily sinks her teeth in, I feel my dick give a full-on salute; she feels so fucking good. *No, we can't go there*. I quickly move her over so she can't feel my body betray me. She stops sucking for a second, then bites down even harder. My body responds instantly. Damn. I want to flip her over onto her back and fuck her. She, in an instant, has stripped me of all of my composure. But, I can't; I refuse to put her into a situation where she is morally conflicted to the point of causing herself more pain. I can't bear the thought of her hurting, let alone being the cause of that pain. Her soft tongue gently licks the wound closed; it is funny how the instincts will take over like that. She collapses on top of my bare chest. Thank heaven that she only shredded my shirt, or we would be in real trouble. Her breathing has fallen into rhythm with mine, and finally, she is asleep. Almost there, my love; you are almost complete.

Soon, she will be able to eat, and then we will move on to training. Some consider my newly-turned vampire training a bit risqué, unorthodox, and possibly bordering on inappropriate, even for vampires. Those naysayers can't argue with results, now, can they? There is a reason my father named me *"Strategos"* or "Major General," by more modern standards. Enforcing the vampire code and security throughout the United States is no easy task. Our race is small in numbers compared to humans, but our primitive drive, and occasional brutal tendencies, pose a threat to endangering our race, as well as humans. All are simple facts that have driven my ruthless methods of enforcement over the years. My name is well-known, and feared, for a reason. What would she think of me if she knew all the cruel, bordering-evil things I have done over my lifetime? Sure, it was all justified, and I could never tell her every detail, but would she judge me for it? Could I bear to be condemned by her? While pondering past deeds and the possibility of absolution in bonding to this little creature, sleep draws me into another realm- one free of dark, lurking shadows.

I awake in a panic, I am so unused to peaceful sleep. Past dark deeds frequently plague my slumber; images of warranted disciplinary actions dominate my dreams. Lying beside her has brought calmness to my being; for the first time in decades, my sleep was not restless.

What time is it? The clock tells me evening has come again. It's been two days already. She should be finished by now. I am starting to worry. She is still alive, very much so, but her transition is not complete. She remains deep in and does not open her eyes. When one is this deep in, you are aware of what's going on around you, but are still trapped in a dream-like state. It is kind of like being stuck in-between hell and the real world. Shit, I better call Erik to do some digging in the archives. Worse-case scenario, he can call over to the European headquarters to get more information. "Erik, she is still transitioning; it has been too long, find me some information," I sternly say into my phone.

"Alright, give me ten," he replies. If anyone needs information, Erik is the one to get it. He has been my most trusted right-hand man for years.

Why won't she wake up? She still shivers, sweats, and moves with the pulsations. She has been lying on her side, facing away from me, and her restlessness has been working her all over the bed throughout the day. Judging by the bumps on her skin, she is done sweating and is now cycling into freezing, so I pull her close to keep her warm. My body heat doesn't seem to be enough to ease the chattering of her teeth. The moment I break our skin-to-skin contact to grab a blanket, she lets out another piercing scream.

"No-no-no, no more. Please, no more," she cries out as she begins to weep.

"Shhhh, my love, I am here," I whisper, and pull her close again. Feeling helpless is NOT a feeling I am used to. Usually, I am the one in control- calling the shots, inflicting the torture. This little being has me feeling so many things that I am not accustomed to. Where the hell is Erik? Maybe I should feed her more. If I do, then I will need to feed sooner than I normally require…. hhmmm. Oh well, it's worth a shot. I bring my wrist up to my mouth and pierce the skin with sharp teeth. Positioning my wrist over her lips, she instantly latches on with a death grip and begins to take long pulls of me into her. Oh shit, not again. My body responds to her instantly, overriding my will, so I grab a pillow and put it between us. Her bare ass rubbing against my sweats does not make this easy. *I would love to bite into* *that ass... oh, how I would love that...*I think as my hand reaches out to stroke the curvature. The thought has my fangs elongating. No, that is not happening. I pull my hand back as my phone starts to buzz.

"Oui?" I answer.

"I found some interesting things that you might want to hear..." She loosens her grip on my wrist and begins to scream again.

"ON WITH IT, ERIK!" I yell, out of impatience and fear.

"Easy boss, she will be fine. She probably will take another day or so, based on what I found. The archives say that vampires who take this long to turn usually do so because there is a good chance that they will have some extra abilities, shall we say... when they are done. The longest transition noted for a gifted vampire is four days, and a shit-load of blood; it looks like you are going to need it too. Would you like me to call Cosette?" he asks.

"Absolutely not. I need you to have Molly make me a tray of food; Gabriel, or yourself, will need to bring it down. No one else is allowed down here, and no one must know at this time, not even Sasha herself.

Comprenez-vous?" I say, as anger and apprehension line my words.

"Alright, I thought that's what you would say. I hope you change your mind about feeding though, no need to kill yourself. I'll be down as soon as the tray is done." Click.

Shit, what have I gotten myself into? A gifted? I have never heard of a half-breed turning into a gifted- most die just from turning! Son-of-a-bitch. Well, that explains a lot about why it's taking so long. Good to know that she is not dying- just turning into something that will make my life a whole lot more complicated than it has already become.

What more does she have planned for me? I think angrily. She has already wreaked havoc in my life and proved to be more of a distraction than I would ever want. Staring up at the ceiling, I find my thoughts drifting to what life *was* like, what it *is* like, and what it *could* be.

Knock-knock-knock. I quickly pull the comforter over Sasha; she is still latched onto my wrist and distracted, so hopefully, she won't shred it in the short time that it will take for the food to be brought in.

"Erik?" I call out just to make sure; my senses haven't been as sharp as they normally are the last day or so.

"Yes." Good, better him than Gabriel.

"Entrer," I answer. Erik walks cautiously into the room, eyes to the floor. Good man. He knows that if he even looks at her, I will lose my temper.

"Put it on the night-stand over there," I bark.

Erik quickly completes the task and turns to face the wall. "Anything else?" he asks carefully.

Please have Molly place some fresh clothes for her just outside the door, and Erik?"

"Yes?"

"Thank you."

I hear his breath catch like I have surprised him; do I really come off that crass all of the time?

"You're welcome, boss; you know how to reach me should you need anything else."

Sasha starts to tense up, bracing herself for another round. Judging by the clothes, robe, and numerous towels she's destroyed the minute they touch her skin, the blanket won't last long. "Quickly, Erik." He nods and promptly leaves. As the door clicks, she begins to claw at the blanket. I better move it before it's destroyed; I happen to like this comforter. I free my wrist, lick the wound closed, and reposition us so I can sit up and eat. It seems that, as long as she has some physical contact with me, her screams are not as bad. Whatever it takes. In the throes of everything, I haven't realized how hungry I am. My mouth waters at the sight of the amount of food that Molly was able to pack onto the tray: roasted lamb, grilled chicken, shrimp, wild rice, grilled vegetables, and there is even a cheese platter. Molly has always been so good at anticipating my needs. Sasha has drained me pretty low; keeping myself sated for this event was far from my mind. I need her to make it through this; I cannot stand the thought of this lovely creature dying because I couldn't provide everything she needed to survive. I feel so protective over her; it must be the bonding that has started. It seems to be making the rules now. I can't imagine how I would feel if we actually completed the bonding; my manhood kicks out at the thought. Fuck me, that is all this situation needs. She doesn't belong to me; I should be okay with that as it is out of my control, but my need to have her in every way possible grows at an uncomfortable speed.

Chapter 12

Weeks, it has probably been weeks of this hell, I think as the pain begins to retreat from my limbs. Despite the dissipating agony, my head still aches something fierce with the innermost workings of my cerebral cortex being in the driver seat this entire time, dictating my transformation. It brings a whole new meaning to, "it's all in your head"; this is some craziness that even I could never dream up. Etienne's body heat is radiating from behind me, bringing remembrance of his constant presence. It is his selflessness that allowed me to live through that tortuous hell. Overcome by emotion, I realize that everything seems to be sharper: my emotions, memory, and sense of smell. They feel so much more powerful. That is not all that feels sharper; it is also as if I can feel the individual threads woven into the sheets below me. I can tell my pillow is made of feathers and almost feel their softness with my cheek through the cover. My entire body feels more alive, like it has been sleeping all of these years and finally decided to arise from a deep and solemn slumber. I want to move, to test the limits of my new body. Fear has me pinned in place. If I move, will the pain come thundering back? That is not something worth living through a second time. So, I wiggle my toes slightly to test the theory. Satin brushes back against them, and the pain continues its slow ascent back up my spine; fortunately, it doesn't come crashing back down. I flex my fingers-still no response from the demon. I wonder if I can open my eyes. I know that I don't have my glasses with me, but maybe, I can make out a blob or two. Opening them just a crack, I can see the room is lit by candlelight. The pain does not get worse, so I open them all the way to find that the room is lined with hundreds of candles. Even from the bed, I can see each one's individual flame, wick, and the beads of liquid wax dripping down the side. Wow! I can see without glasses!

Amazed, I start looking about the room, absorbing every detail: from the wood grain of the heavy-set canopy bed that we are laying in, to the threads of the curtains that drape in four thick pillars around the bed. We are in a large bedroom, but this one is different than the one I was in the last time that I was here. This room's furniture is all made of heavy wood, inlaid with intricate patterns. Judging by the designs, it looks Italian. The walls are creamy, brushed suede and are framed with strategically placed, delicate, cherry-wood molding boxes, extending vertically within a few inches of the floor and ceiling. Ornate, thick, white-molding trims the tops of the walls and leads the eye up to a tray ceiling lined with more decorative box-molding done in the same dark, cherry-stained wood as the walls. The bed is situated with the head touching the back wall and the foot facing the door. Just to the right of the door is a large, built-in, floor-to-ceiling bookshelf constructed from the same wood as the cherry wall-trim. A plethora of books line the shelves, most look ancient, and they are beautiful. I wonder if I can sit up; I really want to explore that bookshelf.

As I start to prop myself up on an elbow, I hear him say with a yawn, "I see you are awake."

I turn to face him, and his vivid blue eyes pierce into my soul the minute they catch my gaze. Their color is hard to explain; they are a vibrant blue with hints of green, making them almost electric. Instead of getting fidgety under the pressure as I usually do, I am overcome with emotion, need, and gratitude.

"Thaaannk you, Etienne," I surprisingly stutter out. Get it together, Sasha. It's still the same guy who pisses you off on the frequent.

"For?" he asks with a grin, probing my emotions; lucky bastard, I can't hide anything from him, can I?

For? For so much! It is because of him that I did not die and leave my children motherless. He stayed by my side and gave of himself whenever it was required; he never asked for anything in return. Turning my eyes to his once again, I say with more emotion than I ever thought possible for me,   "for everything."

I hear his breath draw in quickly as the depth behind my words hits him hard. "Sasha, I would do it all over again for you," he says- his face soft, eyes alight, watching me intently.

I want to caress his face and to run my fingers through his dark brown hair. Seeing how very shirtless he is with his perfect... eight-pack, no, that's at least a ten-pack staring back, makes me acutely aware that I am very naked. *Crap, how did that happen,* I think as look down at my body. No! Did we?

"No, we did not; I would never take advantage of you like that. You couldn't stand the touch of anything on your skin, well, with the exception of my skin...; if you look on the ground, you will see the damage." Peering over the side of the bed, I see a pile of tattered fabric that is beyond repair.

"Oh." Perhaps, I should cover up; this is kind of awkward all of a sudden. We were skin-to-skin?

"Having constant physical contact seemed to calm your discomfort. Would you like to shower before dressing?" he asks, reading into my unease.

"That sounds like a wonderful idea." Really, I just need space to filter through my memories and measure them up against what he is saying.

"The bathroom is just through that door." He points to a door off to our left.

Since we are waayyyy past modesty at this point, I don't bother with covering myself to get up. I was mostly aware of what was going on around me while I was turning; I just didn't give it much thought at the time. I believe him when he says that nothing happened; a hazy memory of a pillow being put between us proves that.

One long grooming session later and a big comfy robe, I feel more human, vampire... whatever. I emerge from the steamy bathroom to find him sitting on the bed with two trays of food.

"Hungry?"

YES! "Famished," I say, bounding excitedly over to join him at the edge of the bed with as much enthusiasm and "pep" in my step as a high school cheerleader. Well, that was out of character for me; I guess it's the "emotions being all over the place" thing. I feel like I am bursting from the seams as I am in sensory overload from all of the overwhelming emotions, sights and smells coursing through me all at once.

We sit and eat in silence- funny how we do that a lot. We're okay with having long periods of comfortable silence, not needing to fill the space between us with useless jabber; yet, we can read each other well. It's like we speak to each other without needing words at all. We finish our meal fast, both probably needing double the amount we just ate. Why does he look paler than normal? His normally bright blue eyes seem to be veiled in a bit of grey now, like storm clouds starting to collect over a bay.

"Are you all right?" I ask, suddenly worried.

"I am fine," he replies in a clipped tone. He quickly changes the subject. "Tomorrow, we will need to begin training your bloodlust; we are behind schedule, and I promised Stephan that I would have you back within two weeks."

He talked to Stephan? I don't remember that; how long was I out? "How long was I in transition?" I ask, confused. He looks at me sideways, hesitant to answer. "Tell me!"

"Five days."

What the hell? "That's not possible; you said it would only be two days? What happened? What went wrong?" I say, panicked, my hand rising up around my throat as I swallow.

"Sometimes, it takes a little longer; you were an exception to the rule, and you drank from me all you needed to survive. Now, here we are."

He's exhausted, no wonder he looks like shit. Wait, if I drank from him for the last five days…

"How often do y… I mean, do vampires need to feed?" I tread lightly, sensing his patience is low.

"One to two times a week under normal circumstances," he says, trying to read where I am going with this.

"I drained you, didn't I?"

I hear him cuss under his breath. *Well, mister perfect isn't so perfect now, is he?* I think with a smile. "Not entirely, but close enough." He quickly looks away from my probing eyes.

He needs blood, doesn't he? Should I offer? He probably already has a source for that. Shit. He probably already has someone who feeds him! The thought of another woman feeding him makes me so angry that I want to take the beautiful tray of fine dishware, chuck it at the wall, and use the shards to rip her throat out. Where the hell did that come from? It's not like me to think like this! Rationality is far from my reach with the mere idea of any woman, even Molly, coming that close to him.

The primitive possessiveness I suddenly feel for him takes over and consumes me instantly as I focus my anger, like a ray gun, on that damn dinner platter. He is NOT allowed to feed from anyone else, EVER! Suddenly, there is a pop sound as the plate cracks open down the middle. Etienne and I gasp in unison.

"Je n'en reviens pas!" Etienne says in surprise.

I have nothing to say; I am pretty sure that I just made that up in my head.

"I must have hit it by accident," I insist.

"No, ma chérie, I am quite confident that you didn't."

"That's not possible; there's no such thing as laser beams shooting from my forehead."

"True, to some extent, but, aren't we past questioning the impossible?"

Maybe, but this one is going on the shelf for now.

"What made you so angry?" he asks, distracting me.

Should I tell him the truth? What the hell, we are way past formalities, and truth needs to stay a constant for us. "The thought of someone else feeding you," I say meekly. He starts to shuffle uncomfortably next to me, reading into where I was going.

"Well, I can't ask that of you; I do not want to put you in an uncomfortable position that compromises your morals; I won't hurt you like that," he says with finality, more so to himself than to me.

I crawl back into the depths of the huge bed, lean back on the oversized, down pillows, and chew on that one for a long while.

I see what he means, and I seem to remember some sexual tension stemming from him, especially when I first fed from him. Damn it, can any of this be a little easy? Is all feeding sexual? Is he sexual with whomever it is that he feeds from? The thought triggers my anger fast, from 0-60, and I can't control it. The tray that once held my food and was innocently sitting at the foot of the bed goes flying across the room, smashing into the bedroom door so hard that it sounds like a gun going off. Instantly, there is a panicked knock at the door.

"Sir, is everything okay?" A male voice sounds out cautiously.

"Yes, Erik, all is well," Etienne says with a stern, dismissive tone. "Sasha, you really must get that little temper under control; I would like you to refrain from destroying my bedroom," he says forcefully, but ends up grinning again.

"It was an accident; I must have kicked it," I say, still trying to keep it on the shelf I put it on. I mentally add a steel vault door in front of it, for good measure.

"I take it that you really don't like the idea of me feeding from anyone else?" He unexpectedly purrs out; oh my, that purr douses my anger fast.

I forgot that I was dealing with an expert manipulator. "Not particularly, no." I say abruptly, trying to shake the effects of his voice out of my head.

"What are we going to do, then?" he whispers, his grin gone, and the ashen grey taking possession over his face again.

"Feed from me; you have been so selfless with me and put your life on hold to help a stranger. This is the least I can do." He starts to shake his head no. "I mean it, Etienne, feed from me!" The thought of him telling me no has my anger starting to simmer again; he senses it coming.

"Sasha, are you sure?" he asks, trying to placate me.

"Yes, I have never been more sure." And that was the truth.

Etienne shuffles back on the bed and lies next to me, grumbling to himself the whole way. He stretches out with a defeated sigh, which is strange for this normally very composed and in-control man.

"Why don't we rest and think about it?" He closes his eyes in defeat.

Ancient instinct drives me, for I can feel his need, and I am powerless to refuse. My long nails seemed to be effective in destroying clothes with their squared-off tips now deceptively sharp. Using my thumb nail, I push into my skin two inches above my collar bone and draw a small line. *That wasn't too bad*, I think to myself as the blood starts to bead up.

"Sasha, no," he says with his eyes still closed, but I swear his canine teeth lengthened slightly through his parted lips. That is all I need. In one move, faster than I thought possible, I position myself so that I am straddling him. Bending forward from the waist, the open wound is now inches from his mouth; he doesn't give in. So I hold my ground, slice it open wider, and let the blood drip onto his lips. Swiftly, I find myself on my back and smothered by a mountain of a man.

"Stubborn aren't you?" he rumbles. I smile back at the sight of him; I can't help it. His canine teeth have lengthened into full fangs, and his gaze is now dark with an all-consuming, thundering storm. His expression is like a force field, drawing me in, without question. In a slower movement, he dips his head, brushes his lips against my neck, and whispers, "I'll be gentle," and he is.

I barely feel his teeth slip beneath the surface of my skin. It is when he tightly seals his mouth onto my flesh that I start to re-think the whole idea, but it is too late. A deep growl bellows out from his chest as he begins to drink, and he is lost in the moment. As if on cue, sexual desire blooms all around us moments later, suffocating us in its intoxicating scent. I feel his length harden along my stomach while at the same time, my entire body becomes flushed with desire. This perfectly-sculpted specimen really wants me, here and now, and doesn't that thought just send me teetering on moral ground. His natural scent is like a homing beacon drawing me in. I find my hands running through his hair, pushing his mouth deeper into my neck. His growl becomes a sensuous groan that has my nipples hardening in response and has me panting hard.

From the place where his mouth meets my skin, I can feel that same white-hot light stemming from him, reaching for me; it's like when we first met back at the hospital. Time slows just like before, and my mind becomes clouded by the thickness of his aroma. The white light dances around the surface of my skin before slamming into me like I am home. There is no pain, there is no fear. The light moves around inside of me, looking for something. Soon, I feel it heading for my heart; *no,* I think to myself. For whatever reason, the thought of it reaching my heart means more than I can comprehend at this time.

"No more, Etienne, no more. Etienne, PLEASE STOP," I yell.

He quickly withdraws his fangs, licks the wound closed, and looks at me with a drunken expression. "Did I hurt you?" he asks through hooded eyes.

"No, it's just... it happened again... I didn't know what to make of it." Cop out, I have an idea on what to make of it, but he is drunk on my blood, and his brain isn't processing very fast.

"What happened again?" he asks with a pause, waiting for his mind to catch up with the news flash. "I zapped you? I'm sorry, I didn't mean to. I didn't realize, I am so sorry, did I hurt you?" he questions me worriedly, sobering fast as the light bulb goes off.

"No, Etienne, you didn't hurt me; it just... surprised me." I have to be as truthful as I can; I have a feeling that he can tell the difference. "Did you feel it at all?"

He looks sheepishly away from me with a little mask of guilt. "I, uh, I was lost in, uh, other... feelings that were taking place, I didn't notice." He just blushed!

Mister in-control just blushed. I'll be damned. I just may be damned, considering where I was contemplating letting things go. He licks his lips and looks at me with blue eyes that seem to glow again.

"Thank you; that was... the best I have ever had." Now it is my turn to blush. The best he's ever had in his 110 years? He has no reason to lie about that or say anything at all about it in the first place. He's far from delicate and usually straight to the point, rarely caring about sparing anyone their feelings.

"I feel much better; I was not aware of how bad I was in need." On that note, he rolls off of me and lies by my side.

"Etienne, what *IS* that?"

"What do you mean?"

"You know what I mean- the light-zapping thing." He ignores me. "Etienne!" With another heavy sigh, he finally answers.

"It's part of our 'destined to be together' issue. Our essence, or the light that you sense, is trying to complete the bond to one another."

Oh! I knew I panicked for a reason when it headed for the void in the center of my chest. "How does it complete the bond?"

"Aren't you the least bit tired?"

"I take it you don't appreciate my inquisitive nature."

He sighs again and finds a good spot under the covers. "Sex usually finishes the bonding, but bonding on this level is rare and not widely known about; it could happen in other ways, but I am not certain."

Well, great, one more reason to learn some self-control; that is the last thing we need to happen.

"Tomorrow, the real work begins; we need to work on your… control," he says as he pulls the covers over us. I ignore his implications.

"Bloodlust, got it," I say, not appreciating his quick shift of moods- from pleasure straight back to business.

"Not just bloodlust, your temper needs work as well. That is not something you can explain easily to a room full of humans, or vampires, for that matter," he says as if he is still trying to process my "temper problem," as he puts it.

"I have no idea what you are talking about; my temper is just fine. But, if I feel angry, I will try not to kick things across the room; a girl just doesn't know her own strength sometimes," I snap.

"Oui, whatever you say, my dear."

With that, we have a good laugh together, lying side-by-side, then sleep claims us.

Chapter 13

"Awake, my dearest Sasha; we must begin." I hear him calling to me through veils of heavy sleep, followed by the brush of tender fingertips across my cheek.

"Coffee." I grumpily demand through hazy eyes.

"Alright, followed by a full breakfast," he laughs.

"What time is it?"

"Six in the evening."

"Wow, we slept a long time."

"Repair we both desperately needed for clear thinking. Come, let us eat. We also have a few friends joining us. We will be requiring their assistance this evening."

Friends? Is it bad that my first thought is *he has friends?* A smarter person would ponder the need for friends to assist in my training.

"Coffee…" I demand again, as I start to get up and head to the bedroom door; who can think clearly at this hour without it?

"May I request that you dress first?"

I look down and realize that my razor-sharp nails left their lasting imprint on my clothes again. "What the hell?" I say out loud.

"I am guessing that you overheat easy. Now, *that* I can say for sure is a *normal* behavior." His words dance with amusement.

"Well, since you're the expert and all." I shrug off the tattered remnants of clothes and walk over to the dresser. Molly apparently stocked a drawer or two for me at *his* request; she also unpacked my suitcase.

"May I suggest something best suited for the gym?" He calls from behind me, probably enjoying the view. I'm glad that I don't have much modesty or this would be awkward.

"Good idea, you did say training. Although, I don't really know what that entails…" I trail off, as I start to dig through the drawer.

"Well, to be honest, we will be... how you Americans say, winging it." I stop what I am doing and turn around to face him, nakedness and all.

"WHAT?" I thought he knew what he was doing!

"Hence the early introduction of my friends; they are the best at what they do. Your long transition and ability to 'kick things' without touching them is something that is new to me."

I start to feel panicked; I thought he knew how to help me with all aspects of this. "So, what you're saying is that I am no longer a human freak, but now a vampire freak, and you don't know how to handle me?!" I yell out a bit too harshly. He might just be right about me needing to learn some control now that I am flying off the handle so easily. I feel as if I have little control over my emotions, when I feel something, it is to the extreme. As soon as the last word leaves my lips, he moves from across the room where he was lounging on the bed to tower over me. His eyes have darkened, and his mouth is drawn tight in an expression that makes the little hairs on the back of my neck stand up.

"I know *exactly* how to *handle* you; do NOT ever question what I can and cannot handle! It is more of a matter on teaching you the most effective way to control yourself, which I can also *handle,*" he says through clenched teeth, and I am the one with the temper!

"Yes, sir!" I say, just to spite him.

The audacity of my smart mouth has the darkness clearing from his eyes, and they are once again their striking blue. I know I have always been a little full of piss and vinegar, but I am on a new level now. I probably need to watch it around him, though he doesn't scare me as much as he should.

"Excuse me, I will see you upstairs when you are ready," he says with clipped words, before taking off upstairs. Well then, I seem to make a certain someone a bit uncomfortable. Does he really think he can intimidate me so easily? If I step back and look in from the outside, I can see how he would come off as scary, but I have seen his softer, more vulnerable side, so that is now all I really can see. The mask of contempt and snarled lip are just a façade.

After throwing on some workout clothes, I head upstairs. On the way up, I am hit with so many strong smells- food being the main one. Hmmmm... I can smell salmon smothered in lemon juice, garlic, and butter. I never knew it was possible to take in this many strong scents at once. Now, I know how dogs feel. It is all too much for one nose; I can even smell the subtle gas from the stove and the dirt left under a pair of shoes by the door, mixed in with everything else. There are so many aromas coming at me that it is hard to focus. A specific scent stops me at the top stair with my hand on the door leading out of the basement. It is musk, but not Etienne's.

I can smell other men in the room. Their scents vary- from earthen mixed with sandalwood, to someone who smells like a smoky campfire, to another whose scent is like crisp-clean lemons that have been sitting in the sun. Three, there are three others. Where is Etienne? I inhale again and find a delicate scent of aged vanilla and cinnamon, Molly; I recognize it from when she came down to leave more linen by the door for us. Reaching out, I try harder to locate Etienne; I cannot go out there without him here, I am already embarrassed being "unveiled" like this to a group of strangers. Aw, there he is. He is in his study, and I can make out his voice talking low as if he is on the phone. "Meet us as the facility," click. "Sasha, please don't be shy, join us." Shit, how does he do that? Then again, how was I able to tell that he was in his study?

Opening the door all the way, I walk forward like a kid caught with her hand in the cookie jar. In the entry, there are three men lounging about- their attention acutely narrowed in on me. I feel my cheeks get hot; there must be a horn in the middle of my forehead, that's why they stare. The shortest one of the three walks forward to greet me; he is the one with the dampen earth smell.

"It is a pleasure to meet you; my name is Antoine." He bows with a friendly smile.

"It's a pleasure to meet you, Antoine; I'm Sasha," I gladly say. What a pleasant ice breaker. He is thick, but lean, and has a baby face with a mop of wavy black hair dancing in all directions. His eyes are brown and quite jovial. Etienne has joined us and is now standing in the doorway of his study watching with scrutiny in his eyes.

Antoine doesn't seem to notice and offers me his arm. "Shall we eat?" I can't help but smile back. I take his arm and let him lead me to the dining room, purposely ignoring Etienne who is now turning a bit red in the cheeks. I guess his plan to scold me like a child in front of everyone isn't going to work. The other two men grin at Etienne's response and silently turn to follow. I look around for Molly on our way in but don't see her. The table is set in medieval-feast fashion with the exception of a giant roasted pig flopped in the middle. There is so much food placed on the table that there is barely room for the dinnerware. I sit down in the same chair off to the right of the head seat as I did the last time I was here, assuming it is okay. The others file in and take a seat, leaving the head for Etienne, who of course takes his time. We sit there waiting for the "master," and I take a moment to try to take it all in. Where is the salmon that I could smell wafting down the staircase? Ah-ha! I watch it sitting right by the head of the table like it could wiggle away at any moment.

Etienne finally walks in and sits. "Sasha, allow me to *formally* introduce you to my comrades," he says, glaring at Antoine. Etienne then nods to the man sitting to his immediate left. "This is Erik, my personal assistant." He is the one that smells like crisp lemons. He is very well kept, not a blonde hair out of place. He seems cordial but restrained at the moment. "To Erik's left is Emile." Emile is the one that smells like a smoky campfire; it's oddly comforting. He is almost as tall as Etienne, with a lean, muscular build, short brown hair that is longer in the front, and a neat mustache that suites him perfectly. His presence is calm and relaxed, as if not much ever really bothers him; I am glad that he is here, we need a calm balance. "And, it seems you already have met Antoine," he says curtly. I ignore him, what is his deal anyway?

"It's nice to meet all of you; I was not aware that Etienne had such a lovely group of friends," I say, with a dramatic tone that suggests that I am surprised he even has friends, just to get under his skin. The others chuckle, and Erik seems to thaw under my humor- a little warmth finally touches his sky-blue eyes. Etienne ignores everyone, including me, and digs into the feast, and we all follow suit. Just as I go for the salmon, Etienne moves the platter.

"Oh, excuse me; would you like some, Sasha?" He asks tauntingly. Frustrating man!

"Oh yes, sir; may I please have some?" I say with a mocking tone.

"Only if you promise not to break my fine china, please."

Asshole! "I shall be ever so careful, SIR, but if it should slip and fall over your head, I do apologize in advance," I say with a condescending tone.

Erik shoots me a grin, and Emile laughs a deep, belly-shaking laugh. "Etienne, she is delightful and fiery- looks like this evening will be quite entertaining." Emile smirks.

"Yes, fiery would be a word for it," Etienne says dryly. Etienne remains quiet and very professional throughout the remainder of the meal, but keeps the salmon for himself. Bastard.

∞

Apparently, I am not to be trusted around his finer things at the house, so they take me to a warehouse off the I-70. The warehouse looks unassuming from the outside, but as we walk in, it is obvious that appearances are not always what they seem. The place is huge and very fortified- so much cement and steel that you would think they were getting ready to test rocket launchers inside. There is an abnormally-large boxing ring off to the side- way bigger than any I have ever seen at the boxing gyms that I have been to. In the middle is a round, sunken arena about six-feet deep into the ground- no stairs, no way to get down there. The rest is lined with typical gym equipment, including treadmills and a very expensive-looking weight set. There is even a long, adult-size monkey bar set up at the back; do these guys do crossfit for fun? That would be unfair to humans.

"Sasha, we thought it would be best to have you spar with Gabriel to begin with." He speaks!

Gabriel is the guy who opened the warehouse door and smelled of a dampened redwood forest. He is a few inches taller than Etienne, which means he is probably, oh I don't know, at least seven feet tall. He also is built like "The Rock," and kind of looks like a Moorish version of him with his long ponytail and dark skin. He is quite nice to look at.

"Spar?" I ask, with my eyebrows hitting the ceiling. This guy stands at least a foot and a half over me; a tank couldn't knock him over.

"Yes, as a newly-turned vampire, you must be tested to see the limits of all of your capabilities- speed, strength, hearing, sight, smell, mind-manipulation, and.... let's not forget about that little temper of yours." For the love of all that's holy! "Dear Sasha, do not be afraid, as we are in the company of friends; I trust these males with my life." Great, call me out in front of all the testosterone, Etienne! Why must he vocalize what I am feeling to everyone?

"All vampires have increased abilities for speed, strength, hearing, sight, smell, and the manipulation of some things with their minds; we all just vary on the level of our abilities. In order to teach you enough control to walk among humans safely, we need to know your limits." Etienne's voice echoes off the cement fortress haughtily as he dramatically paces by the opening of the arena, showing off.

What crawled up his ass? This is not the same man who held me earlier. I am sick of his pontifications; who does he think he is- master of the universe? "Wow,

Etienne, I didn't know you were capable of such long sentences. Well, let's get to work. What ability would you like to test first?" I sass back. Wrong move, Sasha; he is once again in my face with rage emanating from him to the point where it is palpable. Maybe I shouldn't have said what I did. He really can't take a joke and does not like to be humiliated, apparently; well, that makes two of us.

Through clenched teeth, he says, "Well, my dear, why don't we start with mind-manipulation since you are so anxious to get started."

I rise up on the tips of my toes, kick up my chin, and challenge him with a, "BRING IT." I AM feeling feisty.

His eyes darken wickedly in anticipation; a match of wills just sweetened the deal for him.

He puts his hands on my shoulders and lowers me back to the ground. "While most vampires can only manipulate the minds of humans, I have the added unique ability of manipulating the emotions of vampires. You are aware that I cannot read minds, but I can sense emotions as easily as picking them up and touching them. Knowing is more than half the battle, but intensifying what is already there is half the fun," he says with a beautifully cruel grin. Great. Why did I have to wave a red flag around the bull? He reaches forward and caresses my face with more tenderness than he has shown me all night. The touch of his skin sends a distracting wave of heat through me, no doubt a calculated move on his end. Looking into my eyes, I feel him probing, as if he is the very white-light that likes to zap me, moving around my head, looking for something. He is looking for something that he can manipulate, some emotion that, if he intensifies it, can have me crying like a baby in front of everyone. He would like that, wouldn't he- to mortify me. It's not going to happen.

I need an emotion that is so strong that it eclipses all other emotions, making them disappear. What emotion can do that? Don't panic, Sasha; if he senses the change in your emotions, he will use it against you. Keep your cool and simply think; you need to put yourself into a tranquil state. Imagine yourself a blank canvas- void of emotions or preconceived notions, open to whatever comes your way. What strong emotion can cause people to act irrationally? One that can do that would obscure just about any another emotion. Lust? Well, that definitely makes people do stupid things. No, that is short-lived and can easily be turned into a negative. Hate? No, I could see him turning that one around on me fast, but there is a thin line between love and hate. Love, that's it! Love could conquer all other insecurities, and in its purest form, surpass any other emotion.

Shit, his probing is getting stronger, and my thoughts are now triggering emotions. Like leafing through the pages in a book, he is picking and choosing what he wants to torture me with. I need to do something before I lose my concentration and he wins. I need to personify love, let it take over. It has to be some type of love that I can feel; it has to be so strong that, no matter the life situation, it cannot be breached. I don't know a complete love like that other than the one I feel for my kids, but I don't want them brought into this. I, then, remember what I felt coming from him when his white light was reaching for me, trying to bond to me. Use that, Sasha! Use his own emotions against him. The feeling was so pure and unadulterated, it was perfect. Sinking back into a meditative state, I take with me the memory of his light and let it manifest into something that I can feel- something that transcends any other thoughts or feelings until it consumes me completely in its depths.

His probing falters under the pressure of what I am using; upset by this, he comes back at me with all he has. I never let go of the love; instead, I focus so intensely on it that it becomes all I know in that moment. This must be what Buddhists have the ability to do during meditation- let go of preconceived notions and open themselves to truth, to know it on every level of consciousness from the inside out. For the first time in my life, I am able to *feel* love on a new level, unbound and raw. The magnitude of this revelation is so strong that it pulls me into an out-of-body experience; I am powerless against it as it sucks me in through a vortex of space and time. I hold his stare, but can see nothing except the diamond-encrusted tunnel my soul has been drawn into. I originally wanted to take his emotions and use them against him, but in truth, the lines are now fully blurred as I float through this dimension. It is as if I have awakened my own long-lost emotions by manifesting his. The love I am feeling is for this man, even in all of his ridiculousness. The love that is consuming me- mind, body, and soul, in this moment has suddenly shifted into all I have ever known; it is as if the layers of time have unexpectedly lifted, revealing an ancient, unbroken, and bound love that we have shared over many lifetimes.

I revel in the realization, letting it warm my soul instead of fearing it. I let it fill the hole that I have always felt sitting in my heart and allow the once-impossible to place puzzle pieces that have been floating around aimlessly within, to finally shift perfectly into place. His probing stops briskly, the intrusion now gone. His sudden absence pulls me back out of the tunnel quickly; as my vision comes into focus I am met with a pair of troubled eyes that are full of reciprocated emotion. I didn't know that he was paying any real attention to what I was up to; I thought he was so engrossed in his task that it wouldn't sink in.

"Sasha?" he whispers.

"Yes?" I breathe heavily in anticipation. Surely, he will have something profound to say if he tapped into what I just invoked out of nowhere.

"Let's now test speed."

Where the hell did that come from? "Alright," I absently respond while composing myself and quickly put all that love stuff in a box and on a shelf next to the other thing up there. I am stunned at his lack of insight and disregard for what has just happened. I have never had an out-of-body experience like that, let alone, a revelation on that level.

Gabriel jogs over in all of his dark-chocolate magnificence and opens the door for us. Etienne winks and takes off without warning. I guess we are off! I head out trying to catch up with him. Etienne is ridiculously fast; I can barely keep on his heels as we race around the warehouse district in a loop. Just as we are lined up to hit home, he kicks it up a notch and dusts me. I arrive back to base a few seconds later. I am not out of breath like I would expect, my lungs now have an extreme capacity; that is the one cool part about having my ass handed to me. Walking in, I see that he is now lounging in a chair by the arena like he has been relaxing there all evening. The others are hanging around making small talk.

"Guess speed is not my thing," I call out, announcing my arrival; though, they probably already knew I was here but were ignoring me to make good with their boss.

"Ah, no, it is not, but I haven't met anyone in a long time that could keep up with me. You were, however, able to block my manipulation of your emotions, though; you are the first I have met that can do that," he says, trying to offer a win. His speed remains supreme, lightening his mood.

"Moving on, sight, smell, and hearing can wait. At the chance of risking any more china, I would like to move on to testing your gift as it may require more time to grasp its limitations. Into the arena, Gabriel and Sasha."

I walk to the edge and peer down; how the hell am I supposed to get down there? Gabriel answers the question by jumping down and landing on the sand with grace. I follow his example, landing perfectly. I look up; the others have stepped to the perimeter to watch. Etienne has rolled his chair up to watch as well. "Etienne, I really don't think this is a good idea; I don't even know how it happened the first time," I say hesitantly, sizing up Gabriel; I think I should just call him shit brick-house or something, good God.

"That is why we are here; we need to trigger it out of you so you can learn its limits and learn control," he says with such certainty.

"How do you suppose we trigger it?" I ask tepidly.

Gabriel steps forward. "Forgive me," he says and bows. With one swift movement that I don't see coming, he knocks me on my ass.

What was that for? They want to bully me into this? I stand up, and Gabriel comes at me again with a front kick. Finally, a move I understand! I block him and throw a cross-jab followed by a side-kick. The kick knocks him off his balance for a fraction of a second, but not for long, as he is back at me with a round-house kick. I'm back down and planted on my rear, again. At least I am having fun. He is going easy on me, pushing me gently, and I love to kick-box!

"Stop, this isn't working!" Etienne calls out in frustration; he probably senses my joy and wants to squash it.

He never wants to let anyone have any fun, now does he?

"Do you have to pee on everyone's corn flakes? We were just getting started!" I yell playfully at him.

"The goal is not fun, Sasha; we need to trigger your anger," he calls back.

"Well, you do that well all on your own," I mutter; he grins.

"Maybe, we need to channel your primal side," he says, throwing Erik a nod. Erik disappears behind a door and is back in an instant with a bag of blood.

I can smell it through the vinyl it is sealed in. It smells dirty, like the troughs that pigs eat slop out of. Gross, that doesn't smell like any vampire I have come into contact with.

"That smells disgusting; what the hell kind of animal did that come from, a pig?" They all look at each other with raised eyebrows.

"Interesting," Emile says from above.

"Sasha, the bag isn't even open yet; you can smell it?" Etienne asks, not believing me.

"Yeah, and it smells like it rolls in mud."

His grin turns downward. "Erik, another," Etienne says. Erik comes back with another bag, and this one smells like rotten flowers.

"Let me guess, a skunk died and you drained it?" Antoine chuckles then quickly stops as Etienne sends him a "shut the fuck up" type of look.

"It seems that she does not care for animal blood," Gabriel throws out, immune to Etienne's foul mood.

"Animal blood?" I ask, my stomach turns at the thought.

"My dear, that is what we jokingly call human blood. Since some vampires like to feed from humans to sustain themselves, just as humans consume meat, our species has come to coin that expression," Emile calmly explains, throwing me a bone.

"Why would anyone want to drink that?" My face twists up in disgust.

"To most, it smells quite good, but you are once again proving to be out of the ordinary," Etienne calls down; I can't tell if he's perturbed or pleased.

"Yes, I am a freak. Can we go now? This is not helping, and I am tired." Exhaustion is creeping up on me, and I guess that I am not fully repaired from my five days in hell.

"No, we are just beginning," Etienne responds as he pulls out his knife, freeing it from a sheath hidden on his hip. He leans forward in his chair, holds his hand out over the edge of the arena, and slices his palm open. He cups the blood and lets it pool. "Come and drink," he says, testing me. I can't drink from him in front of all these guys. I know I lack certain levels of modesty, but this seems too intimate. The scent of his blood calls to me, and the memory of its taste is imprinted on my tongue. Its aroma has my fangs elongating without my permission. The thought of his blood rolling down the back of my throat makes me quickly bypass any thoughts of being "shy" in front of everyone. Gabriel steps up behind me with tensed arms.

"Come, ma chérie, drink from me," Etienne calls. You don't have to tell me twice. My alter-ego takes over as I try to move to leave the arena but can't. I am cemented in place; Gabriel is holding me with one hand on each of my shoulders in a vice grip. I'm guessing that strength is his thing. The more I try to move, the tighter his grip gets, caging me in. This guy is keeping me from drinking; the thought starts to piss me off, but not enough for me to lose it.

Giving up on struggling, I stop and stand there instead. My effort is futile at the hands of Gabriel. Apparently, my refusal to give in doesn't sit well. Erik walks unhurriedly over to Etienne's cupped hand, takes it, and slowly turns it over for maximum effect. The blood spills onto the ground like it's something that is so easily thrown away. My love's blood is dripping on the ground, wasted. My blood being thrown away like it is nothing. *MINE!* I think as my temper boils my blood to the point of no return. Anger consumes me; its red-hot flame infiltrates my body from the inside out. I try again to get free of the iron grasp, but I can't. The blood has dripped down from the hand it was cut from to the lip of the arena, paving the beginnings of a small red river on the wall that I can't tear myself away from. MINE! WASTED! The intensity of my emotions starts to take on new life as they begin to manifest as vibrations through my flesh like a beat flowing over a tightly-stretched bass drum.

As my skin quivers from the budding power emanating from my body, the arena starts to shake in response- like we are in a small, subtle earthquake. "Do not let her go, Gabriel!" I hear Etienne yell down. The others have backed away a few inches from the lip of the arena, but remain fixated on me like they are watching the best movie they have ever seen. *I have to get out of this place*, I think as I start sizing up all the possible escape routes. The ground begins to quake harder in anticipation of my possible break for freedom. Etienne is no longer able to sit on his pompous ass due to the shaking, so he stands, and the chair slides backward. He doesn't come to me... he doesn't help me make this stop. He just stands there, letting his blood drip down from his clenched hand; each drop joins the others in an effort to grow the long cement-stain now forming down the wall. Ol' shit brick-house's hands can't do the job anymore, so he wraps his arms around my chest to hold on to me. Not quite the embrace I was looking for... though, it isn't half-bad either. The trembling of the earth under us is making it increasingly difficult for him to keep me in place.

He still won't let go of me, damn it! I spy Etienne's chair rattling behind him. Fuck that chair, free to rattle about, with Etienne lounging in it like he can control and do whatever he wants from the comfort of that stupid chair. Stupid fucking chair! As the thought passes through my cortex, the chair goes flying at Etienne, who barely ducks in time. The chair misses him, but it continues toward me at full blast.

"Do not let go! She must not get away!" Etienne's voice echoes down and bounces around the arena. Gabriel quickly turns me around so the chair shatters against his back, his grip still in place. Now, I am facing Antoine and Emile who decided to join us in the pit of joy. The fact that they feel the need to come down here as reinforcements pisses me off more; I am not an animal! Instantly, the burst of a window pane draws our attention upward and is followed by the patter of shattered glass raining onto cement. The few windows located high up near the ceiling are now void of their contents.

Even after exploding glass, Etienne still has no intention of calling off his cronies; he is just standing there with intense curiosity, watching everything unfold. Glancing back down to where we stand, I notice that the sand of the arena is dancing about, thrown around by the quaking of the earth. Damn sand, it doesn't have to worry about all of this nonsense. The sand gets to move around without a care in the world; it's not being restrained like a dangerous beast. No cares, no stress, its life remains the same. God-damn sand, skipping freely…screw all of this. The heat of my anger deepens, causing it to take on new life and become a soft, red, glowing mist that is seeping out of my skin, and is now pulsating around me. Taking a deep breath to register what I am seeing, I study it for a minute. It seems to be responding to me somehow; it ebbs and flows subtly with each of my movements, like it is an extension of me. *Am I doing this? Can anyone else see this?* I look about and see that no one is acting differently, they obviously have no knowledge of the mist; if they did, I am sure there would have been a reaction. If this really is an extension of me, can I move it? Testing the theory, I imagine the mist moving to the left; it obeys without hesitation. My anger has become a freaking glowing mist that I can control, cool!

Captivated, I circle it around the arena in a sweeping motion; the sand underfoot attempts to follow it, caught in its momentum. I sweep the red mist around faster this time; the sand jumps up higher, trying to ride the wave. Increasing the speed of the circling mist without stopping it, the sand is now caught up in the kinetic energy that it has created.

"Antoine and Emile, stay close just in case Gabriel loses his grip," Etienne's voice calls out once more; it is his fault that I am stuck here! I continue to use the red, glowing, manifestation of my tangible anger to move the sand around the pit of hell; it moves so fast and frequent that it begins to rise in a wall formation around us, like we are caught in the eye of a tornado. Controlling the mist, I try to raise the wall of sand higher. I have no idea why I am so fascinated and drawn in when I should be freaked out, but I can't help myself, it feels so right. The anger has triggered a new level of power out of me. The wall of sand is now a foot above the opening of the arena; I think I can do better. Its momentum is moving so fast that a few pieces of the chair have been caught up in it, flying around- ready to strike. Fixated, I can barely hear anything else. No longer am I paying attention to the bystanders; worries about what they will think of my "anger" have passed.

Engrossed in my task, the only sound that is able to penetrate my trance's hold is Etienne. "Sasha, it's time to stop," his voice calmly travels to me through the sand and mist, echoing all around me like a soft lullaby. *Asshole*, I think, as a chair leg swirls by, causing a ripple in the mist. Absorbed by the effect, I forget all about *him* and try to surround the leg to see if I can hold it still and to control it. "Sasha, we don't want to hurt anyone; it's time to stop." I hear again. Oh, but he was okay with bullying me into exploring this thing that was supposed to be in a box on my shelf of denial. I feel a surge go through me, which unexpectedly sends the chair leg I was playing with flying at Etienne. Erik knocks Etienne out of the way just before it makes contact with his head. I didn't mean to actually hit him with it; my power was responding to my emotion, I wasn't in full control. A flood of worry that I have actually hurt Etienne breaks my concentration. The sudden change in my emotional grid forces the wall of sand to respond in an outward explosion all around us. Its glittery remnants travel to all four corners of the building, finding new places to call home in crevices and cracks, coating all of the expensive equipment.

It is evident that I am still locked into the hold of my anger as the ground has not yet stilled under our feet. A distant groan sounds out behind me, but I can't process it. I can't figure out how to calm the rest of this rage. It's as if all of the pent up wrath from the last few weeks is fueling this madness, and every time I try to bring myself down, the enormity of all that has recently happened lights it up once more. The pulsations start to pick up intensity again as I sense the red glowing mist building back up around me. Why won't this stop? I want to be released from this!

It is then that I feel *his* mind reach out to mine, probing around the fury, trying to get my attention. Giving in, I lock eyes with him. "Sasha, listen to me; remember how you stopped me from manipulating your emotions? Can you tap into that again?" He's right! Thinking back to just a few minutes ago, I search deep for that overpowering emotion, which enraptured my soul and fulfilled a long-lost yearning- my soul's ancient love for him. The earth begins to quiet a little; it's working. I call on the memory of the sensation I felt when our past lifetimes reached forward through the sands of time and turned on a switch within me. It allows me to transcend the situation we are in currently and see beyond it. My love for this man will never stop; it will always be. I finally feel more in-control, calmer. Taking a deep, cleansing breath and blowing out the last of my frustrations, the earth quiets under our feet.

Gabriel lets go of me the minute the ground stops and turns to his friend lying on the ground next to us. Oh, no! Emile! A piece of chair seems to have hit him in the head; blood is oozing from a gash in the back of his scalp. Oh God, I didn't mean for anyone to get hurt. Emile attempts to sit up, but the injury won't allow it; he loses balance and collapses again.

"How do we stop the bleeding? What does he need?" I yell, disappointed in myself that I have caused a good man this kind of injury.

"We need to get him to the healer; Kataya is out of town," Antoine responds.

He is losing so much blood that I seriously doubt his ability to make it out of this building. Blood, he needs blood. "Will that human blood work?" I ask.

"No, human blood does not heal us," Erik says, running up with Etienne.

"Can one of you feed him?" I ask, with pleading in my voice.

"It doesn't work like that. He will reject male blood, it must be female blood; vampires require blood from the opposite sex," Erik says.

I caused this mess, I should fix it. Without thinking a second longer, I bite my wrist open and go to press it to Emile's mouth, but Etienne stops me.

"No, you will not feed anyone else," he says possessively.

Well, he doesn't get to decide. I use the few swirls of red mist that are still hanging out around my feet to attempt to push him out of the way. Apparently, it is with too much force because it propels him against the arena wall. The impact only stuns Etienne for a second; he jumps right back up on his feet as I kneel and push my wrist to Emile's mouth, assuring him along the way.

"Here, it is my responsibility to fix this." He accepts my offering and drinks gently.

Etienne growls a piercing, gut-splitting sound that emanates around us and almost breaks my heart. I ignore him as the others back away in fear; he needs to know that, sometimes, things in life are bigger than our own wants or needs. Emile would most likely die or come ridiculously close to death, so why would I let that happen when I could easily do something about it? There is no sexual desire or tension with this feeding; it's not like it was with Etienne. Emile takes a small amount, then closes my wrist.

"That is enough, dear Sasha; thank you." He touches the wound on his head; it has started to close, and the blood flow has slowed to a trickle.

"Are you sure?" I ask, touching the wound, amazed at its quick healing.

"He said he is fine; he is almost healed." I hear grumble next to me. Jealous, much?

"All is well, Sasha. I am well. You just pack quite a punch," he jokes. I take a deep breath, glad that he will be okay.

The relief of his wellness wipes me out. Exhaustion was wearing on me when we first got here; add to that all of this other nonsense, and I quite literally collapse on the spot as soon as I attempt to stand. Etienne catches me and brings me up to his chest. "Erik, take us home, please," he says, as he carries me out to the SUV. I fall fast asleep in his arms on the short walk to the car, unable to deny my body the one thing it needs desperately.

Chapter 14

I awake to find us back in his bed, surrounded by luscious pillows and downy-soft blankets. I decide that the most important thing at this moment is to do a quick check to see if my clothes have survived; nope, they haven't. I am naked once again. A few days ago, this would have really bothered me- waking up next to another man, naked and all. But, it doesn't; it's not like I intentionally did anything wrong...yet. I should also feel awkward, but I don't; I mostly feel unapologetic these days when it comes to the things I need, like, or don't like. How will that work when I go home, though? Stephan doesn't approve of sleeping in the buff; he doesn't want the boys to walk in and get the wrong idea. I guess that he will just have to learn to deal with it, along with this new, more-vocal version of me. For the first time in my life, I feel like I have come into my own. I don't feel scared, angry, or resentful about all that has unfolded; it all feels... natural.

I roll over to face Etienne and find him watching me.

"You really are the most beautiful sight that I have ever seen," he says softly.

I am speechless, this is not expected at all. The last thing I remember is him being his usual asshole self. "And, I apologize for chastising you in front of everyone last night; I really did push you out of good intentions," he continues.

I can't believe that he's apologizing! "Etienne, I know it was for the best; it actually was very effective...Wait, you think I'm beautiful?" I have to go back to that; I'm such a girl! Still stunned and hung up on the fact that this man- who can stop traffic with one look, thinks I am beautiful. I know that I am pretty, but that is not the same. He leans into me and quickly kisses me without permission, his lips feverishly meeting mine as if he has been holding back for so long.

The touch of his lips is like satin, and the feel of his silky tongue has me kissing him back with uncontrolled hunger. God, this feels so good; I need more of him. I cannot get enough! My hands travel up into his long wavy hair, pulling him into me. More, I need more. Stop, Sasha, you are going too far. I don't want to stop and offend him; I don't want to stop at all. I feel this magnetic pull toward him that calls to me, which seemingly takes advantage of my lack of control over my vampire side, all while fogging my human moral. I also don't want him to think that I don't want him, because I do. This is wrong, and I am, once again, letting my vampire side rule, which could push me into a decision that I can't take back. In desperation, I divert his attention with the only thing I can think of; I slice my neck just enough and use his hair to pull him down. He follows my command and takes the invitation, biting deep into me- much harder than the first time. The sting is exactly what I need to clear my head, but just as I think the urges are under control, his sudden firm latch to my neck sends me back over the edge. "Hhmmm... Etienne," I say, as I run my nails down his back in ecstasy and arch my body, giving him all access.

No, Sasha, you need to stop. This is not right. Think of a distraction. The mist, I need to tell him about the mist. "Etienne?" I say calmly, not wanting him to think he is hurting me, which couldn't be further from the truth.

"Hhmm?" he answers, not breaking his seal.

Oh my, he feels so good… focus! "Something happened last night when we were training, something that I think will help," I force out in desperation, as an unfamiliar warm heat begins to build between my legs, threatening my self-control. I finally have his attention! He breaks his seal, closes my neck, and lays aside me. Phew, we really have to stop getting into this position. He looks so relaxed; I don't think I have ever seen him like this.

"Do tell, my love," he says, obviously not realizing what he just said.

Ignoring the "L" word, I hurry on, "When my anger was at its peak, I was able to *see* it."

"Really? What do you mean?" he asks, wanting me to continue on.

"It was like an extension of my body; I could project it and control it. It was like a red glowing mist." I stop there to gauge his reaction.

"It was your essence," he says with confidence.

"How do you know that?" I ask, my curiosity peaked.

"Because, when we started our bond, your light was a beautiful burnt red, like the color of fall, that slammed straight into my heart," he says fondly.

I never thought of what my essence might look like; I suppose it's not something you can see when it belongs to you kind of like needing a mirror to look at your own reflection. Into his heart? Does that mean that I am bound to him, but he is not quite yet to me? Or is it the other way around? Ugh, I have no clue.

"And, yours is buttery white, like sunlight," I murmur.

"Huh, didn't see that coming, I thought it would be dark, even black," he says.

"Why would you think that?" I ask, astounded that he would imply such things about himself.

"Because of my inability to have close relationships with anyone or to love; not to mention, how easy it is for me to perform in my line of work," he says, gauging my reaction carefully.

I avoid the work part, I don't want to know; judging from all I've seen so far, it's probably better that way right now. "Inability to love?" I ask, embarrassed that he already knows my feelings for him. You can't hide that kind of thing when you use it to defeat someone at their own game. I suppose that answers my "who's already bound to whom" question.

"Yes, aside from caring for family and friends, I have never known love."

Shit, this just got more uncomfortable for me, even more so than when he was laying on top of me. He says that he has never known love, which implies that he doesn't currently know love either. And, that right there, hurts almost as bad as when I turned just a few days ago.

"How about breakfast? I could really use some sweet and spicy tea," I say, quickly sitting up. I need to shower- a long, cold shower.

"Sasha, did I offend you?" He knows when I am lying...

"Surprised me, that's all." I try to swing my legs over the side of the bed, but he is now on top of me, pinning me in place.

"Why does that surprise you?" he asks with such interest.

What do I say? Ah, I was hoping to hear that you love me? That is not a can of worms we need to open. Good God, Sasha... what ARE you thinking? "Because it does, you are a good man, er, male. It would be easy for someone to love you." It is the truth, but I wish I had something better to say- something that doesn't lead to more conversations about feelings.

He looks at me surprised, really surprised. "I doubt that," he responds bluntly.

Is he crazy? I thought I was the one who lived in denial. "You don't remember last night very well then, do you?" I blurt out. Damn that broken filter; it's always getting me in trouble.

He still has that quizzical expression in place; after a minute or two of lost in translation, the light bulb goes off. "You mean, when you used love to stop me from manipulating you?" TA DA, he catches on.

I guess that he really can only read emotions and not thoughts; maybe, I'm not as laid-out flat, like a book, as I thought. If that is true, my emotion of love could have been tied to anything, not just him. Shit, can I put my foot in my mouth now?

"Sasha, is that to what you are referring?"

Ugh! "Yes, Etienne."

"Does that mean that the overpowering emotion you threw at me was, in fact, tied to me?"

Now, I know he can usually tell when I am lying, but maybe I am wrong; it has been known to happen once in a while. "I just picked it out, no ties, per se," I say with my best effort.

"Sasha," he demands, reading right through me.

I thought I could skirt-tail it! I guess truth has to remain our constant; we are stuck with one another as it is.

Turning to face him so that I can catch his response, I answer him, "Yes, Etienne, that overwhelming emotion is what my soul feels for you, but you must understand that it is something as old as time; it has always been."

His eyes are suddenly bright, but that ends quickly as surprise and confusion take residence; is that a hint of disgust?

"I thought so, I am going to shower. I will meet you upstairs, and I think I'll only need a few more days of training at this point," I say, as I slip out from under his grip and slink off in disappointment to the bathroom. He is still frozen on all fours, lost in his thoughts.

I quickly shower and don't bother with anything else other than a hair-tie. Etienne is nowhere to be seen once I emerge, so that allows me to get dressed fast. Why am I still bothered by his probable rejection; why does it hurt? I shouldn't care; it shouldn't matter at all. Upstairs, I find breakfast already laid out, and this time, to my delight, it is real breakfast food. Etienne is sitting in his seat, waiting for me.

"Ready for another day?" I ask, trying to move us as far away as possible from the previous conversation.

"Yes, I really think we need to have you hone your gift. You are very close to understanding it- enough to fully control it," he says all business-like.

Great, here we are, back to the master-lackey phase. He begins to eat, so I join him. I can sense that he is still in disarray, not wanting to accept our conversation; that's fine with me. Maybe, going back home and resuming a normal life will be easier this way; his disgust makes it easier to keep it professional.

∞

We head to the training center promptly after breakfast, and his emotions remain masked the entire way. Everyone is already there to meet us for round two. Walking in, I see them all standing around, laughing and joking. As soon as Etienne enters behind me, they fall silent as his mood pollutes their good humor.

"Play-time is over with; WE WILL BEGIN!" he demands, and they all fall to attention. "Sasha was able to make some good headway last night; she was able to see an area where she can gain control of her gift. We will explore this tonight, which means she will need to be triggered again."

The guys start to look at me nervously. I hold up my hands, assuring them that I don't have any weapons of mass destruction on me.

"Guys, I really think I can do this; it's just the 'Entrance' and 'Exit' parts that I need to practice." None of them buy it; while they don't run away, their hesitation to stay speaks volumes.

Erik speaks up, breaking the unease. "I have been doing some research, and, while I cannot find much on this particular gift, I found some other helpful tips that have been used to teach the gifted to gain control." Etienne nods in approval, so Erik continues. "The trick is in the trigger; we need to bring it down a notch. When we go extremes, which is hard for us to refrain from, we elicit a full reaction. Whatever you used to exit the hold of your gift last night, Sasha, you will need to continue that."

Great, nothing like putting your unreciprocated love out in the open for all to see- not that they actually can see it. Etienne is lost in his own thoughts once again- always watching and verbally contributing little beyond his usual barks and growls. Erik continues to drive the ship, as it appears that Etienne is too consumed by some unnamed internal conflict.

"I went to see the healer and got a few things that should help," Erik calls out, as he jumps into the arena... or as I like to call it, "pit of hell."

He starts to pull items out from a paper bag: some dried herbs, some different colored candles, and various other things you would see at one of those spiritual shops. He lays them out on a table that has been placed in the middle.

"Alright sissies, don't look so surprised; we are dealing with old magic, so why not use old magic?" Erik looks up at everyone with his hands on his hips, tapping his foot impatiently.

I jump down into the pit and land gingerly next to him. "So, what's a healer and what do we do next?" I ask eagerly. I just want to get this over with. The sooner I gain control, the sooner I get to go home.

Happy with my response, he takes out a large knife and draws a large circle in the sand around us as he speaks. "A healer is like a vampire doctor who is well versed in all aspects of our culture and spiritual practices. Healers attend medical school alongside humans to learn basic skills, then do a very long rotation with other healers to learn how to apply those skills to vampire medicine, anatomy, and physiology. In the end, you get the combo of a medicine man and a doctor in one." He places four large candles on the circle's line. I am guessing that they are at the North, South, East, and West points based on what little I know of magic. The healer concept sounds pretty interesting; if they spend all of that time learning all of those skill sets, whatever they told Erik should help.

I hope that it helps as I really don't want to lose it again tonight; let's keep it at an even keel. He places the fifth candle in my hands. "Sit here, in the middle," he says earnestly. I follow his command. "Alright, Gabriel, Antoine, and Emile, each of you need to man a candle on the perimeter. Boss?" Etienne looks up in surprise. "Due to your... connection to Sasha, I think you need to be in the center with her unless you would prefer one of us be her blood source." He is just being diplomatic, but the way Etienne looks at him makes all of us cower back a little.

"Alright, I get it; let's all just get into position," Erik calls out. All the males follow his lead and drop into the pit to take their places. Erik lights what I can now tell is a bundle of white sage laced with lavender and places it on a holder in the center of the table. He throws a lighter to all of the guys. "I know none of us have done this since we were kids, but our grandparents taught us this for a reason; we need to think back. When our ancestors needed to channel earth's magic, they formed rituals to do so. Many of those rituals were absorbed into more modern practices, but the basis remains the same. Sasha, our practices are very much aligned with Native American's. We believe our supernatural abilities are tied to the earth and her underlying magical force. We also believe in earth spirits, ethereal-type powers at be who control all that is around us. Tonight, we will be invoking the earth and all of her elements, such as: wind, water, fire, and spirit, which are believed to hold the largest amount of power. We are doing this in hopes of opening a line of communication between us and the spirits world so that we may tap into your power in a more controlled fashion." Erik is narrating so that I can be included in what is unfolding. He walks over and mans the remaining candle. They all, in unison, light their colorful candles and begin to chant in perfect harmony.

The language is like nothing I have ever heard. It sounds older than all modern-day languages, like an old tribal language- one that is long forgotten by society. I do not know what they are saying, but it is beautiful.

Each male's voice harmonizes with the rise and fall of the ancient words, and its rhythmic beat is pulling me into a trance. I can feel the earth below me respond; it feels alive, and its reverberations feel like breaths. The taste of saltwater soon fills my mouth, while the sound of the wind rustling through unseen leaves becomes audible in my ears, and the scent of earth fills my nose. Finally, the feeling of fire skims my fingertips. Those must be the elements of nature being invoked. Taking in what I assume to be all of the elements, I allow them to smother my senses as I slip deeper into the meditative state that is pulling me under. The earth is now humming underfoot as the males' chant grows louder.

Etienne removes his knife, takes my hand, and makes a small cut in the middle of my palm. Blood gently pools in the center, and I am careful not to spill it. I feel the elements swirl around by body, encircle my hand, then return to the greater circle that we have all become a part of. From the blood in my hand, a beautiful burnt-red mist starts to form, floating on top like a gentle fog rolling out over a lake. It is my essence. The old magic they invoked is bringing forward the mist, or the visible form of my vampire essence. I take note of every sensation taking place within my body; I want to be able to replicate what is going on so I can learn to call it forth and ask it to retreat on my whim and not on the whim of my temper.

Etienne cuts his hand open and drips a few drops of blood over my candle's flame. My mist flairs to life; instead of the little cloud that I was caressing, it is now covering me from head to foot. I look around at the faces of all of the males, wondering if they are seeing this also, but they remain unseeing; all are locked into their task. Etienne sucks in air abruptly from behind me, but resumes his chant. I guess that he sees it. I take the mist and practice moving it. I push it away from my body, and it responds. With my mind, I command it to sweep gently out around the circle, and it responds. I do this a few more times to get used to the feeling of manipulating it under my will, not my anger. Back and forth, faster and slower, I take note of its feel: the weightlessness of it, its texture, and its scent. I need to know it inside and out. Pulling the mist back to me, I overshoot the distance and cover Etienne in it. Etienne inhales sharply again, responding to its caress. Through the essence, I can feel his surprise as it responds to him; it wants to call forth his essence... to bond. No, I command. It reluctantly submits.

Retracting the mist back to my hand, I command it to retreat back inside of me. It obeys. Calling on the memory of what it felt like when it first emerged, I try to manifest the same sensations, and it works; the mist comes forward. I think I have it now. I try a few more times, calling it in and out of my hand. I think we can stop now. Considering the intensity of the power that is now building around us, I am afraid to continue on much longer. "Okay, I got it," I say aloud. Etienne reopens the cut that has started to heal on his hand and presses it to my mouth. I drink from him just a little and close his wound. It takes all of my willpower not to latch feverishly onto him, but now is not the time. I can feel the enormity of what we just tapped into clear. The elements dissipate, the ground slows, and the candles go out on their own accord. Everyone's shoulders relax and some stretch after the long exercise as they regroup from being placed into a self-imposed trance.

"Sasha, do you think you have it in you to test the other aspects of your gift now?" Erik asks eagerly; he is as excited as a kid in a candy store. It seems that this round of success has boosted everyone's moral.

"What did you have in mind?" I ask, still a little wary from yesterday's events.

"Call it forth, without our help."

Okay, I can do this. I focus and attempt to replicate what I have just done in the ritual circle, and nothing happens. I try again, still nothing. What am I missing? Biting my wrist suddenly, I surprise everyone, causing Etienne to move closer to me. Males! I focus again on the blood, trying to recreate all of the same sensations that just took place. It works, and the mist comes blossoming forward. I move it around the room, allowing it to brush by Etienne's cheek, then push it up to gently tap the lights before bringing it back down and closing my wrist.

"We are getting there, but we still have a ways to go," Etienne says, then turns to Erik. "Now, what about the elemental response to her emotions?" Etienne probes him.

"Well, now that she is establishing control over her essence, which is half the battle, she can control the other responses by focusing on whatever she did to shut you out of her head. Lucky girl," he jokes, but there is a hint of seriousness. I take it that they hate being vulnerable just as much as he does.

"Should we test the theory?" Etienne asks the guys. They are still unsure of all of this, but nod in agreement.

"Shit, does this mean you are going to bully me into unleashing that thing?" I find myself thinking out loud.

"It is not a thing, dear Sasha, it is a gift; you are magically gifted and should never forget the blessing that has been bestowed upon you!" Etienne lectures.

"You're right, I apologize for allowing my fear to dictate my words. I just really don't want to hurt anyone." All of them look at me in understanding. None of them want to get hurt.

Erik finally speaks, "Instead of pushing you in as fast as we did the last time, let's try bringing it out slowly, then have you utilize your barrier method each time to tame it back."

"Okay," I say. What else am I going to do, run away?

Gabriel takes his position behind me, hands over my shoulders; I won't be able to move, even if I try. My mind starts to wander; what the hell are they going to do to "slowly" trigger me? It is then that I hear the unexpected click of a woman's pair of heels start to prance over the cement of the warehouse. What the hell? I look to Etienne who has jumped out of the arena to meet whoever is coming. She smells of gardenia. She is not human, that is for sure, and she also smells like she smokes too many cigarettes. The click of heels stops at the edge of the pit, and I look up. She is absolutely stunning with long, raven-black hair, big blue eyes, legs a mile long, and she is dressed like a runway model. Who the hell is this? The males around me tense at the anticipation of my reaction.

"Sasha, meet Cosette. Cosette, this is Sasha. She is a newly-turned that we are training."

Cosette? What is she to him?

Erik's words cut off my thoughts, "Boss, you really think this is a good idea right now?" He questions him earnestly.

Sensing my confusion as to who this person is, *he* finally responds. "Cosette is my blood partner; our parents paired us as children. We have depended on each other to feed when needed over the years."

Holy fuck! Did he really just do this to me? Now, here, exposing my vulnerability for all to see? Then, he introduces me as just some new vamp that he is helping; he must really not approve of my feelings for him, and what an adult way to express that. I want to run and cry. The sorrow of his outward rejection consumes me. My heart is now very heavy, and my soul is wounded. It is as if heavy clouds just positioned themselves over me for a storm. I feel the earth's energy respond more subtly than when it was invoked, and I hear the slight patter of rain start outside.

"We will be back shortly; we have a matter to attend. Continue on," he says, as he and Cosette retreat outside.

I do not understand how any of this will help. I can't do this; I need to be alone, and the need to cry is overwhelming. The flood gates are bulging at the weight of my tears, ready to burst forward.

"Sasha, it's pouring rain over the building; you need to channel the emotion you did yesterday to control it," I hear Erik yell. Why is he yelling?

I look up and realize that a storm is literally thundering all around the warehouse; I can barely hear anything over the drum of rain and cracks of thunder. "I can't, Erik; I can't do that, not after...," I trail off.

"You have to try; he just did that on purpose to throw you."

Maybe that is true, he is always testing me. Letting the practicality and clarity of Erik's words sink in, my head clears a little. The need to cry is not as bad now. So, I try to channel the love I felt for Etienne yesterday and let it fill me to the brim. Sorrow fights back, so I push harder to manifest the feelings that were shown to me when I was in that state of transcendence. The rain quiets, and the thundering ceases.

I look up, and Etienne is still not back. Blood partner, it's pretty easy to figure out the jist of all that.

"Good, Sasha, you did it!" Erik says in triumph.

Oh no, is he feeding her right now? Did he leave me to *feed her*? The anger roars to life faster than I can process. MINE! I think to myself as anger takes over once more.

"Sasha, no! This is too much, you need to hang on to your barrier!"

Hang on to my love? How can I do that? The ground is in a full quake below us, and Gabriel, once again, is trying with all of his might to hold onto me. He loses his grip, and Emile and Antoine cannot get to me fast enough. I am up and out of the pit in the blink of an eye. *MINE*, I think, looking for Etienne. The entire building is now rattling, threatening to collapse at the seams.

"Sasha, please try!" Erik calls out to me. Screw that, no way! "I know you don't want to hurt anyone, so you have to try!" Maybe they all should have run away while they had the chance.

I am starting to feel possessed by the rage; it is taking over and clouding my judgment.

"He just doesn't know how to handle his feelings for you, so he would rather sabotage everything!" Erik unwillingly throws out in exhaustion.

"What?" I say, unaware that I have spoken aloud.

"Sasha, look at me. Isn't it obvious? He is acting like a child! He doesn't like being out of control, and you make him feel out of control, so he is trying to gain it back the harsh way." Erik is right; here is this robotic, well-composed man who has just been thrown out of his comfort zone against his will. He is just acting out as a child would. Ha! I laugh to myself as I reach again for the one emotion that calms me. I bring it back into focus, letting it devour me. The quaking calms to a gentle rumble; I almost have it. Just a little more, and I can stop all of this.

It is then that I hear Cosette's laughter travel in from outside. The emotion slips away from me, the ground picks up speed once again, and the building starts to produce sounds of protest. Calm it down, Sasha, you don't want to hurt anyone. I grab for the emotion again, remembering the feelings that it gave me- forgetting the childish acts of the man that the feelings are tied to.

Taking a few cleansing breaths, I try to fill myself to the brim with love. It works, and my blood pressure starts to lower, and my heart slows to a normal pace. I am able to calm myself. The ground is back to a gentle rumble. I make myself continue to process Etienne's acts from a different perspective, not allowing myself to internalize it. Be practical, Sasha, how else would he have survived all of these years; he needs female blood. If this woman has kept him alive all this time, it is only fair that he return the favor. I rise above my emotional connection to the situation and force myself to focus on seeing it for what it is. All falls quiet.

"Good job," I hear Erik pant. I look to see him disheveled, holding onto one of the steel support beams. I look down to the others, and they are all laid out on their asses, laughing in relief. I start to chuckle out loud too- laughing at the irony of it all and the ridiculous acts of Etienne. He must have felt really out of control if he thought that bringing in Cosette just to reassert himself to me was a good idea. Ed was right, I really do unnerve him. I laugh again- so loud and so long that I swear I hear birds chirping in the distance, ready to greet the day in the middle of the night.

"I'm glad to see that everyone is having a good time; it's also good to see that you didn't tear down the building, Sasha," he says smugly from the doorway.

"And, I am glad to see that you could pull yourself away from your nightly escapades long enough to witness the work the guys and I were able to complete." I can't help myself, he deserves it. He opens his mouth to respond, but all the guys shake their heads in warning. He quickly shuts it. "Well, I am done for the night. Thank you, all of you, for helping me so much this evening. Until tomorrow!" I say, dismissing us. Etienne's jaw hits the floor. What can he say? It's time that he takes responsibility for his actions; his final act of assertion this evening is the very thing that relinquished his control.

∞

After we arrive back to his house, I head up to the empty bedroom; I am too tired to eat dinner. He follows me, questioning my choice to go in there; his softer side now shows its face.

"Etienne, I will sleep in here tonight. It is better this way. You are not tied to me, you are not mine, and it's best we start developing a sustainable relationship. I will be leaving in a few days to go back to my life. While we still need to talk about how we plan to handle all of this from here on out, we don't have to do it right this minute."

He looks stunned. "Are you certain? You don't have to do this- drive a wedge between us, we can still enjoy our last few days together," he says, not liking what I have to say.

"No, correction: you wielded the wedge earlier this evening; I am simply complying with your demand," I say peacefully, no anger at all.

"Cosette? She is not a wedge, she has been a part of my life since I was a child; we have depended on each other for decades. She does not have a mate at this time, and if you recall, I have been at your side all week; it was time for her to feed," he says, trying to reason with my practical side.

"Your timing this evening was purposeful, to kick me at my weakest. If you truly just needed to feed her, you could have dismissed yourself discreetly at any time to take care of business. Instead, you decided to throw a tantrum and act like a child. Why, Etienne?"

For that, he has no answer. His shoulders drop in defeat, and with a sigh, he hangs his head. Walking across the room, he sits on the bed next to me. "It is because you make me feel so powerless at times, so weak, and I am not used to that. So, I do... what I know best- inflict pain and gain control over a situation."

I reach forward and stroke his face. "Thank you for telling me the truth; I already knew it, but it is good to hear you say it."

He slows my hand and pushes it firmly against his cheek. "Are you sure that you want to sleep in here tonight?" he asks with hope that I will change my mind.

"Yes."

He leans back on the bed and reluctantly says, "okay."

I head into to the bathroom to get ready for bed. When I come back out, he is still lying there.

"Etienne, I meant that I would sleep alone."

"I know, but I wanted to say 'goodnight' first."

I walk over and climb into bed next to him. "Etienne, we need to get used to being apart, now, before I actually leave."

"I know." He, then, leans toward me and kisses my forehead. "Goodnight, Sasha."

"Goodnight, Etienne."

He gets up and leaves, turning off the lights and closing the door behind him. I know this is the right decision, but it is extremely painful to follow through with. All I want to do is run back downstairs and jump into his bed. But, that is the problem. I have made a choice to go home to my family, so I will have to get used to the emptiness I feel when we are apart.

Midnight Bloom: The Lunar Eclipse Series

Chapter 15

Two more days of grueling training pass. The guys have pushed me and tested me to the point of exhaustion, before having me get back up again for more. I have begun to learn to wield my gift and to use my essence to manipulate things around me. At this point, I no longer need blood or anger to trigger it; I am able to bring it out on my own whim. I've also learned to have better control over my emotions and have started to explore their connection to the earth's magic. I still can't stop the way the elements respond to my emotions, but I have learned better control over myself, which helps keep a calm balance. It's not perfect, but it's enough to keep me out of trouble. By now, they have tested all of my abilities as a vampire too: strength, speed, smell, and hearing. Etienne even wanted a few more rounds of mind games.

Speed still isn't my thing, but it makes it easier to race when your opponents accidently trip over random things that just happen to appear out of nowhere; it's funny how that happens. Some call it cheating, but I call it "leveling the playing field." My physical strength is pretty average for a vampire, I am much stronger than any human, though. I don't have the iron grip of Gabriel, but I can influence the turn of those tables too. It seems that I rank high in the smell and hearing department; even Etienne can't keep up there. Etienne has not been able to breach my mental barrier despite his best efforts either. I have also found that I can actually push him out of my head completely if I drive my metal barrier towards his intrusion; after I figured out that move, he gave up. Apparently, most can't feel Etienne enter their minds, but I can, which gives me a huge advantage. That pesky emotion- love, no longer needs to be clung to and paraded around while we are training. Although, it remains the foundation of my barrier, I don't have to think about it as hard; I can just do it. I also finally figured out how Etienne unlocked that damn bathroom door. It turns out that most vampires have a connection to earth's magic on some level and can do small parlor tricks, like lighting candles and manipulating metal slightly- like to move a lock.

Some excel in certain areas, like Gabriel's strength or Etienne's speed. Erik tells me that to be considered "gifted," one must be able to have a strong ability that surpasses what the majority of the race can do, which is what I guess that I possess. Etienne is considered to be gifted due to his possession of emotional manipulation, but his transformation still only took three days back when he turned. Erik can't figure out why mine took so long and Lord knows, he is trying to figure it out. He tells me that there might be more to my gifts that we don't understand yet; I tell him I am happy with what I have, no more pushing and probing at this time. I don't know what I am going to do with all of this in my normal life around humans; part of me thinks that I should ignore it all and pretend it doesn't exist.

∞

Sitting round Etienne's dining table, we are all enjoying one of Molly's feasts before dawn rises and our vampire "night" begins. It's good to hear the guys all laughing and joking with one another, even in front of

Etienne. He has been kind of out of it since I put my foot down and moved upstairs.

"Antoine, you should have seen the look on your face; I swear it looked as if you were going to pass out," Emile says, razzing on Antoine about our last round of "let's see if Sasha can levitate a vampire with her gift." That was fun.

"Next time, let her try it on you, Emile, and then you can tell me all about it," Antoine huffs. He was not happy about being the first one nominated for that game.

"Alright, I accept your challenge. Sasha, you may launch me next time," Emile says with conviction. Launch him? That was totally an accident!

"Emile, you got it! But that won't be for a while; I have decided to return home tomorrow." This gets Etienne's attention- he has gone from staring aimlessly at his dinner plate to pinning me with one of those stares that gives me goose-bumps.

"It hasn't been two weeks, Sasha; we still have a few more days. You are not ready!" Etienne says, his face starting to turn pink at the unwelcome surprise.

"Etienne, I will be the judge of that. I have other responsibilities that I have to get back to. I would also like to spend a few days at home before I go back to work," I say in refute.

The table has fallen silent. Somber faces surround me. "What in the world, guys? You knew this was coming; you knew I couldn't stay. The whole goal was to make me safe so I can return to my family! Now, you all can get back to your lives as well." I am surprised that they are acting like this; I thought they would be happy to get back to their norm.

"Yeah, time to get back at it," Erik says in disappointment.

"Alright, enough with the hanging face; can we enjoy our last dinner together?" They grunt in response, and all that is audible is the sound of forks pushing food around plates. Guess that is a "no." I will miss them too; they have become the brothers I never had. The last few days have shown me what I have always suspected- that there is more to me and my purpose in life than I have known. It was the bravery and selflessness of all of these guys that led me down that path, and I am forever grateful.

After dinner and some abrupt goodbyes, the guys head home. Their response to me leaving this soon elicits promises from me that I will work with Etienne to set up quarterly refresher sessions, just so I don't get rusty. They like the sound of that.

"Now that we are alone, would you join me for a nightcap in the living room?" Etienne asks. I can't believe that he is asking what I would like to do instead of telling me what we are going to do.

"Sure, I would like that very much."

We walk together down the hall, and it seems like it has been a long time since we have been alone- longer than just a few days. He has remained distant since I put my foot down and demanded that we start to get used to being apart, and I have allowed him to be. We take up our usual spots in the living room, and Molly comes in with the goodies. I smile up at her- I really like her presence, very motherly and calm. "Ooh, Molly, thank you! You brought my favorite tea!" She smiles in return like I just made her day and retreats back to the kitchen.

"Sasha, I must say, you have really surprised me the last few days. Better yet, you have amazed me," he says thoughtfully.

"Thank you, Etienne; I have surprised myself with the speed in which I have grown into all of this. But, I had a good group of teachers." I smile.

A serious expression soon takes up residence on his face as he quickly changes the subject. "About what happened with Cosette- you were right, and I want to apologize to you for how I acted. I was being a bit pompous. I also didn't know how to handle the emotions you shared with me," he reluctantly admits.

"Thank you, I am glad we can clear the air before I leave."

He starts to shift uncomfortably in his seat. "About that, since you have decided to leave so soon, how would you like to handle feeding?"

I don't have an answer. I have been avoiding that topic since the last time I almost slipped and let my libido take over. "I, uh, haven't come to a conclusion on that one," I say.

"How about we agree to meet once a week to feed from each other; what day of the week could you commit to?" he responds, all business as usual. Wait, feed from each other? I thought that he already has a partner for that?

"I assumed you already had your blood needs met; I didn't realize that we need to feed from each other," I say, confused. It had taken me the last few days just to come to terms with that small fact alone. The thought of either of us feeding from someone else is more than I can bear, but if that's what we need to do so we can behave, then that's what we will have to do.

"About that…" he trails off, looking guilty.

"Well?" I question him.

"I have attempted to feed from Cosette recently, more as a way to see what would happen now that things have…changed."

Ugh, I think in disdain. Don't think about it, don't think about it; it's just out of necessity, Sasha, calm down. "And?!" My voice responds with too high of a pitch in it, and the china laid before us rattles slightly. Calm it down, Sasha!

"It didn't work out well; it… now… tastes wrong and made me feel ill after. I think it has something to do with what has taken place between us."

Ha! Take one home for Team Sasha! Wait, don't get too excited; this might make things more difficult. This could mean that I really do have to feed from him. Splendid. "So, we need to feed from each other then, being... connected and all," I trail off, my composure wavering.

"Yes, we are tied together for the rest of our lives, Sasha, whether we want to be or not." He takes a deep breath and leans back; he looks sad.

"So, why do you now look like someone killed your dog?" I ask.

He scoffs and sits straight up. "This situation is not ideal; it possesses a threat to both of our ways of life. Instead of accepting it completely, we are turning our backs on it and pretending it's not there!" He is starting to get frustrated with me.

"I thought that is what you wanted- for me to leave so you could get back to being supreme master of your universe!" I exclaim, responding to his frustration.

"You are the one who decided to go back to your family, to your human husband," he says in repulsion.

So, that is what this is about; he feels like I am turning my back on him to keep my commitment to my husband. What more does he want from me? I have always been honest about my intentions, even if my body has disobeyed me a few times. "It sounds like what you are trying to say is that you are disappointed that I am choosing my husband over staying here with you." I try to say this with as much compassion as I can muster just to keep us from escalating; I don't want to leave on a bad note.

"More or less…," he says softly, but then stops himself and forcefully resumes his dictator voice. "More-so, that you want to resume a human life and turn your back on your species- on everything that you are, so that you can pretend to be something you are not!"

Okay, Etienne, I will let you say what you must in order to make this situation less difficult to swallow. "As you stated, there will be plenty of time later on to develop my gifts and my ties to my species. You have been so distant since our first training session that I thought you would be relieved to have me go."

"That was your assumption, Sasha, not how I felt."

"Then, why did you look disgusted when I admitted to you that those strong feelings I had were tied to you?"

"I am disgusted at the situation- that you claim to love me, yet go running back to your human husband."

"I claimed my soul is tied to you, and that you and I have always loved one another on a level that defies time, logic, or circumstance. I somehow tapped into it when I was trying to block you out, somehow the universe unveiled it to me. I don't understand all of the 'how's and why's.' All I know is that I gave my word to my husband long before I knew you existed, and I must honor that commitment."

"Sasha, do you love me?"

Shit, that's a "damned if I do, damned if I don't" kind of question. Admitting that I love him makes this all so much harder. Telling him that I don't would be a lie. What if I say "yes," and he says nothing; can I handle his rejection? Do I really want to know if he loves me? Do I really love him? How do I know it's not just the bonding making us feel things that are not really there? I have known him for such a short time; how can I be sure that what I feel is real? It has taken years for me to realize that my feelings for my husband are not the deep, everlasting kind- more like loving a friend who's been by your side, but it doesn't go far beyond that. Even with that being true, I feel guilty that my heart is straying. It's so hard to learn that the one person who you thought you would spend the rest of your life with, doesn't quite fit the picture anymore. Etienne is a whole new ballgame. From the moment we met, I have felt that he is my missing piece, that we are made for one another. We balance each other's strengths and weaknesses; he is the Yin to my Yang.

A part of me is really happy to know that we must solely feed from each other because I can't imagine my life without him in it; thinking about separating myself completely from him makes me sick to my stomach. It is with this inner monologue that I finally know how to answer him.

"First, you must know that I have thought a lot about this and have been confused and uncertain about most of it. Though it does NOT change my decision, yes, Etienne, I love you beyond what words or actions can define." He looks stunned that I actually admitted it out loud with no "blame it on the bonding" excuses. "You look surprised."

"I just didn't expect your honesty, your truth. We haven't even completed the bond; yet, you are so certain about all of this, about me. You do not even know me, you might feel differently if you did."

"I don't need a bond to show me what I already know, what the universe has already revealed. Whether I morally agree or not with the life choices you have made in the past, it doesn't change my love for you." He still can't accept it. Is this the point where I ask him if he loves me? Can I handle the answer to that? Part of me thinks that he doesn't even know. Regardless of his answer, it doesn't change my decision or my feelings.

In an attempt to give him an out, I say, "How about Monday evenings; that is a week from today. Plus, I always take Mondays off from work."

He ponders for a moment. "Alright, Mondays, but that means we probably should feed tonight if we are going to wait that long," he says hesitantly.

"If we happen to run into a situation where we need to wait longer than a week, what would happen?" I

267

ask, exploring the waters, really trying to get out of feeding tonight. I am already too raw and doubting my ability to behave in circumstances that strip me down to my most- primitive state.

"We can survive a long time without blood, but it is at the sacrifice of our wellness and self-control. It puts us in a situation where human blood can become impossible to resist. Waiting also puts us quite under the weather."

Alright, I get it; we need to feed tonight. A sudden thrill comes from out of the blue and runs through me at the anticipation, like I have just given my libido permission to have a little excitement after a long drought. The thought of lying by his side for one more night is irresistible. This will be the last time that we will have to hold each other. I feel my heart start to lurch in my chest at the loss. One last night to be tucked away from the reality of my decision. Keep it clean, Sasha, morals need to stay intact. Something deep within shifts as my vampire side begins to push away my moral dilemmas and takes over before I can think twice. I find myself rising from the chaise and heading toward the basement door. I turn my head and call to him, "Well, are you coming?" I feel him tense, not knowing how to respond. Shrugging my shoulders, I proceed by reaching for the door but find myself swept up in his arms instead.

He holds me close and carries me down to his room, and his scent intensifies as we get closer to his bed. Our desire for each other is becoming tangible once more.

"Etienne?" I say with big doe eyes as he lays me out on the bed.

"Oui?"

"Please, we need to behave; just blood needs, okay?" I put emphasis on the behave part. He nods and climbs into the bed before pulling me to him so my head is resting on his shoulder.

"I promise that I will try," he says in a barely-perceptible tone.

"Good, thank you," I say, as I move myself to straddle him. I don't take the time to enjoy the feeling of him beneath me. Instead, I lean in and immediately strike his neck. He behaves himself as requested, his hands resting patiently at his sides. I quickly finish and close. I did it! I didn't give in to the desire! I kept my essence under control and in its place. Phew.

Okay, now it's his turn; we can do this! I sit back on my heels and lick my lips before biting my lower lip, praying we can keep it together. The minute my teeth graze my bottom lip, a rumbling starts in his chest and his beautiful musky scent clouds the room. His blue eyes start to glow, and he props himself up on his elbows as if getting ready to pounce.

"Etienne…, behave!" I can already tell where he is going with this, so I start to back away- too late. In one ridiculously fast move, he snatches me up and throws me down on my back. I start to giggle. His playful side is rare, and it is delightful.

"Oh, I will behave, ma chérie, I really will." With that, he starts to stalk me across the bed with the rumble in his chest deepening a few octaves. I laugh and go to jump off the bed, but can't, as he now has me pinned down by all fours. I squeal as he lunges for my neck.

Quickly, my squeals are cut off as he clamps down onto me and starts to draw me in. "Etieeennnee," I call out- half in warning, half in pleasure. The movements of his mouth are now all I can think about. At the sound of his name, he sinks in deeper. A loud groan escapes my throat in response. I feel his length begin to harden against my stomach. Ignore it, Sasha, count to ten or something. He falls into a rhythm, pulling from my neck and grinding his erection against me- hitting me through our clothes, perfectly, in the wrong place. I feel the remnants of my self-control start to slip away as an odd, foreign heat starts to bloom between my legs. The addition of this new feeling has me calling his name in pure pleasure as I brace myself against the friction. The heat continues to build, along with a delicious tingling sensation. What is this? It's amazing! Moaning while I tilt my hips slightly, I give myself over to the feeling building between my legs. It takes me higher and higher until I feel like I am at a peak, ready to jump off. But, instead of jumping, the sensation takes over. It ignites my core, forcing me to explode into a million twinkling stars, causing my unraveling beneath his weight.

"Oh, Etienne!" I scream as the waves of release hit me.

"Hhhmmm, Sasha."

His response brings my vision back into focus. He is sitting up, licking my blood from his lips. His eyes are on fire, looking as if he wants to tear my clothes off. The sight of him has my moral compass set on "wrong."

My chest heaves as my breathing attempts to slow. He is looking at me, like he is asking for permission to have his way. I can't give it to him.

"What was that?" I mumble to myself, confused; it's not like when he shocked me.

"What was what?" he asks perplexed, hearing me.

"That out-of-body experience that I just had; it was like nothing I have ever felt before," I say, still stunned.

He lies next to me, and a sly smile creeps across his face. "Sasha, are you referring to the orgasm you just had?"

Mental head slap. I can't believe it. I knew I had never had one before, but I didn't know what I was missing out on either. I can't tell him that he just gave me my first orgasm! I feel him probing my emotions, but before I can throw up my barrier to block him, he reads in and finds his own answer. With a purr, he pulls me into him as he lies back and begins to run his fingers through my hair.

"Sasha, Sasha, Sasha, I am honored. I would be lying if I said I am not surprised, though…" He nestles my neck, nipping it gently.

"Why are you surprised? Plenty of women have never had an orgasm!" I say defensively.

"True enough, I suppose. I had just figured, being the age you are and being married, you were versed well enough in the acts of sex," he says smugly, still proud of himself.

I am not talking about my barely-existent sex life with this man. "All I will say is that not everyone is well versed, especially when you have been with only one. I refuse to discuss it further, thank you very much," I say in exhaustion. This is already awkward enough, and it has gone further than I am comfortable with.

"Don't be embarrassed. I apologize for prodding, and I will leave it be. Honestly, I don't want to know anymore," he responds in a short tone, shaking his head at the thought of me continuing.

"Thank you." I yawn as sleep starts to call.

"I will say that I cannot apologize for being your first; THAT, my dear, is something I will never be sorry for."

I figured; he is very proud of himself. Well, doesn't this just add another dimension of difficulty in an already impossible twist of fate.

∞

I wake as the sun goes down. Excitement to get back to my family and back to normal is all I feel. Looking around the room, I try to take in all of its splendor once more. Oh yes, the bookshelf! I still remember the first time I saw it; its magnificence won me over instantly. Still wanting to touch the binds of those old, beautiful books, I decide that now is my chance. Carefully getting up, I slip out from under a sleeping Etienne's arm and head over to it. While exploring the collection, I realize that most of these are first editions, and many are collectors' items. I didn't know Etienne was big on reading.

"They were Edward's- one of the few things of his I decided to keep." I hear from across the room.

I reach out and touch the spine of "Jane Eyre." "You miss him, don't you?"

He sighs heavily. "Yes, terribly. He was the one person I could count on to keep me grounded."

I walk back over to him and sit on the edge of the bed. "I know what you mean; Ang is my Edward. I don't know what I would do if I lost her."

"You really should cherish every moment; it is always *when*, not if. Especially when it comes to humans- we live so much longer than they do, even though we are not immortal," he says.

"How long do we live?" I ask. I really haven't had time to let my brain go there.

"Well, as you know, there are exceptions to every rule; a typical lifespan is 300-500 years, depending on lifestyle and blood choices."

I think I just choked. That is a long freakin' time! I see what he means about our human companions.

Wow, I guess it's better to know now, ahead of time. Life is a gift; we never seem to have enough time with our loved ones, so it is important to cherish every day. "How old was Edward really?"

"I take it that you don't believe he died in his 70s?" Ha! And, I am not really a vampire.

"No, nothing around here is what it seems. Also, how did you two meet?"

He laughs too; nothing has been what it seemed lately. "He was 109. We grew up together in Europe; our family's estates were next to one another."

I have been so caught up in myself that I had forgotten to check in with him- to see how he was doing. I really have been a bad person.

"I haven't even thought to ask more about you. There has been so much going on, not to mention the constant battle of wills we get caught in. I am sorry for being so self-absorbed."

"I am not worried about it, so you should not be either. Fact is, our vampire nature has been dictating our actions; we follow our whim with ease."

"Tell me more- are your parents still alive?"

"Yes, they are, but let us not worry about such things right now. I have actually rather enjoyed the break you have given me. Let us not waste time; how about a meal before you depart?"

Why is he always trying to feed me? I really don't need encouragement for that.

As we are eating, I can't take my eyes off of him. I want to memorize every detail of him; he still seems just too good to be true.

"Why do you stare?" he asks through that thick, deep accent with his eyes dancing in anticipation.

"I am just appreciating the view; I don't want to forget anything."

He cocks his head and grins. "You will find that your vampire mind is clearer and much sharper. Memories are easier to commit and harder to forget." At that, he gives me his full-watt smile. I can't help but smile in return; it still is one of the most impressive smiles I have ever seen. Truth be told, the longer I sit around this house, the harder it is becoming for me to leave. It already is near impossible to control my vampire side and not give in to my every desire. It's time. I need to get going if I am going to catch the boys before they go to bed. At the brink of throwing it all away to stay with him, I stand to go and he stops me.

"Can I selfishly ask for one thing before you go?"

What could he possibly want? A pair of panties to hold on to? "What would that be?" I ask hesitantly.

"May I kiss you?"

Shit, no- that is not a good idea. I promised myself I would stop doing things that are not going to help my marriage. Things have already gotten too personal between us. Hard thing is, being a vampire, I have found what Etienne has described as having a vampire nature to be true. As a human, you use so much psychological babble to rationalize, to justify, and to make excuses. Vampires are more stripped down and raw. Developing self-control is one thing, but maintaining it is a daily battle. Sometimes, I feel like I cannot control myself anymore than an animal trainer can truly ever tame a lion. No matter what tricks I learn, I am still wild to the core.

"Okay, just this once," I hear my voice respond against my will. See, stripped down and true to your innermost desires. It's like I have a rational brain that tells me what to do, but the vampire side will scrap it at any time if it is not pleased with the direction I am headed. He steps into me, takes my head into his hands, tilts my chin up, and meets my lips with a soft gentle kiss before pulling away. It is not fast and furious; it is genuine and thoughtful. It is the sweetest kiss I have ever had.

∞

Erik is the one to drive me home; Etienne didn't have it in him. I understand where he is coming from, so I didn't push the matter. As we drive, I start to think about both men in my life. Is it wrong to love two men? One, I have been committed to for half of my life- the comfy, safe option that is all I have ever known. The other was forced into my life- neither of us asking for it, with both of us happy to remain ignorant to what we were missing. The possibilities with Etienne are endless, but I also know what I have waiting for me at home, and that is something I can't walk away from either. The grass is never greener; it's just usually a different flavor.

Erik pulls up to my house, and the lights are still on upstairs. They must be just getting ready for bed.

"You sure about this, Sasha? We could easily arrange for you to disappear off the grid." Erik asks- half joking, half not wanting me to go.

"You will be fine, you all will; I was just a blip that popped up temporarily," I say reassuringly.

"Blip is not how I would describe it; it was more like a hurricane. You know, he's more of an asshole when you are not around, though, we all know he means well."

A snort escapes me as I laugh out loud. Knowing what I do of Etienne, I can see what Erik means. "Erik, I really am going to miss you. From what they tell me, I am going to be around a long time, so, pretty sure this isn't goodbye, just goodbye for now."

"Yeah, for now... Sasha?" He says, turning around in the driver seat to meet me eye-to-eye.

"Yeah?"

"Just some food for thought: what do you plan to do when time starts to take effect on your husband

and not you? You know, we age very gracefully," he says superciliously.

"Well, I haven't thought that far. For now, how about we go day-to-day." I really don't want to think that far ahead.

"Alright, until next time."

"Bye Erik." With that, I get out and head for my front door with unease, not sure if my decision to return is the right one or not.

Chapter 16

My feet barely cross over the welcome mat when a stampede sounds off heading in my direction. Quickly, I drop my bag and brace myself. Two streaks of brown hair come peeling down the stairs, followed by a cautious-looking Stephan. Not wanting to be obvious about being different, I let the two mops of speeding brown hair take me down in a classic dog-pile.

"Mommy, mommy, mommy!" They call in unison as they smother me with hugs.

"Hi guys! I missed you so much! Have you been good for Daddy and Grandma?" I relish in their affections; I missed this so much. Peering out of the pile, my eyes meet Stephan's; he looks worried and relieved all at once.

"Of course we have been!" Aiden says defensively, which means he probably got in the most trouble.

"And mommy, are you going to come to our basketball game tomorrow?" Ethan asks.

Aiden follows with, "Oh, and I have a science project due next week; can you help me?" And then, they both continue talking over each other, asking question after question; I can see Stephan is starting to feel left out.

"Guys, okay, yes to all of it; mommy is off from work for another few days, so I will be happy to be there for all of it and help with what I can. How about a bedtime story, then sleep? Tomorrow after school, we can skip homework and have some mommy-boys time, okay?"

"Okay!" They call out and run upstairs to get ready. To think, I almost considered walking away from more time with those two. Hands down, staying is the best decision I could have made.

Standing up and dusting off, I walk slowly over to Stephan. I don't want to move too fast, and he looks like he is having a hard time trusting that it is still me. I never realized how hard it was to "move" like a human until I wasn't one. Up until now, I haven't had to, I just moved like all the other vampires do. "Hey, I missed you," I say, looking for an opening- for a hug or something .

"Hey, back...you're still so... you," he says, looking me over like he has a magnifying glass.

"Yup, just a few small upgrades." What else does one say? Yeah, no changes... well, not if you don't count the blood drinking, struggle to maintain self-control, and,... oh yeah, seems I can throw shit with my mind?'

"Wow, okay, I wasn't expecting you home so soon. Etienne made it sound like a longer... process." A shadow of worry is still hanging on his face.

Hurrying on to ease his suspicions, "Apparently, I caught on fast; I was really motivated to get home to all of my boys," I say, sensing he has been feeling insecure about Etienne's involvement with the whole debacle. "Hey, I am okay, I feel better than ever, and I am here now; no more long vacations away without you," I say, moving in for a hug. He allows it, but his hug is stiff and polite; I can sense fear still coming from him. "Well, there seems to be a promised bedtime story; let me go tuck them in, and I will meet you in the room. We can talk about whatever you want." He shrugs in agreement. This ought to be fun.

A million hugs and kisses later, my quota has been reached, and the boys seem satisfied for now. They genuinely missed me and seem to be more at ease now that I am home. They are finally settled, so it's time to "talk." Great. Walking into the room, I find him staring out the window to the backyard.

"Are you going to expand the garden this spring?" he asks, his mind really elsewhere.

"Uh, I had planned on it... Stephan, what do you really want to ask me?" Patience is lower than normal these days, so let's just get it all out here- front and center, no human mind games right now.

"Did you sleep with him?"

Crickets.... Is it me being stunned or feeling guilty for coming close that has me speechless..."Sleep with who? Etienne? I can't believe it! Out of everything, this is what you want to ask me!" Sasha, don't sound too defensive or he really will suspect that that is what happened!

Taking a few minutes to calm myself down and pull myself away from an emotional outburst using the tools I have learned over the last few days, I finally can reply without knocking the house down in an earthquake. "No, Stephan, I did not have sex with Etienne." I hope the technical truth will tuck the shadows away. He exhales the long deep breath that he has been holding onto since he dropped the question, like the elephant in the room has finally left. "Out of everything, is that what you were worried about?" I ask. I thought he would be more worried about…oh,…I don't know…me dying?!

"It was part of what I worried about. When I dropped you off, he was really, really concerned about you; I thought it was odd considering that he just met you. He was also pretty short with me on the phone when we spoke, like he couldn't wait for the call to end. So, once I knew you were doing okay and didn't die, my mind began to wonder."

Wow, Stephan, I didn't have to pull the truth out of you like usual, maybe this *will* all work out. "I would be lying if I said that we didn't develop a close friendship through the whole process. It was really terrifying and painful. He was there for me and got me through it." That is all he needs to know!

"Okay, I'll let it go. The fact that you worked so hard to come back to us as fast as you could speaks volumes, Sasha. I really did miss you and was beyond worried." His emotions finally flood to the surface, igniting my guilt once more.

Focus, Sasha; despite the few close calls and his little parting gift, you didn't sleep with Etienne. That was while you were in the bubble; now that you are back to real life, focus on what is here and now. Pulling him into a tight hug while focusing on keeping my mind in check, I don't realize how tight I am squeezing him.

"Sasha, I can't breathe," he whispers.

"Oh, I'm so sorry," I say, quickly letting go.

"You're stronger- a lot stronger, is that one of the upgrades?" he asks in disbelief.

"Yeah, along with a few others. I still have to remind myself to take it easy sometimes…" I hope he doesn't want to know much more; I can't tell him about my laser beams.

"What other upgrades? Just so I can be prepared…"

"Just things like smell, hearing, and vision being off the charts; I don't need glasses anymore!" I say, feigning excitement.

He laughs, knowing my frustrations with running into things over the years. He moves closer to me and kisses me gently. As his lips tenderly brush mine, I feel the side of me that is hard to control start to buck under the contact. His kiss deepens, searching me, making sure all is still the same. I remember a long time ago, he told me about a show he watched, in which they talked about the science of infidelity. Specifically, it talked about how partners can tell if the other has been with someone else if they sleep with them soon after their indiscretions. My mind starts to wander down this path, hoping that is not his motivation at this time. Carefully returning his affections, I find it difficult to kiss him; my teeth are razor-sharp these days, and humans don't heal like we do. His hands start to run the lengths of my sweater, searching for an entrance. I find myself diverting his hands while trying not to break our kiss. It has been so long since he has kissed me like this that I should relish it. It is hard to enjoy since I am afraid that I am going to hurt him; I can't just let go with him.

My wild side is pulling hard at the shackles I try to entrap it in; it wants to break free and unleash all the pent-up frustrations that have built up this week with Etienne. I have to remember that Stephan is delicate; he is not Etienne. His hands make another attempt and I decide to allow it. Slipping up under my shirt, he quickly finds my breasts, which are all he needs to ramp up. The contact is almost too much, and the urge to throw him onto the bed and latch onto his neck begins to consume me. He strips me bare, lays me back on the bed, then undresses himself before joining me. The sight of him removing his clothes in the same slow, calculated fashion he always has, cools my jets. Being able to predict his every move reminds me of what is to come. There is no rushed passion, or insane longing for one another. It's just the cool and collected routine. He never has been able to let go and be a little crazy. At that, my excitement exits to the left.

"Sasha, I'm so glad your home," he moans as he sits astride me. Leaning in to resume his deep kiss, his hands continue to explore me- making sure all is where he left it. I play along, allowing him to do whatever it is he needs to do to assure himself. What hurts is my lack of interest, my void of feelings. I thought we would have a fantastic reunion- that all my pent-up urges, along with the libido that I chained down to keep some moral ground, would all come undone for my husband. Instead, the repetition of the same initiation, same progression, and predictable ending, along with the knowledge that I can never fully let go with him because I could hurt him, have my heart conflicted, leaving me questioning my decision to return. My body just doesn't respond to him like it does to Etienne, or is it that Etienne inspires a whole new level of response from me?

"So, do you need blood to live?" Stephan asks with sleep in his eyes as we cuddle in the post-coital effect. This feels better- spooning and talking with my other best friend.

"Yes, not human blood though, so don't worry," I reply, not realizing where this is easily going to go.

"Not human? Animal blood?" he questions. Shit. It is a valid question, just not one I want to have in bed with my husband.

"Uh, vampire blood. No worries, it's only needed like once a week; I eat regular food the rest of the time." Double crap, do I tell him *whose* blood? No, absolutely not; I am not bringing Etienne into our bed, his presence already lingers too much.

"Where do you get that? I am pretty sure that's not something you pick up at our local grocery store."

"Every Monday evening, I have an arrangement to have those needs met. I really can't discuss it further. You already know too much, and it is best to keep you in the dark on the details. Can we focus on just being present for each other right now?"

He starts to get restless and breaks our contact by turning to the opposite side of the bed. "Sure, I guess I will just have to learn to live with the fact that there are some things you won't be able to tell me."

Great, we've never kept anything from each other; he really doesn't know how to be comfortable with the sudden need for discretion.

"Is the arrangement with him?" he asks, heartache threatening his voice.

"Can you trust the fact that I plan to continue to honor my marital vows to you and my commitment to our family?" I refute.

"Yes."

"Then, go with that please. *He* does not belong in our relationship, in our bed, or in our time together," I say in misplaced disgust, hoping Stephan reads it as my disgust with Etienne, not my real disgust with myself.

"I will take your word for it, I know you want to protect me and the boys as much as you can." Yeah, or something like that.

∞

I awake to the sun piercing through the half-open shutters of our little hut. The sound of water gently lapping under our floor boards in a rhythmic melody, threatens to lull me back to sleep. I am really warm- to the point of overheating. The air is thick with humidity, and I can taste salt in the air. The sound of a muffled yawn, followed by a stretch, comes from behind me; rolling over to face my lover, I find myself face-to-face with Etienne. "Le bon matin, mon amour," he says with his classic satisfied grin- the one that makes it impossible to be put off by his smugness.

"Good morning to you, too." I find myself returning the grin. We interlace our fingers, content just

293

to hold each other with no limitations. He pulls our intertwined fingers up to his mouth, kissing each one of my knuckles, playfully grazing them with his sharp teeth. Chills shoot down my spine in anticipation. Even though the sun is out, I don't feel the least bit tired. His lips make their way up my arm until he is butterfly kissing my collarbone. His teeth dance along my skin, pausing here and there, teasing me. I start to get goose bumps as my hands find his hair and try to pull him in. He resists and, instead, continues to work his way up my neck. Heat builds in my belly; a low groan escapes me as I arch my back, trying not to move my neck. I don't want to encourage his torture. Responding to me, he takes one fang and drags it back down my neck to his favorite place- about two inches above my collarbone. He strikes quick, and the impact sends me over the edge "OH YES!" I scream myself awake.

Sitting up quickly to take in my surroundings, I find Stephan asleep next to me. I am drenched in sweat. Cold shower, I need a cold shower. Getting up to throw on my sweats, the remorse and confliction start to take over. Why must this man haunt me, and why can't I get back to my life? The clock says 3:00 AM, and there is no hope of me getting back to sleep at this hour. I have become used to being up at all hours, so it feels like it's time to start my day. Walking downstairs, anger starts to flicker as I process the events since I got home. I thought it would be so easy to fall back into our routine, but no! Everything I do, even down to having sex with my husband, is shadowed now. My body and my emotions have ganged up on my logic. My drive and my will to maintain my relationship seem to have downloaded a virus that wants to take over and implement its own coded mission.

Nothing feels the same anymore; it's like this essence has its own agenda, and until I comply with its demands, it will not allow me any happiness otherwise. Has anyone told this thing that it is not a good idea to tell me what to do?

Ommmm, Ommmm, yoga, I need to do some yoga. Tension starts to take residence in my neck, so I grab my phone for a distraction. There is a text waiting. Ang wouldn't text me at this hour- that's crazy, even for her. Hesitantly, I slide the screen unlocked and hit "messages." "You're away for a few hours, and that little temper of yours is already on edge." How the hell does he know that?

"Shouldn't you be inflicting torture on someone else at this hour?" Why do I respond? You want to know why he is like a virus, Sasha? Because, you continually open the spam-mail and invite him in.

"Now, are you implying that I am affecting you from across town? Lucky me." Asshole. That is what I am changing his name to.

I quickly text back, "Absolutely not! Everything is just perfect; it is SO GOOD to be home in the arms of my husband, thank you for making this possible." Fake it 'til you make it, Sasha. Why, all of a sudden, do I feel chilled- like someone left the front door open? Looking over, I see the door is still sealed tight. I check the sliding-glass door and the windows, too; all are sealed shut. Did the heat get turned off? The thermostat reads 74 degrees. I glance at my phone in disbelief as another message comes through.

"It would be wise to watch your words; you wouldn't want to poke a sleeping bear, would you?" Sudden chills, again, as if I can feel the cold blue ice of his words traveling down my spine. Yup, it looks like the possessive asshole can affect me even when we are apart.

My phone beeps at the arrival of another message. "You forget that we are connected. And, you are a bad liar. But, if denial is the path you choose, don't allow me to interfere."

That's what I get for trying to find a distraction. I really need to figure out a way to block our bond, it's annoying. My heart aches so bad right now; it yearns for him. Just the thought of him being within arm's reach is more than my heart can stand.

"Good day, Etienne." Done, cut it off.

He quickly replies, "Try to keep your temper under control so that I may get on with my day without disruptions, please; I really hate it when my day dreams of you are rudely interrupted."

I am not even replying to that.

∞

Waking up to a quiet house in the afternoon can be really nice when you need a minute to take in life's crazy changes, but right now, I need to talk to someone.

Maybe Ang is free? I grab my phone, and as a quick safety measure, I delete Etienne's texts.

"ANNNGGGG, guess who is back and better than ever?"

She replies in no time, "I knew you were back! Little India buffet in 45?"

That sounds really good, plus, one who has a substantially larger appetite can eat on a budget. "Be there with bells on." That gives me ten minutes to get dressed. I haven't been outside in the daylight since this all happened; this should be interesting.

Donning sunglasses and a ball cap, I make my way around the cramped tables to the back where Ang has saved us a seat.

"Why do you look like you're obviously undercover?" she asks with a snide grin.

"It's the damn daylight; being out in it does nothing for the bags under a girl's eyes, not to mention the dull headache," I huff.

"See, nothing has changed," she says with a haughty tone.

"Haha, very funny."

She stands so we can hug; I really missed her. "You smell really good, like lavender with a hint of berries. New shampoo?"

I bend my head and smell my arm; I hadn't noticed my own scent. "Don't think so. So, how have you and the family been?" I ask nonchalantly.

"You are asking me about the same ol' stuff? No, dish on what you have been through!" Her excitement is tangible.

"Not here... after lunch." I really don't want to risk nosy neighbors getting an earful. I get up and go to the buffet to load up my plate; I don't want to talk openly in public like this.

She sneaks up in line behind me and continues, "Shall we talk in code, then? 'Cause I am not going off-topic anytime soon, Mrs. Superhuman." She really never lets up.

"It was horribly painful, I can't even put it into words. He was there the whole time, and he gave me whatever I needed to get through. He held my hand in every sense. After it was over, I had to be trained to act right in public," I whisper, as I continue to heap food onto my plate. At the risk of having my arm twisted to tell her more about *everything* that happened, I hurry back to our table and sit down. The plate of food just magically starts to jump into my mouth as she joins me.

"Not good enough... but, I guess that I'll let you eat first since you are shoveling like you have never tasted food before." She sounds a little shocked watching me eat.

I stop mid-forkful, realizing that I better slow down and act more human, less wild dog. "Alright, I'll talk after lunch!"

She laughs. "Guess that will have to be good enough for now; this smells amazing!" That it does, it has been awhile since we have come here and it is so good.

∞

Walking around the duck pond at our favorite park, I fill her in on all the major highlights of my transition. I talk about my upgrades and even a little about the mind mojo, essence, and bonding. I gloss over a lot of the magic details- like almost hurting a bunch of people with a tornado and the earth-shaking stuff.

"Sasha, did you sleep with him?" She jumps straight to that, even after hearing all of the other stuff that I just told her.

"God! Why does everyone keep asking me that?!" Defensive much?

"Easy. Guilty, are we?" She holds her hands up in front of her, telling me to stop and calm down.

"No, I did not have sex with him; I did sleep *next* to him, but that is it." She looks at me like I am holding back from her, damn our bestie situation... she always knows when I'm holding back.

"Okay, I wanted to, came close, but didn't. Our connection is so deep that it takes over sometimes; it's hard just to come back to the life I left behind and pretend nothing happened, and I am trying so hard!" She nods in understanding. "Ang, I know it's hard to believe but we are surrounded by magic; it is everywhere. One night, I inadvertently tapped into something that showed me my bond to Etienne. In a way, it showed me glimpses of past lives; he is my soul-mate." I hope that she doesn't think I am crazy, as I know this sounds crazy.

"I can see that, and after everything that has happened with you, it's not hard to believe. That sucks, but I get it. That is how Christian and I are- so connected that I can't imagine my life without him; no one could ever compare to him." She really is trying to relate, which means maybe I am only a little crazy.

"Yeah, at least you married your soul-mate instead of marrying a perfectly good guy only to realize he's not the one you are supposed to end up with."

"Life is funny that way sometimes. Sasha, even though you don't think so, you deserve to be happy." What does she mean by that?

"Ang, what are you saying? Leave Stephan? Why can't I just be happy with the amazing man I married? I mean, I know the sex could use some work, but everything else is good; can't that be good enough?" It has to be.

"Wait, you said you came close with Etienne… how close?" Of course, she comes back to that.

"Close enough- kissing, grinding, and feeding is very intimate whether you want it to be or not." Pausing for thought, I carefully carry on, scared to be judged. "Ang, he unintentionally gave me my first orgasm; he barely touched me, and it happened," I say, as I put my head in my hands, embarrassed that I am even talking about this. But, look who I am talking to- my bestie who is so well-versed in sex that she owns just about every accessory sold for it.

"POP! Finally! That only took... all of your life! Amazing, isn't it?" She grins ear-to-ear, probably basking in the memory of her first orgasm.

"Wrong. I didn't need to know what I have been missing out on!" Relief of not being judged floods me.

"You did need to know. Every woman should know firsthand!"

True, I guess. "Okay, Dr. Drew, can we get back to you telling me something profound to help me figure out how to manage this?"

"There is nothing I can say, but I am always in your court. And, that's just it- I am in *your* court, rooting for you, even when you are not looking out for yourself."

"What you are saying is that I am, once again, *NOT* looking out for myself?"

"How you interpret it is up to you," she says, eyes alight. She is right, though; there is nothing she can say to change my mind about any of it. I really need to make these decisions on my own.

"I feel like I cheated on Stephan. Even though I never slept with Etienne, we were so intimate in other ways that it's like I cheated, and I tried so hard to be good. I had no intention of getting that close to him; it's this damn essence driving me to bond to him. It takes over sometimes, and I have to fight hard to control it."

She looks at me like she is going to say something I might not want to hear. "Do you think that you and Stephan would be a lot happier in the long run if you divorced? It would allow him to find the person he is supposed to be with, and it would allow you to be happy too."

And break up my family? "What about the boys? That would tear their lives apart and limit my time with them. I owe it to them, and to Stephan, to try everything in my power to make it work. If it still falls apart, at least I can look my kids in the eyes and say I tried everything." She looks away from me like she disagrees.

"I guess, or you are just setting them up for bad relationships down the road as you are leading by example. You don't want them to think forcing a relationship is healthy."

"Ang, stop. I know you mean well, and maybe you're even right, but this is too much right now; I need a break."

"Easy, Sash, I'll leave it be for now."

I really hurt her feelings... I grab her and hug her hard. "I'm sorry, I just need time to think. Thank you for being here for me and not judging me."

She gasps a little. "Of course, but, Sasha?"

"Yeah?"

"I can't breathe."

"Oops, sorry," I say, as I quickly let go.

"Guess you are a lot stronger!"

"Yeah, upgrades and all," I say nonchalantly. "Ang, from the minute I walked into the restaurant, you have not been afraid of me once, have you?"

"No, why would I be?"

"Well, Stephan was when I first got home last night; he didn't know what to make of me."

"Weird, he knows you would never hurt anyone; maybe, he was just being overcautious because of the kids."

305

"I hope so, it's hard to live with someone who is afraid of you." At that, we head back to our cars; it is time to pick up the kids from school.

Chapter 17

A week has passed since I first came home, and tonight, I have to face Etienne for another feeding. I told Stephan that I wouldn't be gone for long before I left, secretly hoping it is true. Etienne is an easy time-suck, and it doesn't help that Stephan has been treating me like I am a bull in a china shop. I can still sense that he is afraid of me, wary of me, and waiting for something to go wrong.

Sitting in his driveway, logic is telling me that this is a bad idea, and I shouldn't be here. We should have met on neutral ground, somewhere else. The sight of my phone lighting up catches my attention.

"Do you plan to come in, or are you going to sit there all evening?"

I look up to see him standing in the doorway, dressed in black slacks and a blue button-down, long-sleeve dress shirt. The first few buttons are undone, giving me a sneak peak at his thick neck and smooth muscular chest. I find myself staring at him, locked in and thinking about all of the possibilities. He holds my stare, patiently waiting for me to gather myself.

Fighting the urge to run and jump in his arms, I force my legs to get out of the car and approach him slowly.

"Glad you decided to join me, I was beginning to think you would drive away," he says, with that sexy smile of his.

"I thought about it, but you kind of have my hands tied with the whole 'needing your blood' thing," I say, pushing my way past him into the house.

"Hhmm, oh how I would like to tie up those hands." I hear him say under his breath from behind. I have nothing to say to that.

"So, shall we get started?" I am trying to change the subject. I am already on edge being here, and to have my body spring to life in his presence isn't helping matters.

"Impatient, as always; don't we get to enjoy some time together first?"

"No, we don't have a lot of time." I really am a bad liar; I'm sure he can tell that I am nervous.

"I see, after you," he says, motioning to the basement door.

"Could we go upstairs instead?" He frowns; it is not what he was expecting.

"I guess that would be okay; after you." As we ascend the stairs, I start to think that we should wrist feed; that wasn't sexual when I did it for Emile. We arrive into the room, and he hurriedly closes the door behind us.

Turning to face him, I have every intention of telling him that we should feed from the wrist, but my words are cut short as he is staring at me with that same hunger in his eyes that he had the last time I was here. Heat starts to pool low in my belly as if my loins have a direct line to his motive. Why is my body betraying me?

"Behave...please!" I plead, as he starts to stalk me across the room. It is like I never left... and like I never have to leave if I don't want to. All I want is this, right here, with him. He pins me in a corner of the room, up against the wall.

"Every time you tell me to behave, it makes me want to behave even less," he says with a low deep voice as his lips skim my neck. It's just like in every dirty dream that I have had about him this week. I find myself tilting my head back further, giving him more exposure.

"Hhmm, Sasha, you smell more amazing than I remember," he says, as he strikes without hesitation, startling me. The heat that has been building in my belly responds by spreading down my thighs as my fingers bite into his shoulders, tearing his beautiful shirt. Find a spot on the ceiling and focus, Sasha, don't give yourself over.

I try to ignore him- to just think about the wall pressing uncomfortably into my back or the garden I am planning for the backyard. Time passes slowly, threatening to pull me under. Waiting for him to finish without giving in to my urges is torture. After what seems like an eternity, he finishes and closes my neck. Wrist feed- try it, Sasha. Before he can move back, I find myself grabbing his hand and running my nose along the soft inside of his wrist. I can feel the vibration of the blood coursing through his veins; it's as if it is singing me a hypnotic song, drawing me in. Sinking my teeth into his flesh brings forth the familiar velvety liquid I have been craving all week. With each beat of his heart, the blood comes willingly. He repositions us, moving behind me so he is caressing my back. Embracing me tightly from this new position, he buries his nose in my hair, inhaling deeply.

Being this close to him is so hard, and feeling his front pressed to my backside makes me want to rip my own clothes off. I guess the wrist isn't helping. The familiar heavy satisfaction fills me, signaling the end. Closing his wrist, I turn around to face him without breaking his hold.

"Thank you, I need to get going," I say gently, trying not to be rude.

"So soon? If you must," he mumbles with a heavy sigh, but doesn't loosen his tightly-wrapped arms around me. "I missed you, and it was very difficult to get through the week; I was looking forward to this time together." He reaches out with his emotions, trying to trigger my longing for him before I can put up my barrier. Damn it, he knows that I am out of practice being away for a few days.

"The feelings are not one-sided, but my mind has not changed; the longer we spend together, the harder it is on both of us." He continues to probe, but I am able to get up my faltering barrier and kick him out of my head. I don't need any help from him with conflicting emotions.

"Well, Mother always said that I was a bit of a masochist." It is weird to hear him talk about his mother.

"Your mother? Do your parents live here?" Maybe, changing the subject will distract him from trying to play with my emotions; who knew that a week of ignoring my gifts would have me struggling to remember how to use them.

"No, they reside in the south of France, why?" South of France?!

"It is just weird to hear you talk about anything personal."

He shrugs his shoulders. "Maybe, if we had more time together, I could divulge more information." He raises an eyebrow at me as a tortuous grin slides into place.

"As tempting as that is, another time." If I don't leave soon, I never will.

"Is this how it will be- a beautiful ritual made to be rushed, forced even?" He pursues. He's trying to guilt me, such a bastard. Looking into the depth of his eyes, resisting the urge to cry, words seem to fail me. The week's struggles at home with trying to prove myself to Stephan, and all of this here, is just too much.

"Sasha…" Conflicted emotions cloud his eyes. I let the barrier down so he can see for himself. "Sasha, I understand. If this is the only way I can have you, then I will take it."

What do I say to that? "Thank you for understanding. Can we try meeting somewhere neutral next time- like a parking lot or something?" He looks at me like I just smacked him. I'm sure that it has something to do with him being upset about me suggesting that we perform an intimate and sacred act in a car. To my surprise, he holds back on lecturing me.

"Sure, if that is what you need," he says, as he buttons up the collar of his shirt. Crap, he caught me staring at his neck again; I wasn't aware that I have been doing that this whole time. He takes his thumb and wipes a drop of blood off the corner of my mouth, and before he can retract his hand, I take his wrist and bring his thumb into my mouth, sucking the remainder of his blood from the surface of his skin. He draws in a quick breath and holds it, trying not to show any response. The main thought driving this primal action on my behalf is simply, *that is mine.*

Chapter 18

Etienne

Frustrating female! Parking lot? She wants to engage in our race's most intimate act in a parking lot! I can't believe that I even agreed to such a demoralizing act. It is amazing how this little creature can blur my boundaries- have me agreeing to do things I never would have considered doing before meeting her. Being away from her is the hardest thing I have ever had to do, yet being with her has begun to hurt even more. Last night's feeding was all I could think about; the anticipation proved to be a large distraction all week. While I feel physically replenished, mentally and emotionally I am not; it is as if I am depleted. The very knowledge of each other's existence is beginning to cause us both more pain.

Ring…Ring…Ring. Pulling out my phone, I realize who is probably calling me. "Hello, Ummum." I really am not in the mood to take this call.

"Hello, Son. You do not sound so pleased to hear from me upon this hour." She is being so formal; she must have heard that I am not coming to visit. "Your Abum tells me that you are not coming for the Lunar festival? I needed to hear it from you directly. As you know, we have not seen you since you first decided to go to the states, and you did give your word that you would come home for our most celebrated holiday."

She really is upset with me; why did father have to tell her? I was going to tell her myself, eventually. "Ummum, please do not be upset with me. Taking a vacation from my responsibilities is not something I can do right now." Leaving for a two-week vacation is not an option; what would Sasha do without me? She is too fresh to be testing the limits of her thirst.

"Emile is coming with Kataya, and Emannuelle and David are going to come stay at the estate with the twins. The only one of my children who will be missing is you, my son." So, she will try and guilt me into coming. She would still be missing one of her children, even if I did come.

Don't dredge up the past, Etienne. "I would love to be there, but two weeks is simply too long for me to leave right now." I hope that she can leave it alone.

"So, it is true; you have started to bond to someone."

Shit, fucking Emile. Talk about a vampire lie-detector- Mother is gifted in truth, and she would know the minute I tried to hide it. Even with my abilities, I have never been able to get anything past her.

"What else did Emile feel the need to bring to your attention?" I figure that I had better judge how much room I have to work with.

"Just that he has never seen this side of you. Oh, and that it happens to be with a half-breed whom you turned." Her distain is audible.

So, most likely Emile slipped about the bonding, and she grilled him for the rest of the information. "Are you more upset that I didn't tell you myself or that she is a half-breed?"

She sighs in an over-the-top dramatic fashion, "Etienne, I have never in my life seen you remotely close to being interested in a female of any species, let alone ours. While you know how I feel about half-breeds, that is not what angers me. It is that you kept all of this from me; these are serious, life-changing events taking place. You have always been my distant child, but I had hoped that you would want to share these things with me!" She sounds as if she is going to cry. I hate it when she does this- uses whatever she can to manipulate a situation to her advantage, even if her intentions are usually good.

"Ummum, the situation is extremely complicated. It is not as if I can just sweep her off her feet and bring her to France with me. I cannot tell you any more than that; please understand and respect my boundaries. Due to the delicacy of the situation, this is what is best for now. If, at any time, things change, I will call you, myself, and tell you." I pray to Nannau that she does not start prodding the situation for more information; she is good at interrogating her connections throughout the world for any information she wants. Talk about friends in high, as well as low, places. She can be quite intimidating.

"Alright, my son; I will respect your truth and do as you ask. Would you, at least, consider coming for the first week of festivities? I would love for you to partake in the opening ceremony in Turkey with the family. Then, back with us to the estate for just a few days?"

Maybe a few days away would be good; it has been almost a year since I left France to head up the division here in the States. "I will think about it. I need to facilitate a few things on this end to make that possible..." She cuts me off immediately at the possibility.

"Oh, I am so pleased that you are considering it!"

"Yes, remember, considering it."

"Son, if you don't mind me asking, what is this female's name who has touched your heart?"

Give her that, and she will run a mile with it. "Ummum, please, no details right now; it is too difficult as it is."

"Okay, well, I will call you in a few days' time to confirm!"

"Okay, have a good evening, Ummum." Trepidation lingers on my goodbye. What in the world am I to do about keeping a close eye on Sasha halfway across the world? What if she falls ill or injured and requires blood sooner than seven days? She needs a backup- someone she can call upon. Who do I trust enough for that task?

It would have to be someone who knows boundaries, respect, and self-control. Antoine? Absolutely not, he would fall for her in a heartbeat, and then it would be required to deploy him to another post in a distant part of the world. He's too good to lose over something like this. Gabriel? Possibly, he has good self-control, and he is popular with the females... a little too popular. Erik? Yes, perfect. Erik is one of the few that I can trust without a doubt. He, above all, understands the importance of maintaining respect and not crossing boundaries. Plus, he is infatuated with one of the new, young females he helped turn recently.

"Erik, please come to my study," I call out over the house intercom. It would be best to have this conversation in person. True to his prompt nature, he arrives in a flash.

"Yeah, Boss?" he asks with a quizzical expression on his face; I must have interrupted one of his sessions with his new fling.

"I have a delicate situation that I would like to discuss with you; I need you to do something for me, with your permission, of course."

Erik leans against the doorframe with his brow lowered in thought. He is not used to me "asking" him to agree to do anything; usually, I just give the order. "Such as?" he draws out.

"I have decided to go home for the Lunar festival, just for the first few days; I will most likely be back by the sixth day. Should Sasha need…," he cuts me off immediately.

"No, absolutely not, sir; let me stop you right there. I know what you are going to say, and I refuse to volunteer to feed her- not only would it make her weak, it would also be a threat to my job."

I appreciate his dedication, but he is the last male I would risk losing at this post. "Erik, there is no threat to your job; it is as secure as it always has been. I know it would weaken her to feed from another after a bond has been started, but it wouldn't kill her. I would rather have her weak than out on a blood-lust spree because I was held up in France. Evolution has allowed even fully-bonded vamps to get to a point where they can still feed for survival, especially after losing a mate- just with less than optimal results."

"Yeah, well, what if she rejects my blood or any other male's for that matter? Then, you leave her not only ill, but at risk for losing her hold on her self- control, endangering all those humans she immerses herself in."

He has a point; it is rare to fully reject blood, but she has proven to be the exception on more than one account. "What if I go for just the first few days? Then, after the main ceremonial open in Turkey at the sacred grounds, I head back? There is no one else I trust more to keep her safe in my absence than you, Erik. Emile told our mother about her; It was all I could do to talk her into respecting our privacy on the matter. If I do not go, she may start probing her sources for more information. What are we to do if Sasha's gifts get back to her, then back to my father?"

Erik strolls over to the heavy leather chair across from my desk and sits back, legs crossed, ankle to knee. "Boss, that would suck, I am not going to lie. Your father would love to leverage her somehow. You're sure that Cosette didn't suspect anything when you set Sasha off? She could be a liability if she did."

Thank goodness, no; she would leak all of this back to headquarters without a second thought. I never could trust her. "No, once I could sense she was fully triggered, we went up a few blocks. Sasha only affected the direct surroundings of the warehouse. Plus, Cosette is usually only focused on one thing when we are together." She is a life-long friend, true, but she has always wanted more. She has never been able to be happy with what she has, plus, she is very insecure.

"True, Boss, she seems to have been on a mission to land you ever since her last mate jumped ship. Maybe, if she cut back on the after-hour's scene, she could keep a male around. Anyway, okay, I'll keep an eye on Sasha. As long as you promise to come back right after the opening! Should it come to anything else, I will call you first; that is all I will promise."

Well, that sounds better; at least I will have fair warning first should something go astray. Not that I wouldn't be able to sense it, even if there is an ocean between us. Our essence has not even fully bonded, and I can still draw on it at any time to check on her wellbeing. "As for her safety, and the safety of those she surrounds herself with, as you say, we need some sort of emergency alert system in place just in case she loses her temper." The last time we were together for a feeding and she let down her barrier, I dove a little deeper to see how things had been going at home. Her husband's fear of her is concerning.

"You want me to bug her house?" Erik replies, not too keen on the invasion of privacy I am suggesting.

Perhaps, a full bugging would be too much... "How about giving the husband an untraceable, anonymous phone number that forwards to your cell?"

"Are you sure that is such a good idea? Going behind Sasha's back and all? If she were to find out..." I cut him off.

"Her husband is afraid of her, which is causing her more grief than necessary during this rough transition. Giving him a security blanket might ease the tension, thus, reducing the risk that he will set her off." I hate bringing the human into this world any more than he has already been submerged, but if doing this small deed reduces Sasha's stress levels by even a fraction, it is worth it. I may not be her mate, but it is still my job to look out for her. If she accidentally hurt any of those humans who she cares for, she would never forgive herself.

"What if he takes the offer as a reason to be more afraid?" Erik refutes.

"True, that is a risk. Play it off as a precautionary measure that The Guard takes with all newly-transitioned. Sell it, Erik; it's a simple manipulation of the feeble human mind. Just make sure that he understands that Sasha is not to know of your discussion or the security measure put in place."

"Alright, will do. It is better to be safe than sorry considering her improved, yet, short fuse, I guess."

"Yes, it is, especially considering her young ones that are involved. I have a feeling that they are the main reason she stays. If it were not for them, she most likely would not have returned."

"Maybe, we don't know for sure. I'll call the husband first thing in the morning before I head to bed."

At that, he gets up and leaves, most likely not wanting to discuss the circumstances that influenced Sasha's choice. It is a sensitive subject for all of us, especially me. No telling where a debate in that topic would quickly go. I am just pleased that I got him to agree to look out for her blood needs in my absence. It is going to be extremely difficult to be away from her, but I have no choice. If I do not attend, my absence could set into motion a terrible domino effect at the hands of my mother.

Chapter 19

"Ang! I can't go meet him tonight! Maybe, I can try to put it off- I am pretty damn strong. I bet that I could go longer than a week!" I say, pleading with myself more so than her.

"You said you talked him into meeting on neutral territory. That should help, plus, we are going for Monday mojito night with the rest of the girls. Javier's man is playing tonight, so, we get free admission! And don't forget the salsa dancing!" She says this with so much enthusiasm that it becomes contagious.

"Okay, you're right; we are going to have a blast tonight- especially, considering that the kids are at grandma's, and she's taking them to school tomorrow so I don't have to. Stephan also said that he is going to join Christian for poker, so there is no time constraints, for once. What should I wear? I haven't been out salsa dancing in forever, Ang!" I can hear her rummaging through her closet over the receiver.

"Wear the girls' night out dress we found at the mall last year- you know the one you found for the New Year's party." Great, that dress gets me into trouble every time I wear it. The dress makes me feel extra sexy, and that's why it is dubbed the girls' night out dress. Whatever happens on girls' night out stays lost in the night, never to follow us home. She wants me to wear *that* out to a salsa club on a Monday night? Ahhh, what the heck. I have had no intimacy from my husband since I first got back home, so it has been at least two weeks? "Girls' night out dress it is; feeling sexy might just be the pick-me-up I need. See you there at 9:00."

"Yes, you will, because if you don't show, I will come find you!" She would too, she hates any threat to girls' night out; we only get to do this a few times a year.

I walk to the back of my closet where all of the dresses that rarely get worn are all lined up- waiting for the day someone will come and dust them off. I unzip the grey garment bag, and ruffled seafoam green chiffon flows forward, happy to be free. I skim my hand over the soft fabric before removing the dress to look it over and make sure there are no stains or rips in it. The last time it had a night out, things got a little crazy. A hazy memory of a drunken truth-or-dare episode on a hot summer's night comes to mind. The girls thought it would be a good idea to liven up the boring bachelorette party we were at. It got exciting all right; let's just say that daring a girl, who has had way too many sex on the beach cocktails, to kiss a random guy who wasn't really there alone isn't always a good idea. I barely remember any of it except a little bar fight... and a security guard throwing me over his shoulder before hauling me out to our limo.

Ang says that I tried to talk some sense into the girl who was coming at me ready to brawl, but she threw the first punch and that was all it took. I believed Ang's play-by-play; it sounded about right. I try to be rational and calm in heated situations. My dad also taught me to never start a fight, but to always finish one. I woke up the next day in our hotel room without a scratch on me; Ang says that the other girl wasn't so lucky- hell if I remember. Thank goodness, my dress is still in one piece and looking better than ever. Come to think of it, that guy at the bar seemed to forget that he had a date at the time too; it was the power of the dress. Ahhh, good times.

The halter straps are braided in a Greek fashion, and the bodice is fitted with gold thread and beaded details. The chiffon spills out from the waist line, accentuating any movement one makes from within the dress. The back is open, dips low, and stops right above my butt crack. Fashion tape is much needed back there. The dress comes down to a few inches above the knees and hugs my body in all the right places. This is why I am glad that Stephan has just left to take the boys to his mom's, leaving me to get ready alone. He doesn't need to know what I have decided to wear out on the town—not that he would say anything, but I don't want to add to his insecurities. He's been having a lot of those since I got back. So, why wear the dress? Because a woman likes to feel pretty and sexy sometimes, and that is what this dress does for me; I feel fantastic whenever I wear it.

Finishing my hair and makeup first, I blend a little gold and turquoise into my eye shadow to pick up the colors in my dress. I put my hair up into a French twist with a few loose tendrils falling about my neck and face. I prefer my hair up when dancing; it's annoying to have long hair sticking to your back on the dance floor. Time for the dress. Stepping into it and pulling it up is like sliding a fitted masterpiece into place. I tie the halter up behind my neck, slip on my gold stiletto heels, and step back to look at myself in the full-length mirror. I look amazing, not too formal, but perfect to fit in with all the dressed up Latin hotties at the salsa club. The women there really like to go all out, even on a Monday night. Looking at the clock, it's going on 7:00 PM; I better get going if I am going to meet Etienne beforehand. We agreed to meet at City Park; it is on my way downtown and still close enough for both of us to get to easily.

On my way there, I realize that I am going to meet my wannabe lover dressed like this. Shit. I was so excited to wear my favorite dress and go out dancing that I didn't even put two and two together. This will be interesting. At least, Ang will call if I'm running late; she would drag me out of hell by the scruff of my neck if I tried to get out of our night out.

Turning into the park, I round the bend onto one of the odd little streets you can park on. His large, black

Infiniti SUV is just up ahead; I had forgotten how huge that thing is- like a mini bus. I pull my Audi A8 up behind him. Before I get out, I find myself checking my reflection in the rearview mirror; ugh, I'm such a girl. Maybe, I should skip out and meet him way later- after I have gone home and changed into sweats or something. Sitting there contemplating turning around and rescheduling, I feel my thirst come on hard.

My fangs begin to elongate a little, and my mouth is salivating. Being this close to him and knowing what he has waiting for me ignites my other half to take over. It's time, let's get it over with. I quickly get out of my car, unable to hold back. Walking to the rear passenger door, I open it without pause. Looking up, he is in the backseat waiting for me, gazing at me with curiosity, most likely because of the dress. I didn't bother with a coat- they overheat me too fast these days. Perhaps, I should have grabbed one before coming here. Hitching up my dress, I climb up next to him, and his delicious scent draws my fangs out all the way. Erik is in the driver's seat reading a book.

"Erik, I will let you know when we are through," Etienne says, without taking his eyes off of me. The thought of being alone with Etienne has me looking around nervously. I try to avoid his stare, and suddenly, I feel naked in his presence. As Erik's door closes, the air becomes thick, making it hard to breathe.

While I am fighting the suffocating feeling I am now experiencing in his presence, I find that I can't stop focusing on his neck- my stomach is burning with hunger.

"If you wanted to maintain strict boundaries, why on earth would you come to me dressed like that?" His sexy grin is wide, and his eyes are still undressing me. I'm too hungry at this point to care that this might end with us finishing what always starts when we feed.

"Girls' night out, salsa dancing... dressing up comes with the territory," I nervously rush out. Why am I this hungry? It wasn't this bad last week. Still trying to avoid his eyes, I settle for looking straight ahead, my heart is now beating as fast as a hummingbird's wings.

"Hhmmm, Sasha, you mean to tell me that you are going to go salsa dancing with friends, which means that you, most likely, will find some casual dance partner there, only to dance a very sensual dance with them. I must say that I am rather uncomfortable with that, especially considering how ravishing you look at this moment," he says greedily in his deep voice, while pulling me over into his lap.

His left hand is now skimming my bare back in a downward motion, stopping at the low seam of my dress- an inch away from my bottom that is barely covered. The dress also has a built-in bra, so aside from a thong, I am not wearing anything else underneath. I shiver under his touch, and my body begs for permission to bend under his will.

"It is just harmless fun, then back home right after. Why does it matter?" I say, challenging his need to control.

"Isn't it obvious? I don't like to share," he says forcefully, as he takes my right hand and pulls my wrist up to his mouth, gently kissing the posterior side. Biting down gently, he starts taking of me immediately, not able to contain himself. His left hand is still tracing the outline of my back, playing with the low seam sitting atop my rear, threatening to tuck his fingers under and explore just how little I am wearing underneath. It is all I can do to hold on.

Sinking my teeth into my lower lip while sucking in deep breaths through my nose, I focus on my plans to finally go out dancing and have fun, not on what is happening right now. He finishes and closes the wound with heavy contentment. As I am about to move off of his lap, his eyes suddenly narrow and focus on my lower lip- to the place where I bit down so hard that it is now bleeding. Leaning in, he runs his tongue along my lip, closing the cut. The contact of his warm tongue sliding like silk across my skin sends a lick of fire through my loins. Before he retracts his tongue, I automatically part my lips to release the breath that I didn't know I was holding. He takes that as an invitation and claims my mouth as his, kissing me hard.

He comes at me so fast that it is impossible to resist. No longer able to hold onto my control, I dive headfirst into his pool of desire that is now bubbling up from the depths of his normally-cold exterior. His kisses are deep and feverish, and I can't get enough. It is freeing not to have to be so gentle with him; he is a big boy who can handle all of me, no matter how wild I get. My fang inadvertently nicks his lip, sending an explosion of flavor across my tongue. God, he is lusciously good. Pulling his lower lip into my mouth I draw more of his decadent taste. I run my hands up through his hair and bring him in closer. I feel his hand travel up my back to my neck and release the halter. The front tumbles down, exposing the tops of my breasts. Shocked by his quick hands, I close his lip and try to sit back. He doesn't allow it; instead, he pulls me in closer and cups my breast through the bodice. My head falls back to let go of a groan as his forefinger and thumb begin to tease one of my nipples through the fabric as his mouth softly kisses the tops of my breasts. You need to stop, Sasha- feed and then leave! My voice of reason pleads.

"Etienne... I need to..." Just then, he frees my left nipple and takes it into his hot, wet mouth, forcing me to finish my sentence with a loud moan. His right hand is now up and under my dress, grasping my bare thigh. Take me. No really, please, take me right now! No, no. "Etienne, please stop," I say, in a pitiful attempt to get him to stop, not really wanting him too. He doesn't listen. He takes my nipple deeper into his mouth, sucking hard, as his hand creeps up to the crease at the top of my thigh. The heat in my belly responds; instead of hunger, it now burns with desire, ready for his hand to move closer. Yes, this is so right; I need all of him right now. I dig my hands into his hair and pull him away from my breast. Hitching my dress up higher, I quickly straddle his lap.

Memories of how he looked last week with his shirt open at the collar force my hands to rip his shirt wide and go for that mouth-watering neck. He bucks under my strike as his length stands at attention, trying to break free from the confines of his pants. My lack of restraint has sent both of us over the edge, and our passionate need for one another has taken over. Before I can finish feeding, he pulls me away from his neck and lays me down on my back with his hands pushing up the length of my dress to my panties. "Ring...Ring...Ring...," my phone sounds out.

"Ignore it," he calls out, as he loops his fingers around the elastic of my thong.

Shit. Grabbing my phone from my small purse on the seat, I answer in a breathy hurry. "Hello?" I say, as I close my legs to him and slap his hand away, the fog quickly clearing from my brain.

"Sasha! Where are you? Its almost 9:00, and you are not here!"

Where did the time go? It definitely was not lost in a deep conversation with this private man! Apparently, all I can think about is sex and blood around him. Wasn't meeting in a car out in public supposed to help? No, it didn't in the least. "Okay, I am just leaving- be there in a few," I say, and quickly hang up before she can respond. Etienne has stopped and is now sitting back glowering at me. "Why are you looking at me like that? I have to go, and we are both to blame for letting this get out of hand… again," I say, as I scowl back at him. Both of us are disappointed at being pulled back into reality.

"These are not to be weekly lover sessions; we need to behave," I lecture on. He doesn't answer, but instead, pouts as he goes to button-up his shirt, only to find that it is shy of all of the buttons. "Oops, sorry about that," I say in a giggle, laughing away the tension.

"You really must stop ruining all of my clothes," he says sternly, but quickly gives over to the lightening mood. His laugh is deep and wholesome, as well as infectious.

"You laugh like Emile, whole-heartedly; it's beautiful," I say, dazed.

He stops laughing and straightens up, tucking what is left of his shirt back into his pants. "He is my brother; it is to be expected that we have some things in common," he says matter-of-factly. Emile is his brother? Wow, I didn't see that coming; Emile is so calm and laid-back. Etienne is uptight and usually has everyone on edge.

"I didn't know that you have a sibling," I say, surprised.

"I have siblings; Emile has a twin sister."

It's hard to imagine him as a child playing with siblings. Maybe, he was the one who played off in a corner by himself, plotting world domination. "Do you have others or is it just the two?" I ask, now wanting to know more- surprised to hear him admit to having family. His mood suddenly darkens, eyes greying over in sorrow. "Etienne? Are you okay?" I run my fingers along his jaw, trying to comfort him through touch.

"Fine, I had a twin sister; she has long since passed." His voice now holds a touch of sadness.

"What happened to her?" I ask, hoping he will keep talking.

"Her bloodlust was strong back during a time when our race was not as patient with young, irresponsible vampires; she was killed for her actions. I really don't want to talk more about her if you don't mind. She and I were very close, and her loss is still a burden on my heart," he says with finality. Guess that's it about that subject. There is still so much I don't know about him. Over the last few weeks, I have had time to think about everything, which means my list of questions has grown.

Considering how we end up every time we feed from one another, I haven't had the courage to call him. Sitting up tall to straighten my dress, he reaches forward and pulls the thick braided straps back up and around my neck to tie them.

"You really are not wearing much under that dress, are you?" he asks darkly. I can tell that he is trying to mask his emotions with sex and control.

"Hhmmm…wouldn't you like to know. I have to get going- my dancing shoes have been antsy all night to hit the floor," I say, thick with anticipation. If I stay a minute longer, this will end with me on my back again and hating myself in the morning.

"Well, don't let me stop you, my love. Until next time?"

"Yes, see you Monday." I quickly get out and walk back to my car, running my hands over my dress the whole way, tracing the imprint his touch has left.

∞

Heading down the hidden alley toward the club's entrance, I realize that I would have missed it altogether if it wasn't for the long line of people up against the brick wall. I don't see my friends anywhere.

"Ang, where are you guys?" I text.

"We're inside by the bar; your name is on the list."

Oh, Javier- Mr. Magicmaker. I met Javier a few years ago in a cooking class that I spontaneously decided to take when the kids were toddlers and I was determined to cultivate my inner Martha Stewart. He wanted to be a chef and still does. He says that he is just taking the scenic route. He has his hand heavy in the club/restaurant scene doing marketing and promotional gigs here and there, and has found it hard to change careers. His reputation precedes him everywhere he goes. He is highly desired in his current profession, and I think it will be a long time before he is ready to walk away from that. He also has amazing taste and is the one who talked me into this dress the last time Ang and I went shopping with him!

Walking up to the front of the line, I give my name to the large bouncer who is flanked by two cops. After about five minutes of being looked up and down, he lets me in. It was taking so long that I was surprised when he actually decided to let me in. Descending the narrow staircase into the belly of the seedy-looking basement, I barely am able to spot my friends through the dim lighting when I cross the threshold. They are in the back by the rustic-looking bar, circling a cocktail table… building up their liquid courage. Thank goodness for super-vampire vision.

"Sasha! Darling, you made it!" Javier bounces up to meet me at the door with two mojitos in hand. He hands me the pineapple mojito, my favorite. "Don't you look to die for! I told you that dress was amazing. You *make* that dress, honey!"

"Thanks to you, the bouncer and his flunkies just eye-fucked me forever before he would let me in. This dress is nothing but trouble!" I joke.

"True, but being bad sometimes is just more fun," he replies with a little sashay in his step.

I almost spit out my drink at the irony of that statement, considering how I have been acting the last few weeks. We pass through the crowded entrance over to the rest of the group. Monique, Laura, and Ang are all on their second- well maybe third, drink. It is starting to feel packed as more people begin to fill the place.

Monique and Laura are Ang's friends from high school. We hit it off at one of Ang's backyard fiestas and have been cool ever since.

"I can't believe the amount of people here on a Monday night!" I yell over the music.

"It's like this every Monday; this place is so underground that all the hard-core people come in waves to get their fill!" Laura yells back.

The place is small as it is; add all the people and it makes me wonder how there will be any room to dance.

Ang whispers into my ear, "What happened? You got held up a long time; you said it wouldn't take that long!" She eyeballs me suspiciously.

"Let's just say that I got a little carried away, but your phone call came at the right time. What? Don't look at me like that- it's the dress's fault! I am almost certain that I would have behaved if I wasn't feeling all frisky!" I say, feigning innocence.

Her look screams "ya, whatever" as she booty bumps me.

"Ooh, the live band's coming on-stage; that means it's almost time!!" Monique says with excitement. Her feet have been tapping along the concrete floors to the DJ's happy-hour music since I walked in. Knowing her, she is ready to find a partner and work her charm; men have always responded well to her. Laura chuckles next to her, cheeks rosy from the rum, and her short blond bob is perfectly framing her face. She is pretending to listen to us, but is really fixated on a handsome guy at the table next to us.

"Laura, just go talk to him!" I yell, calling her out. She blushes, always the more reserved one.

"There's my Tony!" Javier screams as the musicians start tuning, making sure everything is ready. Tony waves back. He is super cute- tall, muscular, skinny, and very Italian. The band thunders to life with a warm-up tune, telling us all to find a partner. That is all Monique needs as she is off already with someone she probably picked out the minute she walked in. She is very straight-forward- no games, but pulls it off with grace. Laura grabs Ang, and they head to the table next to us to make conversation, or more like, stake their claim. This leaves Javier as my partner, which is great because he is an awesome dancer.

The beat picks up and all couples hit the glossy, wood-planked floor, warming up with basic salsa footwork. It's been at least a year since I have done this, so the slow start is good. Step forward, replace, shift your weight, other leg… remember to lead with your hips. I concentrate as I fall into my dance groove, getting the basic steps down. Javier and I switch to a side-step, continuing the warm-up. Thank goodness that Ang and I are always looking for new things to try to keep our workouts going. Dance, yoga, kickboxing... we are always up for a physical challenge and love trying something new. Last winter, we took a bunch of dance lessons just for fun.

The beat picks up a little faster this time as the band roles into another song; Javier and I step into dancers' position and start moving around the floor. He is leading me perfectly. The two mojitos that I just had have loosened me up a little. Javier is picking up speed and starting to lead us into turns. Having a good partner to dance with makes all the difference. If your partner is bad, the dance is bad, and tripping is almost certain.

As we are dancing in and around the other tightly-packed couples, I start to sense other vampires in the room- males. The air is thick, causing everyone's scents to blend in the heat, so I didn't notice them right away. I have no clue how I can pick them out, but it's like I can tell their scent is not human- that their genetic make-up is more akin to mine than our counterparts. Looking around, I spot them by the bar, watching the crowd. I don't recognize them, but decide that I should keep an eye on them. Etienne says that vampires walk alongside humans, but something tells me it's not always a symbiotic relationship. Reaching out to see if there are any others, I sense one other female dancing on the other side. She seems harmless and is focused on enjoying herself. I wonder if all vampires can sense each other. Javier slows down, leans in, and motions for a drink. He looks like he needs a break. I think that I was moving a little too fast, and I almost knocked him over a few times. It is so hard to act human these days!

Despite my need to slow it down, we all are having so much fun. Even Ang, who doesn't typically like to dance with anyone but her husband, is getting into the vibe with her partner next to us. Walking up to the makeshift tin-sided bar, I see the two vampire males that I spotted earlier sit a little taller around their table as we near. They are staring at us with the intensity of a moth drawn in by a flame; it must be the dress again. Javier doesn't notice them, but how could he? It is dark in here. If I was still human, there would be no way that I would be able see much past what is right in front of my face. The bartender places our drinks in front of us, and we thirstily drain the glasses. I am ready to get back out there.

"Sasha, you are pretty graceful for someone who claims that they haven't danced in a long time! I am afraid I won't be able to keep up with you much longer!"

I knew I needed to act more human, poor Javier. "I have a lot of endurance these days…. If I wear you out, just let me know, and I guess I'll just have to find someone else to wear out."

"Ha, very funny!"

"Ready to give it another try?" I ask eagerly; he reluctantly nods in agreement.

Turning away from the bar, I catch a glimpse of one of the male vampires who was staring rudely slam a few tequila shots then get up too. He quickly approaches us before we can weed through the crowd back to the floor.

"Hello, my name is Tristan; would you care to dance?" Even my ears are ringing from the music's vibration off the cement walls, so I am surprised that I can even hear him. There is a mischievous glimmer in his eyes- he can tell that I am not human.

I open my mouth to explain that I am already dancing with someone when Javier pipes in. "She would love to! I need a break and was just about to go catch up with some friends who just walked in," he says with a wink and takes off. Damn it, Javier! I don't need to be dancing with some hot vampire guy named *Tristan*.

He is taller than me- about six feet. He has sandy blonde hair that is short and a little tousled, green eyes that miss nothing, and his scent is like crisp, fresh-fallen snow. Though he doesn't scream "threat," there is something about him that bothers me a little. Could it be the fact that I don't trust easy or the fact that he seems to love all of the attention the ladies are giving him- many just throwing it at him as they walk by.

"Sure," I say with a shoulder shrug and weak smile, trying to play it off.

"Excellent." He holds out his hand, inviting me along as the music flows into another set. I place my hand in his. His warmth is friendly, and he has good energy; he just likes the ladies. Womanizer, that's probably what's off about him. He glances back and blushes like he knows what I am thinking. Hmmm, focus on the music, Sasha, just in case he can read thoughts or something.

Tristan quickly pulls me in close, hip to hip and takes the lead. He makes it easy to follow and to add my own little "something special" without worrying about being tripped. We don't start slow and work our way up like Javier and I did. He leads us straight into quick steps and open-arm turns. My hips, once again, find their rhythm, and my arms follow. He is smiling the whole time, watching me move, probably enjoying the view. Tristan sure is cute; it makes it easy to let him get away with his little flirtations. It's sweet, but not a turn-on, much to his dismay. Being with him shows me how nice it is to dance with a non-human- someone I don't have to worry about hurting. He adds a little more flick to his wrist on the turns, and I am able to push back more when our hands meet. We playfully add a little more zest to each step, both knowing that we won't injure the other. I must say, dancing like this with someone who isn't so breakable is really fun. He pulls me in close, slips a leg between mine, then dips me back. His nose brushes my neck before he slowly rolls me upright; oh yeah…what a flirt. He changes the steps up, adding a little tango flavor in- very smooth, Mr. Ladies' Man. He crosses his arms over and pulls me in so that my back is pressed to his front, and my hands are still in his. My hips dip and nudge him hard before I make my way into a little downward shimmy. I would have knocked a human over with that one. Rising back up, he crosses our arms over again, turning me back to face him. The air has become increasingly humid from all of the pressed bodies, creating large amounts of kinetic energy. I find, due to my slick skin, that I have to hold on a little tighter to Tristan's hand. He smiles big as he takes my hand and pushes me out into a wide, open-arm spin. As I turn out, a few tendrils of my hair escape the front of my up-do and fall, framing my face. For some reason, this inspires me to really flick my free wrist out behind me and add a little sashay to the beat like I am a professional or something. I have no idea where that came from. I do know that I sure like this more live-out-loud version of myself. A familiar touch grabs my free hand from behind; I feel Tristan immediately release the hand that he has been holding and see his face turn pale. I find myself being forcefully spun in the opposite direction, never breaking the rhythm.

Turning into the familiar man who just stole me away from Tristan, I can't help but smile. "I didn't know you danced, and I don't remember telling you where I was going for salsa, either." He looks upset that I was just dancing with Tristan, who by the way, has a shocked, as well as embarrassed, look on his face.

"And, I didn't know how cruel a woman could be on the dance floor until I saw you dancing with one of my lieutenants." That explains why Tristan just looked like he saw a ghost.

"Don't be jealous, Etienne; we were just having a little harmless fun. It's hard dancing with humans, being afraid you will break them and all." I purr, as my body and hips take on new life, moving to the music and newly inspired by *his* lead.

Our chemistry is undeniable as we begin to express what we have wanted to do to each other from day one through dance. Never have I danced so close and personal with someone. With every move, we stay close- our bodies moving in synchronicity with one another. His muscular build is intertwined with my soft curves. Sweat starts to glisten across my chest as heat claims what is becoming lost in a few stolen moments of pleasure. Each step flows forward from our joined hips, matching the rhythm of the band's intense Latin beat; it is hard to tell where I begin and he ends. He is enjoying being in control, and I am lost in the surrender. Our typical match of wills is nowhere in sight. We both are hypnotized by the deafening music and the movement of our bodies engaging in, what resembles, upright sex.

After a few songs, it becomes obvious just how well we would do together in the bedroom- not that my imagination needs any help in that department. My desire for him is becoming too much. Watching how he moves effortlessly on the dance floor, elegant yet masculine, makes me want to tell him to handcuff me to his bed and have his way with me. Wouldn't that be something, to be tied up and vulnerable to his will.

"I'm thirsty. Let's take a break?" I pant.

He nods, takes my hand, and leads me through the crowd back to the bar. Tristan and his friend are sitting at full attention at their table, eyes averted, like they are waiting to be reprimanded.

"So, what really brings you here?" I push, wanting to know the real reason I am being stalked.

"There were a few things that I needed to discuss with you before you left, but I didn't get the chance earlier as I was a little distracted."

I laugh and perch on a bar stool, and he leans in close so we can hear each other better. Pineapple mojito in hand, bravery starts to take up residence again. "So, stalker, what would you like to discuss? Let's try to keep it light-hearted, though. I would like to dance more at some point before the night is over," I say spiritedly, knowing how fast his mood can turn sour.

Thankfully, he plays along. "Stalker? You have no idea." Something dark flickers across his eyes for a moment. "On to 'light-hearted' as you requested. I am going back home to France for a few days; it is our race's biggest holiday- the Lunar festival."

"Lunar festival?"

"Imagine Thanksgiving, Christmas, and New Year's all wrapped into one. It is usually a two-week long celebration..."

I cut him off before he can continue. "You will be gone for two weeks?" My anxiety shoots up at the thought.

"No, I will just be going for the first few days; it is important that I attend, but I also don't want to leave you for too long either." What if something happens while he is gone? Should I tell him about my increasing hunger?

"I will text you Erik's number should you need... anything." Does he mean blood?

"Anything? Nourishment included? I thought that would make me sick?"

"It could. It could also just tide you over until I am back, should it come to that. It is good to have options in case of an emergency," he says, reading into my emotions once again.

Imagining feeding from someone else makes my stomach cringe. It makes sense, though. "Okay, if you will be back by next Monday, then I think we will be just fine. Tell me more about this Lunar Festival; it sounds amazing."

His face takes on a euphoric peacefulness as he speaks. "We celebrate our birth from Mother Earth, or Nannau, as we call her. Our magic- our existence, is all tied to the earth. The Lunar Festival is a celebration of our race, our new year, and our commitment to our ancestors. It is not taken lightly." Fascinating. This information has my wheels turning, quieting my nerves.

"You said the earth gifted me; you meant Nannau?"

"Oui, ma chérie."

"Nannau doesn't sound like a French name."

He laughs. "Our ancestral language is not French; it is something along the lines of Sumerian. All vampires speak our ancestral language, but, most choose to speak the native tongue of the country in which they grow-up in- needing to fit in and all. Although, many become multilingual over the years."

Duh, Sasha. "Sumerian? Isn't that a really old language from Mesopotamia or something?"

"Yes, it is thought to be the world's oldest written language. While it was at one time a common tongue, it was quickly replaced with other dialects, and its primary use has become one for sacred, ceremonial, and scientific purposes," he says, and adds a wink at the end.

"Let me guess, vampires created the language."

"As I have said, our influence in human society runs deep. Our ancestral tongue influenced the development of Sumerian, which is why they are so close, and many translations are exactly the same." Of course they are.

I could listen to him talk about his culture- well, I guess our culture, forever. Looking into his eyes and watching him speak in such a relaxed manner is wonderful. This picture of him will be forever engrained in my memory; it's far from the icy, cold-hearted tendencies that he usually exhibits in public.

"Obviously, I can't go to the library and pick up a history book, but I would love to learn more, Etienne." He looks pleased with my inquisitive nature for once.

"Talk to Erik; he can give you access to the digital archives."

"So high-tech, I just might do that."

"Why wouldn't we be privy to modern technology and take full advantage of it?"

"It's just hard to imagine something so ancient and secretive being uploaded to the World-Wide Web- out there for anyone to hack into."

"You are forgetting how ingrained we are into modern-day human society. You really think the super hackers who make the national news for breaking into secured government servers are human?"

"I thought they were."

He looks at me snidely and replies in an aristocratic tone, "Ha! Humans?! Please! You would be wise to reconsider your theories." Well, it is obvious how he feels about the human race.

"Don't bother hiding your disdain for humans or anything." Does he forget that I was one?

"Disdain isn't really the word for it." Ugh, his cocky SOB side is alive and well. I need a drink.

One thing is evident at this point in the evening, vampires need a lot more booze to get and keep a buzz. That must be why Tristan and his friend were shooting straight tequila. It is then that Erik decides to approach from the shadows with a bottle of Patron and a few shot glasses.

"Well, Sasha, if you really want a buzz, you gotta hit the hard stuff," he says with a smile, reading into my disappointment about my soberness.

"Now, where did you come from?" His smile is bright and mischievous.

"I am always around, not to worry. Here you go, boss; after seeing Sasha dance with Tristan, I figured you would need two glasses." Etienne's eyes narrow as he clenches his jaw.

"Ha, ha," I say, as I punch Erik in the arm.

"Easy, Sasha!" Erik fake cries, but quickly begins to rub his arm. I thought it was lightly... guess not.

A bottle of booze, paired with shot glasses, at your table is like waving a flag; here come all of my nosey friends from the woodworks, ready to partake.

"Sasha, where did you find these handsome men?" Javier asks, and Monique and Laura bob their heads along. They are looking at me like, "how the hell do you know these attractive men?" Ang looks perplexed and a little annoyed.

"These are my friends, Etienne and Erik; I just ran into them, go figure." Ang isn't buying it, so I pull her aside. "Ang, don't worry, he had to tell me that he is going out of town; we were a little distracted earlier, and he forgot."

Her arms are crossed, and she now looks pissed. "Uh-huh, okay, isn't that what phones are for?"

"Don't worry, he won't ruin our girls' night, plus everyone is off dancing with different people and having fun."

"Okay, as long as you don't leave me hanging and run off with him."

"Deal! Shot?"

"Yes!"

Four shots later, I feel my little buzz coming back around while the girls and Javier are verging on straight drunk. It used to only take me two drinks, and I was good for hours.

"Let's dance!" Monique slurs as she trots off to find the good-looking African guy she has been with all night. Javier and Tony head off too; the live band has been replaced by the DJ for the last hour, giving the musicians time to dance. Laura and Ang ran off to find the bathroom. Seeing the humans flee our table, Tristan and his friend decide to approach. They have been soberly sitting at their table, watching us this whole time.

"Sir, I apologize. I didn't realize when..." he chokes out, trying to figure out my name. But, he never asked, so how would he know?

"Sasha." Erik corrects him.

"When Sasha attempted to tell me that she was with someone, but was interrupted, I didn't realize that she was here with you." Tristan's fear is obvious, and he is sweating bullets. Etienne is enjoying watching him struggle. I feel his cruel side creep out as he reaches out with his gift and starts to use it on Tristan- no doubt to maximize the guy's fear and unease. I elbow him hard to make him stop.

"Etienne!"

"Oui, Sasha! Alright... alright. Tristan, all is well. Please, leave us and carry on."

At that, Tristan, who now looks like a gorilla just jumped off his back, and his friend turn and offer to take Laura and Ang who, coincidently, choose that moment to walk back up, onto the floor for part two. They gladly accept; the combination of booze and intense hot guys are too good to say "no" to. This leaves the three of us back at the table by ourselves once more.

"You dance, Erik?" I say, teasing Etienne.

"Not usually, but I make exceptions," he says, knowing that it's making his boss uncomfortable. Erik also knows that he can get away with a lot more when I am around. At that, Etienne grabs my hand and yanks me off of the stool.

"Come, let me show you how a real male leads a female on the dance floor." I follow along, allowing him to express his dominance. Purely, because I find it amusing; it's not like I can't knock him on his ass at any point if I wanted to.

The DJ turns the music down a notch, telling us all that the night is coming to an end. The bodies around us have slowed into a Latin form of dirty dancing. All are glistening with sweat and pressed firmly into one another amidst the dense air. Usually, I would have long been back on a bar stool, feet barking from my heels, but I have more stamina since I turned. Etienne pulls me in close for the slow dance- not that we can get much closer at this point.

"I haven't had this much fun in a very long time, Sasha," he murmurs sweetly, as he nestles his nose into my hair.

"This new dimension of our friendship is nice-having fun in public," I say, as he turns me out, then pulls us back together.

"You will find that we are compatible in just about every aspect you can imagine," he whispers in my ear. Why must he always go back to what I am missing out on, rubbing it in constantly. Or, maybe my subconscious knows how right he is and is just waiting for me to get a clue.

"Etienne, please, let's not talk about what we could have together; I already know."

He pulls us closer, lips brushing my ear. "Why fight it?" he dares.

"You already know I refuse to abandon the promises I have already made; the grass is never greener, Etienne. Stephan is a good man, and he deserves more than what I have been giving him." It is true, and he knows it.

Running off every Monday to the arms of my dark lover is not fair to Stephan. From here on out, I will show up in a trash bag, if necessary, so we can keep it strictly business.

"You have outgrown him, don't you see that?" That's enough.

"It's time for me to get going; I'm going to go say goodbye to my friends." Breaking our embrace, I head over to Ang and Javier to say goodbye. Monique and Laura remain immersed in their partners; Laura is still dancing with Tristan's friend! I need to ask Etienne if she is safe with him; the last thing I want is her getting her heart broken, or drained, for that matter. Hopefully, our association with boss-man here is enough to keep her in good hands.

"Hey, I am going to take off." Sadness is now threatening my eyes. Ang comes around the table to me.

"You sure you're okay? Maybe, we should go to Pete's and eat after those two peel themselves off of those guys?" She always knows what to say, but I need to get away before I lose control over my emotions, as that never works out well.

"No, I need solitude. I have had such a blast; thanks for setting this up, it was a perfect evening."

"Well, it was your birthday; wish you would have let us have a cake."

"Shhhh, Ang, no one needs to know it was my birthday! You know I didn't want a big hoopla."

"Thirtieth birthdays are supposed to be big, but don't worry, there isn't a cake with a horrible amount of candles hiding anywhere."

"Thanks, Love; I'll call you tomorrow." We hug, and I take off toward the door. It was amazing to be showered like a princess on my birthday- minus the singing and people making a big deal. All in all, it was the perfect night.

I don't look for Etienne on my way out; my need to be alone to ponder the significance of my 30th birthday rules the direction of my feet before my better judgment can catch on.

"Sasha, did you forget something?" I hear come from behind me. Crap, I don't want to see him right now. My eyes have already sprung a leak.

"Etienne, I need to be alone right now." I keep my back to him as I wipe away the tears.

"Why didn't you tell me that it was your birthday?" His voice sounds hurt that I didn't include him in on the secret.

"Because, I didn't want a big production; I just wanted to have a good time, and that was more than accomplished," I say, turning around to face him, forgetting about the streaks through my makeup.

"Birthdays are important. It is a celebration of your existence- a day to be grateful for your birth, a day to celebrate... you." Not him too. The dry winter air around us starts to thicken and become damp as the clouds overhead darken.

"True, it's just not what I wanted today. I am grateful for every day that I get to embrace, not just one day a year!" I cry out. The emotional enormity of our relationship is just too much at this point. A light rain starts to mist us where we stand. Breathe, Sasha, calm down. He starts to take in my emotions; I leave my barrier down on purpose this time. I don't have it in me to put my feelings into words, so showing him is best.

"Can I at least take you for a meal before I leave for the airport?" Sounds innocent enough in theory- sitting and just talking with him would be lovely, but it is never that simple.

"If I agree to do that, there is a very large chance that I will get on the airplane with you and never look back, especially since my humanity and morals have become easier to dismiss ever since I turned." He seems to get excited at that possibility, but nods his head in understanding. We walk together up the street to where I am parked.

"Until Monday then, mon amour."

"Have a safe and wonderful trip." We hug a simple, non-threatening hug, then he opens my door for me, letting me get in without question or asking for some form of physical contact that will send me over the edge. Driving off with him in my rearview mirror is a pretty obvious metaphor. I have been flirting with the idea of asking Stephan for a divorce over the last few weeks, but that is not what I really want. I want to get control over my wild side and not be so beholden to a stranger who has turned my life upside-down. I want to fulfill my marital commitment to my husband and to our children. I want to be everything he deserves as he is always so selfless with me and the children. We can make it work; we all just need a little more practice.

Stephan is already in bed, smelling fresh from the shower. Discreetly returning my dress back to its hanger, I opt for a shower too, before crawling into bed. Screw pajamas tonight; I know how Stephan feels, but I hate them so much. He needs to get used to me having more of an opinion these days instead of just going with the flow all the time if we are going to make this work. Sliding into bed next to him, he wakes up and pulls me in close.

"Felize cumpleanos, mi amour," he mumbles as he holds me.

He is a good husband. He respects my limitations and boundaries. He let my birthday present be a girls' night out with no quarrel or guilt trip. Falling asleep in his arms is a reminder that sex isn't everything in a relationship. Our level of intimacy can be enough if we nurture it.

Chapter 20

"Sasha, what do you want to do this weekend since you have it off? We could have a belated family day for your birthday." Stephan asks while we all are finishing dinner. The boys have started to fling peas at each other, reiterating the point that we need to take them to do something fun.

"Guys, you are going to clean all of that up!" Yelling at them gets them to stop and begin picking up the green globs. "Should we head up to Loveland for the day? We could get up early and head out by 7:00 AM." Taking the kids skiing would wear them out for not only tomorrow, but part of Sunday too.

"Sure, we haven't done any family activities in a while. It will be nice to spend the day together. Wait, will you be okay to be up all day?" he asks, while trying to be cautious of his words around the boys. We agreed in the beginning that we will keep this from them for now. Later on, when they are older, we will figure out how to explain why mommy doesn't age like the other mommies.

"I should be good. If I'm not, I will head to the lodge and wait; just keep your phone on you." Fatigue has been plaguing me already this week; I hope it goes well. I need to stick it out; I cherish these times when we are all together as a family. "Alright guys, go get ready for bed and lay out your ski clothes for tomorrow; we are going to go have some fun!" At that, they take off upstairs like two little hellcats. It would be nice to figure out a way to bottle all of that energy so the adults could have something to help them keep up.

"Babe, you sure you will be okay? You look a little grey around the gills."

Fake it until you make it. "It's all good; if the altitude plays tricks, you will know where to find me," I say with a smile. We wash the dishes together and pack the cooler for the morning. "I can't remember the last time we went skiing together; this will be an excellent birthday present," I yawn out.

He shakes his head at my stubbornness. "Why don't you go on up to bed and get some rest; I will be right behind you," Stephan says, as he shoos me out of the kitchen. He is right; things have been going so well this week between us that I don't want to ruin a family day because of sleepiness.

∞

"Wake up, my love; it's time to get going," Stephan says, as he gently shakes me awake. I don't even remember falling asleep. I crack my lids to see 6:00 AM staring back at me; I better throw some clothes on and start breakfast.

"Ugh, okay, I'm up; meet you downstairs in a minute." Have I mentioned how mornings are not my thing? Who, in their right mind, agrees to wake up at this hour; it is unnatural. Throwing on my ski base-layers, I quickly comb my hair back into a ponytail before heading downstairs- forget the makeup at this hour. The boys are already up and dressed, playing video games. They crack me up; they know that if they are dressed and ready without us asking, they can talk us into a little video-game time. Stephan is out packing up the SUV, so breakfast is the last detail that needs attention.

Scrambled eggs, toast, and fruit served up for four; then we are on our way.

I love going up to the mountains at any time of year as they are always impressive. Nature at its finest-proof enough that Mother Nature has so many secrets and wonders that we barely understand. Loveland is the perfect spot to ski for the day; it isn't too far away, it's easy to get to, and it is a quick drive home after. The boys have been bantering with each other on who is going to ski the fastest, or get the most runs in, the whole way up. These two are so competitive. We pull up and park.

"Alright, we are here!" The boys squeal in unison. They fly out of the car to the nearest parking lot snow-pile before we can even get out.

"Ready, mi corazon? The boys have already beat us to the first powder." He winks.

"Let's do it!" I say, with too much enthusiasm.

Getting out in a hurry isn't the best idea as the sun and altitude hit me like a time bomb. I thought that being a vampire meant you had more stamina; this is ridiculous. I am supposed to be stronger than this, damn it! Pushing through, I pull out the kids' ski gear and call them over to get it. This will not get the better of me.

"I'm all suited up; here's your gear, Sash." As I reach for my skis, an extreme wave of nausea hits me like bulldozer.

"Stephan, I think I might hang back for a little bit; you guys head up for the first run, and I'll meet up with you." The air is too thin up here; that's what the problem is. Plus, I am out in the sunlight; it always makes me feel off.

"Are you sure? We can hang back and wait for you; the boys are having fun in that pile of snow," he says worriedly.

"No, I'm okay, no need to wait."

He gives up and nods in agreement. He knows it does no good to try and persuade me; I don't usually bother with expressing my needs unless I absolutely mean it. "Si, but call if you need anything or if you change your mind about being up here."

"I will, don't worry so much; take the boys to run off some of that energy." With that, he gives me a quick peck and heads off with the twins.

Leaning back against the Mercedes, I take a moment and try to recover. It's no use, the ground is starting to move- tilting this way and that way. Reaching for the passenger door, I manage to climb into the back, lock the doors, and lie down. What is this shit? I've been up during the day before, and it has never bothered me this much. Looking at the vehicle's carpet, I can see every fiber swirling around to the beat of soundless music. Did someone slip some 'shrooms into my water? Closing my eyes, sleep takes me fast, which is a hell of a lot better than trippin' off of the thin air in the back seat.

"Sasha, wake up! What happened; are you okay?" Stephan asks urgently, as he wakes me.

Peering up, I see him and the boys staring at me through the open door. The sun has begun its descent in the sky, and all of the skiers are packing up for the day. How long have I been asleep? I prop myself up and try to sit up. "Yeah, I think it's the flu or something; did you guys have fun?" The boys chatter on about how well they did- beating daddy a few times down the hill. Stephan is looking like he wants to drive me to the hospital or something. "Guys, load up your gear while daddy gets the cooler out; you can eat on the way back

374

and tell me all about it." Stephan takes the cue and gets the kids settled while I climb to the front of the car. Checking my phone, I see a few missed calls from Stephan and a few texts from Ang, checking in. "Sorry, babe, I didn't hear my phone ringing. I must have been really tired."

"I figured you went to the lodge or something and forgot to call; we were going to drive up and get you," Stephan says, as he gets in. The boys have already opened the cooler and downed part of their sandwiches while simultaneously turning on the DVD player and putting on their headphones; they are ready for zone-out mode- talented little creatures.

"Do you need to go see him?" Stephan asks out of the blue. Him, who? Oh! Does he mean? Do I? I am not due to feed until Monday; I just fed a few days ago. Well, it was a partial feeding... maybe that is what is wrong. Being dropped off there, again, by Stephan is not going to be helpful. It has taken us weeks to get to this good place that we are in, and I really don't want to ruin it. Our peaceful family life this last week is what I needed to remind myself why I stay; I would never want to tear this family apart. Nor, would I want to do that to my boys. "I don't know what's wrong; I would rather that I didn't at this time."

Stephan shakes his head. "You obviously are not okay, and I can't take you to an urgent care. Maybe, he knows what is wrong." Silence… "Sasha, can you feed from me? I know that it's not ideal, but if that's what the problem is, and it helps you…" I don't even let him finish.

"Are you kidding? I could accidently kill you if we open that can of worms!" I appreciate his offer, but I told him long ago how this has to work.

My vampire side already likes to rear its selfish side enough as it is. The last thing I want to do is test my self-control on human blood- the equivalent of vampire crack. The smell repulsed me, but what if the taste doesn't? He lets out a long sigh; I am guessing that he is relieved by my refusal.

"Maybe I do need to go; I don't know what's going on with me, and he is the only one I know who might be able to tell me." Stephan tenses up next to me. His need to take care of me and his inability to do one simple thing, such as feed me to sustain me, is hard for him to accept. "Hey, easy, this might happen once in a while- things we can't explain might come up, just as needs change based on environmental stresses. I did work extra this week; maybe that was too much... and I can't risk hurting you. That is one factor that brings out a whole new side of me- one that I don't want you to see. " He already treats me differently as it is, I can't imagine how reserved or fearful he would become if we ever experimented with that side of things... if he actually survived it.

"I told you to stop picking up so many extra shifts; we don't need the money. What if you make yourself really sick?" His irritation over the situation is rising.

"Relax, I do it because I like to help out my team when I can. If you drop me off, I can get a ride back. You want to watch that movie tonight? I'll make us some stove-top popcorn." I am trying to encourage him out of his mood.

"I didn't think I would have to go back there after the last time I had to take you," he reluctantly says.

"Stephan, it's not like this is a picnic for me either, but it is better than being laid up like this, or worse, losing self-control!" I hiss under my breath.

"Then, let's just try having you feed from me. I am your husband; I should be able to take care of you." I thought he would be relieved not to have to do that.

"You are really willing to risk everyone's safety because of your insecurities?"

He rolls his eyes and continues, "I knew we would have to adapt and that it would take some time. But, you're different now in some ways, and it's hard to understand; I thought you would still be the same."

Different? Looking back I see the boys still have their headphones on for their movie. "How am I so different?" This should be good.

"You just are- like sleeping naked, eating a lot, and you're more aggressive."

"I hadn't noticed any big changes in my personality, but yes, I hate pajamas; I always have. I just kept them on for your comfort. My natural body temperature is higher these days. Aggressive? That is just plain silly- missing a filter or two, sure, but I was tired of those anyway. You should be happy that I am getting better at telling you how I feel or what I want instead of bottling it up."

He keeps going, letting it all out, "And, when it comes to... relations... you are more distant." Gee, wonder why, Mr. Vanilla.

"It is because that has become boring and predictable. Like, we are just going through the motions; it has been like that for years. I guess it just bothers me more now." He has nothing to say to that; he knows that it is true, and that it has been a struggle for me- even before I turned. My changes have just put a spotlight over what was already there. "Stephan, we need to grow together; change is going to happen in life, period. We have to learn to adapt, together; that means going outside of our comfort zones." Sex, why is all of this coming down to sex... again.

"And, I have told you that when it comes to relations, I like it simple and straight-forward. I don't like kinky, and I don't need it either."

"Well, I do like it and need it!" I say forcefully. He looks at me stunned; I have never been so brazen with him. Usually, I'm just passive when it comes to our intimacy, never wanting to offend him. I also have never wanted him to look at me like a freak for wanting some kink added in. Who knew…I am a freak, and I like it.

"And, for the record, I am burning all of my pajamas." His face is full of resolve, he is set on his mission to drop me off. He doesn't broach the subject of me trying to feed from him again. He probably is hoping that his passive little wife will return after she has her blood fill. "Stephan, I have always been vocal about my opinions on things when I felt it was necessary, but these days, I just have more to say."

"Yeah, I got that. I have always loved your honesty, but never has it been so out and in my face. I hope you can control yourself around my mother; she is more sensitive, you know."

Yeah, he never lets me forget how very sensitive she is, as well as very religious. I love her to pieces, but I never have been able to be myself around her. Come to think of it, I have never really been myself around her or any of his family. Ever since I turned, I am more myself now than I've ever been.

He pulls up in front of the beautiful old craftsman home. "You got your phone?" he asks, without even looking at me.

"Check. I'll text you when I am on my way back." He doesn't even reply, just looks straight ahead. His hands are clamped tight around the steering wheel, ready to take off. "How about that movie later?" I offer as an olive branch, trying to break his foul mood. He doesn't respond. The boys are asleep, so I get out, foregoing the goodbyes, and close the door. Stephan drives off without another word. I can't wait to go home to that! Forget it, I refuse to tuck Sasha away anymore just so he can be happy.

Walking up the front path, I see that all of the windows are dark; maybe he is still gone? Knocking on the door, there is no response. Molly is usually here... maybe this is a bad idea; I feel like I'm intruding. The ground starts to tip left and right as I back down the walkway. Shit. I better see if someone is home or wait until they are. I head around to the side of the house where the garage is. I need to look and see if there is a granny unit or something in the back that Molly or Erik live in. Coming around the side of the house, I see a studio over the garage that I hadn't noticed before. Since you can't really see the garage from the driveway, it is easy to miss.

The lights are on, so I decide to head up the stairs and see if anyone is home. I think that this is where Erik lives; I am pretty sure that Molly has her own quarters within the main house.

The door to the studio apartment is slightly cracked. Peering through the slit into the candlelit room, I see a semi side-view of a naked male with a muscular back, holding onto a slender female body with full, bare breasts from behind. The sound of clinking metal draws my eyes upward to a long chain suspended from the rafters. She groans in ecstasy and tilts her head back into his shoulder as his hands continue to work over her nipples. The chain being jostled draws my eyes up again, and this time, I see, at the end of the chain, a pair of handcuffs linked around slender wrists. Wow, I shouldn't be watching this. I should tear myself away, but I can't. Their sounds of pleasure are intensifying-muffling any other sound. He caresses her body with his, as his hands slide down and gently cup her sex, sending her into a wave of tremors.

She is locked in place at the wrist and can only move her legs. He moves a leg in-between hers and spreads them apart. Dropping to the ground, he pulls two shorter chains with cuffs out from under the bed, and fastens them around her ankles. She laughs in anticipation and leans back into her restraints. "Oh my, you do pull out all the stops for a lady, don't you," she purrs out. I shouldn't be seeing this. I quickly close the door all the way to give them some privacy and head back down the stairs. As my feet hit the ground, I hear the door open from the studio.

"Sasha?" Hoping the voice has pants on, I slowly turn around and am relieved at the sight of a mostly-dressed Erik.

"Uh, hey, Erik; I was looking for Etienne. I saw the light on so I came up... the door was ajar. I really didn't mean to intrude." I hurry on, embarrassed that I hadn't been able to pull myself away from the peep show.

"Doesn't bother me- sex is a beautiful thing. Is everything okay?" Thank God that he is moving on from my breach into his privacy.

"Apparently, I didn't feed enough the last time, or my feedings are not lasting as long as they should. We went up to the mountains today, and I have felt like I am on drugs ever since."

He starts to laugh a "duh, Sasha" kind of laugh.

"Alright, I get it," I say in good humor; I probably should know better by now.

"He's not due back until tomorrow. Can you make it until then?"

Great, probably not. "I hope so. It's just the damn ground is still on a tilt-a-whirl, and all I can do is sleep. And I am told I am being more aggressive these days too," I say with a huge sigh; the weight of the car ride over here is evident in my words.

"Here, go inside to the main house, and I'll meet you there in a minute." At that, he quickly unlocks the back door to the main house and heads back up to his previous engagement.

Sex is a beautiful thing, he says; like, "hey, whatever, who doesn't fuck whenever, wherever, or however they want." Erik has become like a brother, so the realization that I just saw him doing the nasty is now a tad bit disturbing, even though his methods were hot.

The back door leads to a small hallway, which opens up into the most beautiful kitchen I have ever seen. It is my dream kitchen. Antiqued, beveled, white cabinets with polished, dark-cement countertops, all stainless appliances, and a huge island in the middle adorn the kitchen while Moroccan-themed tile work sits proudly above the counters as the backsplash. The hardwood floors are done in cherry and match the rest of the house. I could live in this kitchen- it was so large. The refrigerator is impressive too. It looks like a double-wide, it must be custom. Of course it is. Curiosity has me opening the handle to the fridge, and I am greeted by an entire grocery store.

"Hungry?"

I didn't even hear him come in! "Uh, no, food doesn't sound so good. I'm amazed by this kitchen, I would love to cook in here," I say startled, trying to wipe the picture of a naked Erik from my mind.

"You cook?" he asks with skepticism.

"Do I cook? Funny question- no, I create!" I say with a cocky smile. He has no idea how I can tear it up in the kitchen. Cooking is my outlet, my craft. Blending flavors and textures to create a mind-blowing meal is my passion.

Erik, now fully dressed, saunters over to the island bar stool and sits down. "Good, you can make us something to eat, then; I've worked up an appetite." Ugh! How is it that he can make that sound so gross and wickedly appealing, all at the same time?

"No can do; I think I need to just lay my head here in the fridge for a while, sorry." I think I am turning green again; the smell of the refrigerator's contents have started to overwhelm me.

"Sasha, do you want to try and feed from me? If you do, it's fine. It just might make you feel worse. It's your choice." Great, I don't need to feel worse.

"Erik, do all vampires get sick unless they feed from a certain… vampire?" I really need to know why I can't just feed from whomever I damn well please. I am getting pretty sick of depending on one male for this shit.

"No, only those who bond, which rarely happens. Those of us who are unbound can feed from whomever we please."

Isn't that nice. "You're just full of good news, aren't you? Guess if it's a rare thing, it will probably happen to me. Fucking ridiculous." I was obviously starting to feel very bitchy.

He looks at me smug. "Of course, it's like your 'thing.' You are a puzzle that even we experienced vamps are trying to figure out... what *will* she do next?" It is my turn to laugh.

Laughing makes the ground start to spin full-force, forcing me to reach out and grab the island to support myself.

"Come here and sit down on the stool, rest your head on the cold surface before you blow chunks," Erik says, as he gets up and puts me on the stool. My cheek hits the cold countertop without needing any encouragement.

"Uuuuhhhh, Erik, let's just try it; I can't do this anymore." I see him pull out his phone and make a phone call.

"She's here, she needs to feed; how far out are you? Fuck, really? Alright, ALRIGHT! We will give it a shot. Yes, I will call you back after." He puts his phone on the island. "You know who that was; he thinks that we should try it. I wanted to make sure that he is still okay with it beforehand. He is just boarding his plane, so he won't be here anytime soon." Erik looks nervous, like he is afraid for me and for himself.

"Don't be a wimp, Erik, just give me your wrist." I am fed up with everyone tiptoeing around the boss man's feelings; he's an asshole, it's not a news flash. He leans onto the island and puts his left wrist in front of my face, and his other hand disappears into his pocket. Does he plan on punching himself in the crotch if his other head gets the wrong idea? "Feeding isn't always sexual, you know!"

He scoffs. "I'm not taking any chances, baby-cakes." I crinkle up my nose at this response. Okay, let's get this over with.

His lemon scent is strong, but not repulsive; I think I can... I think I can. I lift my head up slightly and begrudgingly pull his wrist over to my mouth; my stomach is already starting to flip out the nearer he gets. Hey now, you don't know that you don't like something until you try it. With that, I go against my better judgment and bite down. Erik holds still, but he is tense; I can hear him grinding his jaw. His scent is decent, but he tastes like metallic lemonade- as if someone made a batch of overly-sweet lemonade and left their change in the bottom. Just keep going, I tell myself. After a minute, my head stops spinning; it seems to be helping. Erik is starting to get fidgety, and that hand in his pocket looks like it is trying to hide something. Men! Thankfully, the feelings aren't mutual. After a few more seconds of taking long pulls, I stop, close his wrist, and slowly sit up.

The ground is where it belongs, the walls have stopped pulsating, and my head is still good. Erik looks uneasy, like he's waiting for something bad to happen. "Why are you looking at me like that? I feel fine."

"You sure? You didn't take much."

"That's because you were fidgeting like a squirrel in a nut-house!" And, he tastes bad.

"Let's just wait here for a minute and make sure that you have your sea-legs back."

"Oh, I didn't plan on jumping up." We are going to take this nice and slow.

"You wanna watch TV or something? I think you should hang for a while, actually- like an hour or so. You being the unpredictable type and all."

"Thanks for the reminder, smart-ass. Sure, let's go." See, such a big brother. After about thirty seconds, I swing my legs out to slide down from the bar stool. The sudden movement has my stomach quaking. I stop and lay my cheek back on the island's surface in an attempt to get it to settle back down. It doesn't help at all. A sharp pain shoots through my gut. Oh God, this isn't good.

Without my permission, my stomach heaves, and before I can make it to the sink, it decides to reject all contents in one large, fast, forceful evacuation all over the beautiful kitchen. The white cabinets that are in my projectile range find themselves now sprayed a shade of red... and tuna sandwich. Did I mention that Erik is standing right next to me, too? Horrified at what just happened, I turn to take in the painted Erik.

"Sweet Mary and Joseph, I am so sorry, Erik!" He has his lips pressed tight, and his face looks like it is going to blow. "Erik?"

He bursts out laughing so hard that he falls back against the fridge. "Molly is going to have a stroke! This is great, it's like a horror flick in here! I gotta take a picture of this; the guys will never believe me if I don't!" He picks up his iPhone and snaps a rolling video of the room and my expression, then flips the screen to capture himself covered in gore.

That stuff came out of me with so much force that it was like a fire-hose coated the joint, and he is laughing.

"I am glad that you are so amused. I don't see how this is funny! It's your fault, you know, you taste like shit- like someone threw a handful of change and a pound of sugar in one glass of pink lemonade!" I say defensively, but end up laughing. His mood is infectious. Of course, he caught that on camera too before shutting off his phone.

"Hey now, I've been told I taste like a summer's day, delightful even!" he replies, trying to look hurt. All of the excitement has put me back at square one.

"Yeah, that's it. Hey, listen, the room is still dancing like a bad trip. I'm going to go crawl into the shower. I will help clean this up once I know that this," I sweep my arm out over the mess, "isn't on the verge of happening again." I go to stand as Molly walks in from the back hallway, looking quaint in a crisp, white blouse and khaki skirt. Her greying hair is pulled back into a neat bun. Her face is still young-looking and has just a few laugh-lines. Right now, she is showing more lines than usual as she is frowning in a very unpleasant manner.

"Molly, I am so sorry; I will clean it up." She holds up her hand to silence my rambling.

"Hush, child, you will do no such thing. Erik, don't you dare move; if you track this mess even an inch, you will not eat for a week. I need to get some towels, and you will need to strip here in the kitchen!" She jumps to action, fetching supplies.

"Molly, relax, I will help you." Erik laughs as he starts to slip off his shoes.

"Erik, Sasha, are both of you alright? No one is injured, right?" Molly opens a trash bag and motions for Erik to put his clothes in. He starts to unbutton his shirt, revealing his perfect abs. I don't need to see this!

"Sasha seems to have rejected my blood, that's all."

"Apparently so! You should know better; she is bound to the master!" She huffs while shaking her head in disbelief.

"He is the one who told us to try; she's running on 'E' and needs to feed."

"Well, then, he should know better. Go on, Sasha dear, I will tend to this. All of your things are still in the master's bath downstairs," she says, dismissing me with her motherly British tone.

You don't need to tell me twice- the thought of seeing Erik naked again might lead to part two of painting the floors in red.

Walking gingerly to the doorway of the kitchen with one hand tracing the cabinets to keep my balance, I remove my shoes and leave them there, just in case. Molly might not care for me so much if I track blood throughout the house. I head out the kitchen door and down to the basement bathroom. I haven't been down here in weeks; everything is the same. Memories of my time here are still at the forefront of my brain. I feel the wall all the way to the bathroom; I am afraid to let go of any surface. Surely if I do, the floor will suck me down hard. Once inside, I quickly find the shower and climb in; the hot water feels wonderful. Leaning back against the stone, I let myself slip down to the floor and sit in the steamy spray. The stone walls start to pulsate around me and shift like tiles on a board game. It was a bad idea to come in here; the steam has intensified my symptoms and is making everything worse. As good as the hot water feels, I decide to quickly soap up and head for the bed. After I am able to crawl out of the shower and pull on one of the fluffy robes, I grab my phone and dive into Etienne's bed. It is obvious that I will have to wait here until he gets home. I wasn't really excited to go home anyway.

"Hello, Sasha? Where are you?" Stephan's worried voice sounds out through the receiver.

"He isn't here; he's out of town. His driver let me in to wait. He won't be back until the morning, and no one here knows how to help me right now; they think I might need to feed."

"Should I come get you? I can bring you back in the morning once they know for sure what to do." He sounds desperate to get me away from my current location.

"No, I just threw up a lot of blood. I will wait here with the housekeeper; she will take care of me until we figure out what is wrong. His driver will bring me home as soon as all of this stops. I don't want the boys to see me like this, or you, for that matter."

"Will you be okay?"

Of course I will be. "Yeah, think of it like a vampire flu."

"Can the driver call a vampire for you to feed from to see if that helps? Or can he feed you himself?"

I can't tell him the truth about the bond. That is not something he will understand and that could shatter him. We are too delicate as it is right now. "The driver is a she, and she is trying, but it's not that easy. There is no guarantee that it will work or make me better. I need to stay here until this passes, whatever it is." I have to lie; there is just no other way.

He hurries on. "Alright, I am just worried about you. Plus, I was looking forward to having that movie night. I am sorry about earlier, Sasha; I just feel so helpless sometimes, and I hate that."

"Trust me, I know. We will have a movie-night tomorrow; we should have this figured out by then. How about you take the boys to your mom's tomorrow and go play golf for the day?"

"Yeah, that sounds good; we'll keep busy until you get home." He feigns excitement.

"Stephan, I really am going to be okay; sleep well."

"Ya, sure. Goodnight, see you tomorrow." Click. Even the world's most patient man has his limits. His wife, staying the night at another man's house, is one. Curling up in the bed, surrounded by Etienne's scent, I fall into a dreamless sleep.

I feel him before I hear him. His presence is strong the minute he comes within a few miles of the house. The closer he gets, the stronger his essence is. It is like he is a blinking light on a map- a grid I can see without using my eyes. The car pulls up in the driveway and doesn't even shut off before he is out of it. In a flash, he is in the room. Speedy little thing, isn't he. Standing at the foot of the bed, he looks at me with worry.

"I'm still in one piece, not to worry."

"I knew you didn't get enough the last time."

"I seem to remember someone removing me from their neck before I could finish." He takes off his coat, shoes, and scarf before joining me in the depths of his plush bed.

"I see that you're just as spry as ever, even when you are ill," he says, as he props a pillow behind his head so he can sit up against it. Spry, aggressive... I guess it depends on the source. My head hasn't left the pillow all night, but now, in his presence, my body responds to him without needing to be told twice. Screw the wrist, I crawl onto his lap and unbutton his shirt slowly. He just watches me, enjoying the sight of me going to work. He is taking satisfaction in providing me with what I need.

His shirt parts open, unveiling his neck and my favorite spot. My fangs elongate at the sight, and I go for it without hesitation. He tastes amazing as usual- his blood perfectly designed for me, far from that shit I tried last night. My stomach sits quietly, taking in its fill without protest. After a blissful, non-sexual feeding, a sated feeling takes over, signaling me to stop. I close his neck and lie back on the bed, happy that the bad trip is over.

"Better?" He has no idea how much better I feel! It's nice to be able to pick your own head up off the pillow without the room spinning.

"Much!"

"Mind if I take a turn?"

I roll onto my side facing him and lay my wrist across his mouth in response, no words needed. He bites down and takes his fill. Before long, we are languidly laying side by side, basking in the post-feeding effect. It is like we just ate a Thanksgiving turkey and have the "itis." The lingering of his fingertips on my skin as he runs them down my arm does nothing to motivate me to move.

"Hungry?"

Does he really need to ask? My stomach is grumbling loud enough for the neighbors to hear. I love to eat and haven't liked the fact that I wasn't able to for the last 24 hours.

"Yes."

"Let's go. Molly most likely has the table laid out." Hmmmm, I wonder what she has made.

"Let me put some clothes on. I already appalled her once this weekend, let's not add to it," I say in a huff, as memories of the gory scene flash in front of my eyes. At that, he starts laughing- a deep, bellowing laugh; I guess that someone already told him. "Let me guess, Erik showed you the video?" He nods while still trying to get himself under control. Glad I could give everyone a good chuckle. I pull on the clean clothes that Molly, apparently, now stocks for me in the armoire. "I'll see you up there; you look like you need a minute to recover," I say haughtily, and head up to the dining room. I still don't get what is so funny.

The smells hit me long before I get to the table. It is full of all my favorite breakfast foods: pancakes, French toast, huevos rancheros, fresh fruit... and a few versions of fried pig- yuck; I am guessing that is for Etienne. I grab a plate and dig in, not bothering to wait for his highness.

"Starting without me, already?" He sounds out from the doorway.

"I didn't know how long you would be, and I haven't eaten anything that would stay down in the last few days," I grunt, no more justification needed.

"You must admit, it was funny. Even Molly had a good laugh after it was all cleaned up," he says, as he stifles another chuckle.

"Yes, in hindsight, I guess it was- especially the sight of Erik covered in his own, foul-tasting blood. Ugh, I don't think I will be able to drink lemonade for a while." My face screws up tight at the thought.

"Yes, he was a little hurt that you found his blood to be unappetizing, but that is just a sensitive subject for vampires."

"I am sure he will find a way to get over it."

"I would be lying if I said that I wasn't pleased with the results, selfishly speaking and all." Pleased? At that, I release my essence and send it toward his plate to seize up a piece of his nasty sausage. Using the mist, I encircle the meat and launch it off his plate and into his face without moving my eyes from his. He sits back, looking a little stunned, before a cruel, yet playful grin creeps across his face. "I see someone has been practicing." He leans forward slightly like he is about to jump out of his seat.

"Yes, I have; I started to get bored on my days off. Etienne... I have been practicing a lot!" I warn, as I slowly push my seat back. He stands, trying to be casual, but I can sense that he is anything but. Instead of sticking around to find out, I bolt, heading for the upstairs. He is on my tail, but before he can grab me, I jump over the banister and land gracefully back on the first floor. Heading for the basement, I can tell that he's inches away. Running into the bedroom, I go to close and lock the door, but I am too late; he gets his foot into the threshold. Being stronger, he forces the door open with ease, catches me mid-run, and throws me onto the bed. In a split-second, he has me pinned down.

"Etienne!" I squeal as he threatens to tickle me.

"What to do to you...uhm... tickling you would be too easy; tying you up would be more fun, then I would have full access to do as I please," he says menacingly.

"Don't you dare, I will unleash my own little beast if need be!" I threaten, knowing damn well there is little I can do to stop him from binding me up without possibly hurting him. I am still practicing and tend to forget my own strength. But, that could be fun too; I still owe him a good one for the last training session we had. He starts to tickle me, but now the problem with that is he knows all of my worst spots, as well as the perfect pressure to induce mass tickle overload. On the verge of peeing my pants, I use my essence to pick up the nearest pillow and wack him hard across his face... stunning him for a second.

"Oh, that's how you want to play?" he asks as he turns up the tickle torture. I have got to get him off of me! I try to move my legs to kick him off, but it doesn't work. I am really going to pee my pants from laughing if he doesn't stop soon! I throw my red mist at him hard, hoping it will make this stop. It takes him off of me all right- right off of the side of the bed with me in tow. We land in a disheveled heap on the ground laughing, and his wholesome laugh booms out, dancing around the room.

"Okay, you little devil, you win for now. For the record, next time, I won't be so nice." He jokes, but I know that there is some truth lining those words. His wickedness runs deep.

It is good to know that he has a playful side. As everything quiets down around us, I remember that he just got home from an important trip.

"How was your trip?" He looks at me like he really doesn't want to talk about it.

"It was… really good to go home, I hadn't seen my family in almost a year, well, with the exception of Emile." The way he tacks on the part about Emile suggests that he isn't too happy with him.

"Do you have any nieces or nephews?" I ask, evading the subject of Emile; I don't want to be in the middle of whatever it is.

"My sister has a set of twins."

What's with all the twins? "Are twins a big thing? It seems like everyone is one or has a set." Including me…

"Vampires rarely decide to procreate; when they do, twins are a common byproduct. The Elders also say that it's because of our high-mortality rate- before, and right after we turn, so there is a better chance of repopulating the species." Interesting. I can see how the selfish vampire side would want to evade anything that would impede its self-indulgence.

"Do you have any children?" His face turns bright pink as he strains under the directness of my question.

"No! Why would you ask that?"

"Just curious. It's not like you are an innocent virgin, and things happen."

"Not like they do with humans. Females only ovulate once a year, and it's a big production. Everyone around her knows it is happening- sure as if she was waving a red flag. Most males steer clear. We are selfish in nature, and procreation is not a common goal of ours."

"Fascinating." That explains why I haven't started my period this month. Do I really want to discuss that with him, though? The workings of my female plumbing is something I should know... maybe Molly can fill me in.

"Fall- it usually takes place in the fall. Ovulation is followed by a few days of heavy bleeding if fertilization does not take place. Most take a long weekend away; it is something that females like to do in private. Then, it is back home for a much-needed feeding." Awkward, but I should have known that if I let my thoughts stay on one subject too long, he is going to figure it out.

"Good thing I can't have more children; that is one less thing to worry about if I am to expect a few days of hell during that time."

"You can't have more children?" He suddenly is way too interested in this conversation.

"No, I, uh… had my tubes tied after the twins."

"Ha! You still need to be cautious; your transition probably corrected that."

What? You're kidding me, right? Great. That is all I need, the risk of getting pregnant. "Good thing that I rarely have sex, then," I mumble. As soon as it slips out, I realize that the dialogue I thought was running through my head came out of my mouth. Turning rosy-red in the cheeks, I quickly get up; play time is over. "I better get going- it's already noon, and I need to get stuff ready for the week." I offer him a hand to pull him up, and he takes it; I leverage him up with ease.

"Sasha, are you alright?" he pries.

"Good, thanks. Just gotta get back to the grindstone." He looks like he wants to say something more but decides against it.

"I didn't see your car out front, may I give you a ride?"

"I thought Erik did all of the driving?" I'm hoping that he will change his mind and have Erik take me.

"He is out at the moment."

Of course he is. "Well, let's go then." Nothing like an awkward car ride home to end this perfect moment.

Instead of dwelling on my verbal diarrhea, I decide to prod him about his trip. "How was the festival?" He looks surprised at my question and hesitates before answering.

"It was good. I opened... I mean, I participated in the opening at our most sacred grounds." He looks as if he is trying to recover from almost telling me something that he shouldn't.

"Sacred grounds?"

"Yes, at Göbekli Tepe."

"In Turkey? I thought you were going to France."

"I did, for the first few days, but we, as a family, go to the ceremonial opening at Göbekli Tepe."

"I have always heard how amazing, yet mystifying, that site is. It's thought to be the oldest religious site in the world, but no one can figure out how it got there. Guess it all makes sense now."

"Humans! Yes, they think their primal ancestors built it... how little they really know."

"Humans have completed some amazing feats over time too."

"Possibly so, but most have been influenced by our kind in some way or another. You still underestimate just how integrated we are into the masses and how much power we really hold."

Well, as true as some of that may be, I would rather move away from the narcissistic turn of this conversation. "I loved studying the carvings at that site in one of my college art history classes. I can't even draw a decent stick figure, but I have always loved art-especially learning the history of man through art." He senses that he went too far, once again, on his anti-human spiel.

"The carvings are just one of the many visual highlights; you should feel the sight with your vampire senses. It is other worldly to someone with our level of awareness."

Images flash through my memory from the ceremony that the guys performed when they were first teaching me to harness access to my gifts without needing strong emotional ties to do so. The earth felt alive. It was as if I was breaching the surface of something so deep and so powerful that if I were to move too fast or ask too much, there would have been grave consequences beyond my comprehension. I can't even imagine how a ceremony like that would feel on a site like that!

Chapter 21

I skipped out on our Monday-night feeding; I was full from Sunday and figured that I could wait until next Monday to get back on track. He, of course, replied with a nasty text when he got my message that I wasn't showing. Whatever, I really don't care to deal with his mood swings right now. Come to think of it, for the last few days, I have been in a post-feeding bitchy mood and haven't wanted to deal with anyone's crap.

Today, I am meeting Ang for an evening kickboxing class; it feels good to be doing something fun. The cocky meat-head instructor is teaching today. Oh well, we will just have to work with what we have. "Line up with your bag, ladies, let's get to it!" Meat-head calls. Personally, I think that he thinks all women are pansies; I would love to go a round with him in the ring and drop-kick him- just to teach him a thing or two about how strong women really are. The vampire super strength would also help prove my point. We start the warm- up with some simple kicks and punches. It's hard to hold back, but I know that my real strength is too much for these humans to handle. Meat-head walks over to Ang and starts criticizing her technique. "Do you really want to be here? I've got plenty of ladies on the wait-list who would like to take your spot! Pull your form together!" he yells at her. That's it! I move around my bag so that it is in line with the douche-bag and front-kick it so hard that the heavy bag goes flying over, and knocks him flat on his back with a loud "THUMP!" Pretty sure that I heard the air get knocked out of him too.

Ang is beaming over at me while meat-head is still staring at the ceiling, trying to figure out what just happened. I decide that I should be the bigger person and pull the bag off of him- they *are* pretty heavy. "Hey, you okay? Sorry about that, accident," I say, with a "no biggie" shoulder shrug and offer him my hand to help him up. He looks at me stunned and shakes his head, preferring to get up on his own. The other women in the class are trying to suppress their grins, but it is hard since we all have been verbally abused by him at some point. It's the gym and the rest of the instructors that keep us coming back, not this guy. For the remainder of class, he stays on the other side of the room and only calls out the routine, not his unsolicited criticisms. It ends up being the best class he has ever taught! Post class, Ang and I walk over to the smoothie bar to get a sugar jolt.

"Thanks for that; it helps having a friend with super powers."

"Ha, super powers. Right. He's an ass- the gym should have gotten rid of him years ago."

"Something about him being the owner's nephew keeps him around."

"Great, well, let's skip his class next time then," I say, as I gently nudge her; she is the one who usually decides what class we go to. Walking over to a small table, we sit to enjoy our "healthy" smoothies.

"Can I ask you something?" she asks, treading lightly.

"Shoot."

"Are you happy these days? With your choices?" She doesn't need to say more; I know where she is going.

"Ang, I am happy enough. Fulfilled? No. Stephan is as distant as ever, but he is trying. It's like we are just going through the motions for now." I suck down my tropical-fruit, sugar infused drink, not wanting to talk anymore about my apparent unhappiness.

"Why stay then? Neither of you seem very happy these days."

"It's that obvious?" I didn't think much had changed; we try really hard to act like everything is going great.

"Well, to me it is. Christian and the rest of our friends don't notice it, but I do. It's like you two are just hoping that by sticking it out, things will line up and work."

"You know Stephan's ultra-religious mom doesn't believe in divorce, and neither does Stephan, for that matter." Do I dare add that, if I left Stephan, he would probably take the boys far away from me?

"Isn't happiness worth ruffling a few feathers? I would just hate to see you two end-up making each other more miserable."

"We don't make each other miserable; our relationship is just like an old, comfy pair of sweatpants that you can't throw out. They fit right, they're safe, and they work for your general needs." She looks like she's not buying it.

"If it's so comfortable and safe, how do you explain your mood swings these days? I don't think you realize how bad you are sometimes."

"Gee, thanks!" I huff.

"It's true; someone has to tell you."

I guess that I haven't noticed. It isn't like me to be like this. I am usually the happy, go-lucky type who just goes with the flow.

"It's worse toward the end of the week, like today, for instance. The longer you are away from him, the more short-tempered and bitchy you become."

I try to open my mouth and have something profound come out. "I…" I got nothing.

"Moving on, do you think you are setting a bad example for the boys, modeling a so-so relationship?"

Don't hold back, Ang, just let it all out. "The boys will be fine; they know their father and I love each other, and more importantly, we shower them with affection. They have good standards set in that department."

"Do they? I just can't help but think back to the woman I saw on the dance floor, living up her thirtieth birthday; you were lit-up from the inside. I have never seen you so happy."

I miss that woman too; she was a lot of fun. "Truth is, Ang, I am going to live a long time- longer than you or Stephan. Sacrificing my happiness for now is worth the time it gives me with my family. That carefree woman will have years to be as selfish as she wants to be. Who knows, maybe even explore things with her dark lover. Now is not the time."

"So, you are basically just going to wait until Stephan dies, then you can start caring about yourself again?"

Yup, that sums it up well. "Basically."

"What a waste of time. Locking that fun-loving woman up in a closet, for the next however-many decades, will do nothing but make you cynical and mean."

I look away from her as she continues; she is starting to tear up as she spills her guts. I never could stand to see her cry.

"Fine, say you stick it out. What are you going to do when age starts to catch up with him and you still look like you are in your twenties? Are you going to go around in public and hold his hand, kiss him, and make love to him in his frailty?"

Oh no, not this again. "I don't have the answers for that right now; I am just taking it day by day!"

"Easy, I just am saying that you might be hurting each other more by sticking it out. You might do him a favor and send him on his way to find someone who he can grow old with, someone he can have a deep, passionate love with. You are not the person to give that to him. Everyone deserves a chance to experience that kind of love."

"Thanks for the insight, Gandhi; I will take it into consideration." I can't stand to listen to this anymore, and my bitchy side is on the verge of rearing its ugly head.

"I hope you do- someone has to look out for your best interest, and his."

I know she means well, but swimming in a river of denial is all I am capable of at this time. I want to relish in watching my children thrive and grow. If

Stephan wants to walk away at any time, I will let him, but I will not lead him. The only lead I will follow right now is time's. Time sets into motion all of nature's biological clocks, and time also reveals the truth when one is patient enough. Knowing how little time I have left in this life before I am phased out of it, brings me to a standstill. For my truth is on the horizon, and it will come when time deems it fitting.

∞

    Heading back to the car, Ang's words just keep echoing over and over in my head. She is right about a lot of things, but I don't have the capacity to accept them right now. The biggest question on my mind, at this time, is what to tell my sons as time passes and they come to realize that mommy is "different." I also feel bad that I might be holding Stephan back in some way. She is right about my attitude being worse toward the end of the week, too. The fatigue has also been showing a bad trend by that time as well, just to top it off. Damn it, she is right about everything. Maybe, I need to step-up my feedings... ugh! I wish there was some blood alternative. I quickly shake my head at the thought of trying anyone else's blood- that didn't go over so well the last time. Leaning back into my leather seat, I sit and think about what I should do. It is Thursday night, and the boys are at home with Stephan, getting ready for bed. Should I try to go find Etienne? Another feeding might set my head straight for the weekend. I have to work, and I don't want to risk biting people's heads off there too. I must be getting bad if Ang stepped up and said something. Glancing up into the rearview mirror, I can't stand the person scowling back at me. That's not me, that's not Sasha. Sasha is the smart, sexy, fun, and witty woman who only comes out these days when she is embracing her vampire side. When she is trying to fake a human existence, she becomes closed-off and emotionless. What is happening to me?

I decide to test the waters and see if I can even pick up on Etienne's essence. I might be able to track him the way he always tracks me; if not, I will just go home. I close my eyes and picture the city of Denver and its surroundings as a grid; better yet, like a blacked-out map with green streets running their course. Nothing. Taking a step back, I picture his house to see if I can sense anything. Nothing... again. Huh, how does he do it? Thinking back to Sunday when my blood need was strong, I was able to pick up on him before he even got to the house... that gives me an idea. My essence is what was able to pick up on him. That's it! Send out the one thing that is bound to him to find his location! Releasing the beautiful burnt-red mist from my body, I tell it to find Etienne. The small cloud that forms over my open palm quivers under my direction and shoots off through my windshield without making a dent or sound. It travels through the city like a beam of light. I can see what it sees- it is an extension of me. Anything it brushes past sends the same sensation through my body, as if I am the one ghosting through. It starts to head to the outskirts of town toward the warehouse district. I think I know where it is headed now. I haven't been there since I first turned. It stops just outside the familiar building where I had spent a few days learning how to control myself. I can sense him inside. Should I bother him? What if he is busy? If I send the mist into the warehouse, he will know. Calling my essence back to me, I start the car and head home. I am happy that I was able to succeed at my task, but I don't want to spend any more time than I need to with the one person who I yearn for the most.

I really don't want to see him right now. What I need is a hot shower and sleep for at least a few hours. As I near my street, I keep driving past it in a daze. Before I realize where I am going, I find myself driving up Quebec Street, heading toward his warehouse. Great, guess my subconscious has other ideas. Pulling over, about a half-mile out from my destination, I park my Audi in a nearby lot. What am I doing? I should turn around and go home. I could make it another four days or so. Being this close allows me to pick up clearly on his essence and his emotions. I have found that, while I can't manipulate and fully read everyone's emotions like he can, I can pick up on emotions pretty well- especially his. He is preoccupied with something serious. I can tell, through our partial bond, that he doesn't feel me near. Come to think of it, it is the same thing that I sensed through my essence when I sent it out to look for him. He is deep in thought, and a darkness surrounds him as he continues on... amused with his task. Strange, these are emotions I have yet to fully experience from him. Sure, I could pick up on a trace of them occasionally when he was being cruel, but it always dissipated quickly. Curiosity pulls me in, and I find myself out of my car, zipping up to the warehouse on foot.

As I come close, I can tell he is not alone. Something is wrong. The whole vibe of the place is different. Quieting my breath and closing my eyes, I try to sense what is going on inside without using my mist. Most vampires can't project their essence like I can, but plenty can still use their senses to "taste," "smell," and "hear" what is going on. I have also found that I can sense a vampire's or a human's aura, or energy; it's kind of like I can tell if they're bad or good- what their true nature is... or, something along those lines. I usually can do it best when I have some sort of physical contact with that person. I am not sure how helpful it would be right now from a distance. Erik and Etienne don't know about this little added feature to my upgrades, and I haven't divulged the information either. They don't need to know, and I just figured it out myself. The night that I first met Tristan and could tell that he was, without a doubt, a womanizer was my first clue. I have been playing around with it since. My theory is that it has something to do with my deep connection to the earth's magic- that is about all I have.

Etienne is inside, and his emotions are clouded in black. He is vehemently angry about something. I can smell a little of his blood, but it is old- like an old wound. My heart beat picks up pace at the thought of him possibly being hurt. Calm down and take a deep breath, Sasha; get a full picture before you go running in. I catch a hint of coppery lemons- Erik, he has old blood on him, too. What is going on? Crisp snow… Tristan, no blood. Damp, redwood forest… Gabriel, no blood as well. Smokey fire pit… Emile, once again, no blood. Yet, there is a sixth vampire covered in blood. This one smells of damp hay, like what horses eat. His spirit is strong, and he is badly hurt, but does not bend under the will of something that is trying to overwhelm him. None of this makes any sense. Creeping around the side of the building, I look for a crack or window to look into. My vampire senses, while strong, are still young, and I am getting impatient trying to use them.

I can sense that there is no fear, so that is a plus. Good thing I am still wearing gym clothes; stretchy yoga pants and a workout top make it easy to creep in the night without making a lot of noise. Halfway around the building, a piercing scream lets out, followed by the scent of a new wave of fresh blood- Etienne's. Screw the tiptoeing, I think, as I call forth my essence and flash to the front door. Etienne is hurt, and so are some of my friends; that is all I need to know. Instead of knocking first, I burst in, ready to take on whatever I find, or so I thought.

I wasn't prepared for what I see, but I can't say that I am surprised either. Tristan, Gabriel, and Emile are surrounding the perimeter of the pit. I stop a foot back from Emile, but I can still see Etienne and Erik in the pit, next to a table full of wicked-looking instruments. Etienne has blood dripping down his forearm. They have a nasty-looking friend down there too. He is the biggest male that I have ever seen in my life; he is even bigger than Gabriel. He is chained to the north side of the pit's wall. He looks as if he has been tortured. His skin is littered with small cuts and what looks like acupuncture needles. Is that bamboo shoved up under his fingernails? His face is bloodied and bruised- one eye is swollen shut.

"What are you doing here?" Etienne calls in disgust. I look around to see who he is talking to, and judging by all of the eyes now trained on me, I can guess who.

"Sending in a female to do the job you cannot?" The Clydesdale of a man banters out to Etienne before spitting on him. Holy hell, that just pisses me off more. I feel my anger flare.

"Answer the question!" Etienne demands from me.

"I heard a scream and smelled the blood." What else can I say? I already feel like I have walked into something that I am not supposed to be seeing.

"Leave!" he orders me.

Tristan, Emile, and Gabriel start to walk toward me, and the look in their eyes is one of determination. Their boss has ordered me to leave, and they are going to make sure that I do.

"What, my Lord? You are making her leave? What else am I to play with once I break free?"

What did he just say? My senses sharpen at the threat, and I can hear his muscle fibers start to tense under pressure as he pulls at his chains. The metal is groaning in protest. That set up is not going to hold him.

"Keep trying. If you cannot stay put and behave, you will be put to your death," Etienne warns the menacing man.

The others are still walking slowly toward me in an attempt to circle me, but I ignore them. Tristan is moving the fastest, and I take it that is because he has no idea how much I do not like being told what to do, or forced against my will. The other guys know me well enough, and will most likely try to rationalize with me before putting a hand on me. All of them look like they want to get me out of here and fast.

"Here, kitty-kitty; daddy needs a new pussy to play with." the prisoner calls out, as he pulls again on the chain. This time, I hear a faint pop, as part of the hinge on his wrist gives. No one else in the room responds to it; they don't hear it.

"Fucking unbelievable," Tristan mutters under his breath. He is now off to my right, Emile is circling to my front, and Gabriel is flanking my left.

"I suggest that you apologize, or I will take the gloves off and stop going so easy on you!" Etienne threatens.

The giant man's face clamps down into an evil grin as he pulls again at the chain that has weakened. NO! I outstretch my hand and send my essence full-force into his direction, pinning his wrist back against the cement wall just as the shackle falls free.

"Interesting... very interesting. I suggest that you let go of me or it will not end well when I am free!" He angrily screams out. I feel him straining under my hold, and I am not sure that I can keep it up.

"Do not let go of him!" Etienne barks at me. Oh, now he wants me to stay and help! Tristan is frozen in place and looking at me like "what the hell?" The other two have jumped into the pit to provide Etienne with back-up. The beast is pulling hard on my hold, and I am falling weak.

"I can't hold him much longer, Etienne; do something!" I call in fear. I have a feeling that if this monster gets free, it won't be a good thing.

"Yes, my Lord, do *something*. This is getting boring, and I have other business that I need to attend to," he snarls out. That is not a good look for that evil face.

"Oh, but killing you would be too easy, now, wouldn't it?" Etienne chimes back. He is in his element, and I can feel no fear or loss of control from him.

"True, and you never liked the easy way out, now did you? Even if it might cost you everything?" he says, and glares up at me through his half crusted-over eye with his mouth drawn tight over razor-sharp teeth. He heaves his arm that I am holding and breaks through my hold.

"AHHHH, HA!" he screams as he takes his now free hand and latches it around the shackle that is binding his left wrist and pulls it off with ease.

"Males, hold your weapons. I would like to refrain from killing him!" Etienne calls, as the beast leans down and pulls off the chains from around his ankles with ease, as if it is nothing more than taking off his socks. This is bad, this is really bad.

"Why must you fight it, Aksel?" Etienne asks him, as the beast sizes up Etienne, ready to claw his way out.

"Humans are our playthings; they always have been and always shall be. Your escapades are ridiculous," he laughs out in a deep growl.

"I am sorry that you feel that way. Even after three- hundred years, you haven't changed a bit," Etienne calls, remaining calm as ever.

"And, I never will, no matter what torture you inflict," Aksel spits back, as he edges closer to the table with weapons.

The other guys have palmed up their knives; where are the guns? Wouldn't that be better?

"Then, I guess you leave us no other choice," Etienne says in defeat, and turns his back to Aksel as the others close in. Is he stupid? He just left himself vulnerable! I call up my essence again, and intensify it, just in case. The guys are circling Aksel, who now has on a mask of pure madness. Etienne is just outside the circle, projecting his gift, trying to mess with Aksel's mind. I don't know what he is trying to do, but it isn't working.

"Keep trying, my Lord; I have no fear left," Aksel calls out. "Oh, but I do have plenty of lust left- especially for females that are well-endowed," he says, as he glowers up at me. Shit, this is really starting to piss me off. Tristan lunges at Aksel and goes for the ribs, but Aksel is too fast. Aksel grabs a knife off of the table and slices Tristan horizontally across his shoulder. His aroma floods the arena, and the scent has my fangs elongating. I guess it still smells good, even though it probably tastes bad.

Etienne has now taken up Tristan's stance with a sword.

"Ah, good to see you have finally joined the party," Aksel mocks, before lunging at Etienne in one fast swoop, but this time, Aksel isn't fast enough. Etienne is able to dodge the strike and respond with a swipe of his sword into Aksel's right kidney.

"Fuck! You are going to pay for that!" Aksel screams, as he lunges again and catches Etienne by the throat with his bare hands and lifts him off the ground. My anger erupts instantaneously and fills the room down to the last crevice.

"Put him down," I warn Aksel as my essence swells around me, responding to my normally-caged emotions.

"Or what, sweetheart? What do you think you can really do about it?"

The ground around us starts to subtly shake under our feet in response to his question. My words have become lost at this point; I am sucked in too deep. Even while immersed, I am trying to keep it somewhat under control. If I give myself completely over to the emotion too fast, I might hurt everyone.

"Ahhh, gifted, are we? But, you are so young still that this is nothing but a parlor trick!" He laughs and squeezes Etienne's throat tighter. The guys move in, but Aksel tsk-tsk-tsks them and holds the point of his knife over Etienne's heart. I need to knock this guy away from Etienne; what can I do to get him to release his hold? He is a ginormous beast! Nuts! Wait... I take my mist and power it into Aksel's male parts full-force. The contact drops him to his knees and forces him to loosen his grip enough for Etienne to break free.

"You will do nicely as a new plaything!" Aksel motions to stand, but before he can, I launch my essence, once again, and flatten him against the cement wall. Now that he is away from everyone, I let my anger flow freely and feed into my strength, pinning him under its crushing weight.

An evil, demonic laugh bellows up from Aksel's core. "End me now, for this is your last chance!" He continues on laughing. I can't stand the sound of it; it is like nails on a chalkboard. If only it would just stop- make it stop! My essence responds and closes in around Aksel's throat, cutting off the sound, and replacing it with a wet, gagging sound.

"Gabriel, do the honors, please," Etienne calls out from somewhere. I cannot see anything but red mist at this point. I hear a knife being drawn and the fall of Gabriel's heavy footsteps. I feel Aksel struggle more under my hold as Gabriel's footsteps approach. The footsteps stop and the sound of Gabriel's knife being quickly sheathed in flesh sounds out around us. The struggling stops. Aksel is now lifeless. Fear that he isn't really dead, that he could attack again and possibly make it out of the pit, has me unable to release his body.

"Sasha, my love, all is well. You can release him," Etienne calls up to me. No, I can't release him; what if his heart still beats? I don't want to be attacked by him. Did Etienne hear the threats that he was making? I hear the muffled sounds of the others, but nothing makes sense. I feel Etienne's hand out of nowhere, tenderly running down my bare outstretched arm. "Shhhh, all is well; calm yourself." His touch and his voice do the trick, and in one deep breath, I call my essence back into my open outstretched palms. I hear a loud thump as Aksel's body falls back down to the ground in a sickening heap. I am still breathing fast, but my vision is slowly clearing. As the fog lifts, I see a pair of piercing blue eyes looking straight into my soul.

"Etienne!" I squeal and jump into his arms, happy that he is alive and well.

"Oui, mon amour, I am well." He holds me close and takes a deep breath of his own; the weight of the evening falling off of his shoulders. He is one hell of a poker player. It isn't until now that I can feel his unease and fear. After a long embrace, the sounds of the other men begin to register. Etienne puts me down and turns to the noise down in the pit.

"Jesus Christ! What is the King going to say?! We have to send the body back overseas and her magic is all over it!" Erik says, in disarray.

"I will deal with it, Erik," Etienne says, as he jumps back into the pit.

"How?" Erik challenges.

"He is right, Etienne. Mother will detect Sasha's magic imprint, which she will report," Emile joins in.

Gabriel and Tristan have fallen back against the south-side of the pit, trying to stay out of the way. Tristan keeps glancing up at me in disbelief. I feel like jumping at him and saying "BOO," but I hold back. The thought of what his reaction might be has me chuckling to myself.

"Mother wouldn't even know about Sasha if it wasn't for your big mouth!" Etienne shoots back.

Emile holds up his hands in innocence. "I did nothing of the sort. Kataya overheard me and told our dearest sister, which promptly earned me a phone call soon thereafter."

Etienne stares at him in disbelief. "So, it was gossip that inspired this tell-all? To whom were you gossiping?"

Emile shakes his head like he doesn't want to say but gives in because it is useless. Gabriel and Erik shake their heads "no," however, Emile doesn't listen.

"The guys were over for dinner one night, and it came up…"

Etienne skewers Gabriel and Erik; Tristan avoids the attention. "Well, maybe if you pansies weren't so busy taking tea together, you would have detected when this one snuck into the area before obliterating a whorehouse!" No one has anything to say. I think it is time I go; this really is none of my business.

Backing toward the door, trying to be sneaky, I hear Etienne yell angrily up at me, "Stop right there!"

"Alright!" I yell back, pissed that I was caught.

"Prepare the body to be sent back home; they cannot tell whose magic is imprinted. They can tell that it was the knife's blade that inflicted death. We did our job- he had an immense barrier ability that no one could get through, except for Sasha. No one is to blame; we were just doing what is expected of us. If anyone asks, it was Gabriel's blade that brought him to his demise, nothing more!" Etienne lectures the men. They all nod in agreement. "Erik, just to be safe, research 'reclaim of imprint'."

"Yes, sir." Erik takes off to the back office.

"Tristan, you will forget what you saw Sasha do, understand?" Etienne presses. Tristan is starting to squirm under the pressure, like he can't quite comply.

"Yes, sir; I just don't understand why... and how she..."

Etienne cuts him off and is suddenly in his face, towering over him. "There are things in this world that go beyond how and why. If you are so interested in studying gifted, take that up with Erik on your own time. As for the why..." he quickly glances at me and mumbles something to himself... Did he just say "forgive me?" "If it gets back to headquarters somehow, it will be sent to the King. If that happens, Sasha could be taken away and used for military purposes." Tristan turned ghost-white, Etienne's words are sinking in deep. What the hell, I can't just be taken and used like that... could I?

"I understand, sir; I am sorry for questioning your reasoning," Tristan fumbles. He is being sincere. He is also still bleeding. I jump down into the pit to assess the damage. Etienne is almost healed, but Tristan is not.

"Tristan, you're hurt pretty bad," I say absently, as I reach forward and brush back the tattered shirt to reveal his wound. Once I am able to peel my eyes away from the blood trickling down his arm, I can see that his shoulder's flesh has been parted enough to see bone.

"He will be fine; he just needs to get to the healer," Etienne growls, sensing where I could be going with this. Tristan is looking pretty pale, but the blood flow has slowed down. God, he smells good; biting into him would be like drinking a tall glass of freezing cold, ice-water on a blistering-hot summer's day. I feel my fangs fully lengthen.

"Sasha?" Etienne calls, but I can't hear him. All I can focus on is the trickle of blood rolling down Tristan's arm. Erik smelled good too, at first, but he tasted horrible; I don't think I will ever be able to drink lemonade again. If I try Tristan's blood, it might ruin my stomach for water... period. "Sasha!" Etienne demands.

"What?!" I yell back, tired of his attitude. Tristan and Gabriel gasp at my tone; they would never dream of talking to him like that.

"Tristan is stable, and Gabriel will get him to the healer. Let us go," he says in a softer tone. Tearing

435

myself away, I follow his request and jump up out of the pit and head out the front door. I need to get as far away from Tristan as I can. I must be hungry if I am thinking about risking my stomach for Tristan's blood, especially with Etienne right there.

Chapter 22

"Hungry already, are we?" Etienne calls from behind. I stop at the curb and wait for him.

"I don't know what you are talking about." I know that I can't lie to him, but that doesn't stop me from trying occasionally.

"Uh-huh." He puts his arm around me and lays his cheek on top of my head.

"First thing, first, shall we take care of that ferocious appetite?" At least he is being nice about it; he must be figuring out that I don't respond well to his dictatorship-type tones.

"After you." I motion for him to lead. He, instead, grabs my hand and takes off running at lightning speed to his Infiniti parked around the corner. It's more like he's pulling me in tow; show off. He opens the back passenger-side door for me. The last time that we attempted this in his back seat, it almost didn't end well. I doubt that will be an issue tonight- a mangled corpse killing the mood and all. I hop up and scoot way down the bench so he can join me.

"Sasha, do you need to talk about what happened first?"

No, I don't. I need to feed, then eat, then maybe. I shake my head "no." He pulls me over into his lap and unbuttons his shirt. I can see his jugular vein, vibrating with each beat of his heart, ready and waiting for me. I am not feeling frisky or animalistic. The strangulation marks on his neck squelch that. I move gently so that I am straddling his lap instead. Brushing his neck, I gently kiss the marks before pausing my lips over the pulsating vein. Slowly slipping my fangs into his skin, I make myself keep calm. The relief of being here in this moment is almost too much. Our night could have ended so much differently had that beast succeeded in his threats.

There is no sexual tension, just need and concern for one another. He wraps his arms around me and lets me take my fill without rushing me. As the sated feeling takes over, I close his neck and move my long braid off to the side. Tilting my head, I give him permission to take his turn. He returns the feather-light kisses along my neck before biting down and pulling me in tighter as he feeds. This is a new level of intimacy for us. A level beyond sex, one I thought that we were both too bull-headed to get to. Deep rooted love and compassion for one another are all that lingers. An even deeper need to care for one another on every level necessary dominates. He has never told me that he loves me, but that doesn't seem to matter anymore.

"Sasha, thank you," he whispers, as he closes my neck and sits back into the seat.

"You're welcome?" I reply, confused on his gratitude as we are way past saying "thank you" for feeding each other.

"For assisting tonight. For 'saving my ass,' as you would say."

I can't help but laugh; his French accent makes it even better. "Etienne, I would do just about anything for you. I also wasn't fond of what he was insinuating, either," I say, with a disgusted smirk, the demon's words echoing in my head.

"I had hoped that you would never have to see my… work."

"Work? That was work?" He looks put-off by my question.

"What do you mean? Of course it was," he says with skepticism, as if he shouldn't tell me more.

"Torturing vampires is what you do for work?" He shifts me uncomfortably off his lap.

"Hungry? We should get something to eat."

"Changing the subject?"

"No, I am willing to answer all of your questions, but I need you to be rational, which means that you should eat first."

"I suggest you watch it. If I was completely irrational, I would have run screaming into the night our first night together."

"True, but where to?" He isn't going to budge.

Fine, since we are actually going out in public, we better go somewhere I want to go. "Stella's down by DU; it's my favorite late-night spot."

"Isn't that a coffee-house?" He questions. He seems disappointed in my choice as he gets out of the vehicle and heads to the driver's seat.

"Yeah, but they have food too," I call back and climb up to the passenger seat, foregoing the opening and closing door issue.

"You're the boss," he says, as he takes the driver's seat.

This makes me smile, again… his frequent attempts at Americanized inflections are hilarious.

"It is good to see you smile."

"It's good to have a reason too; apparently, I haven't been the friendliest these days."

"Says who?" No need to give him any more reason to try and encourage me to run away with him.

"Oh…everyone. Especially by the end of the week."

"Is that why you came to find me?"

"Yeah, I thought that I needed a bump."

He raises an eyebrow at me. "Bump? I don't understand that one."

"It's drug-slang, like addicts need a 'bump' or 'hit' of cocaine."

He smirks. "Are you referring to me as your drug?" Ha! Wait… that would fit the picture, wouldn't it.

441

"Apparently so… is it normal to need blood this often?"

"Yes, especially considering your gifts, I am not surprised," he sighs.

"I was trying to make it on just the once-a-week schedule."

"I know."

"So, you suspected that I may need more and didn't say anything?"

"Would you have listened?"

Probably not. "Fair enough. Are you going to get back to my original question about your work?"

"Eventually. Why were you trying to fight your needs?" He answers my question with a loaded question.

"Because, the more I am with you, the more tempted I am to leave my husband. I am trying to make it work. You do not help the situation at all."

He looks at me sideways. "What have I done? Seeing you an hour a week hardly constitutes as monopolizing your time."

"Smart-ass."

"What? I truly don't understand. If you want to be with your husband, then just be with your husband. I have not intended to make that a difficult decision for you."

"Are you kidding me? Our level of chemistry? You don't understand how hard it is for me to distance myself from you. You don't see how I might be a cold-hearted bitch, longing for you but trying to make my marriage work?" I feel my blood pressure skyrocket. Breathe one, two, three, four, five....

"It is what it is, Sasha; we are not a couple, and you are not betrothed to me. I do not own you; you are free to make your decisions as you please- just as I am free to do the same."

What is he saying? "I don't understand how you don't understand."

"I understand longing for something that you cannot have. I cannot have you because that is your choice, not mine. You could have me at any time, it is impossible for me to deny you. You are the one who has to live with your decisions. Your choices affect someone negatively no matter how you decide. Can you see how I might be affected negatively?"

He has a point. I have never thought about his feelings before, mainly because I was certain that he didn't have many. "I do. It was selfish of me not to have thought about that beforehand."

"So, seeing you more frequently is just as much a knife in my side as it is yours."

Ouch. But, I get it. It seems that staying with my husband just causes everyone more pain.

We pull up to Stella's and head up the wooden steps into the cute old home that has been converted into an Indie coffee-house. The line is long, even at 9:00 PM.

"What is good here?" Etienne asks, while pondering over the selection.

"I like the burritos or sandwiches… and desserts of course." I wink at him, which, in turn, gets me rewarded with a grin.

"This is all cold food; how about I take you to a nice restaurant?" Not a chance.

"Do you realize that I am still in workout clothes and you have dried blood down your arm under that jacket?" I whisper in a tone so low that only vampire ears could hear. "I also happen to love this place and am perfectly happy with a heated-up burrito and some amazing coffee or tea."

"Alright, burritos it is." I am glad that he is being so agreeable.

"What can I get you?" The barista chimes. Etienne goes to order for me, but I cut him off immediately.

"I'll have the bean, cheese, and green chili burrito... the vegetarian one, along with a mocha- nonfat milk, and some of that caramel syrup in it too, please. Oh, and a brownie." She looks at me with a cheesy smile before training her eyes on Etienne and blushing as she asks him what he will have.

"I will have the same," he says with pleasant manners, ignoring her stare. He's probably so used to it that it doesn't even faze him. We stand off to the side and wait for our order.

"It doesn't even affect you, does it?"

"Come again?"

"The women, falling all over you." He shrugs his shoulders in indifference.

"There was a time when I paid attention, but that was a long time ago. There is much more to life than lust, which is all it ever ends up being." Jesus, if they only knew how good he is with his hands, they would damn well fall in love on the spot.

Picking up our order, we head around the corner to find a cozy spot. I love all the twists and turns, bookcases, and people working on computers or just playing chess. We find a two-top table in the back corner on the other side of the library wall.

"This is an eclectic choice of food, Sasha, and I thought you preferred tea?"

"You didn't have to order the same thing, and I happen to be a little too exhausted for tea." Glad to see that he is back to giving me a little sass, that is much better.

"Why the vegetarian burrito?"

"I avoid pig on most levels, and green chili is usually made with a form of pig."

"Interesting…"

"Here, try some hot sauce on that burrito!" I excitedly push the bottle toward him. He takes it suspiciously and puts some on his food.

"Hmmm, pretty good."

Hot sauce makes all reheated burritos better. "Of course, they are not as good as mine, but they will do. And the coffee is wonderful here."

"You cook?" I realize from this question how little we really know about each other. We have been so intimate on many levels, but our basic knowledge of each other's likes and dislikes, as well as our daily idiosyncrasies, falls short.

"Do I cook? No, I create... experiences that dance across the tongue and ignite the taste buds," I say with pizazz, talking myself up. I am tempted to add some jazz hands with it too, but hold back.

"Sounds intense. I had no idea that you are so passionate about food. I did notice your healthy appetite, though," he says with another sexy grin. I kick him under the table.

"That is why I have always exercised a lot, never wanting my taste buds to get my hips into trouble."

He lowers his eyelids and looks at me with a smoldering look that melts the whip cream right off of my mocha. "I can attest that your hips are quite perfect."

That is the first event of the evening to kindle the heat in my belly. "You are blushing."

"It is not every day that I get compliments like that." He mutters something to himself with a huff. "What was that about?"

"Nothing, shall we get back to the conversation about me being your drug of choice?"

"No, we will go back to when you were going to elaborate on your line of work. I believe that you were trying to justify torture?" I lower my voice again on the last part, sparing the human ears around us.

"Let us refer to it as an effective instrument in overcoming the difficult learning curves of a vampire. A behavioral modification, shall we say."

"It didn't seem very effective this evening."

He narrows his eyes in defense. "That was an exception; much like you, he had impossibly-perfect barrier methods, along with brute strength. We have been trying for years to capture and retrain him, but he has eluded us." I am surprised that he didn't put one hand on his hip and the other up in my face with a "No you didn't" while he delivered that one.

"Why did he need to be sent back to 'headquarters'?" I say, trying to stifle a chuckle.

"Let's just say that he was the brother of someone important. He decided to change his lifestyle and disappear, and might I add, taking many, many innocent lives with him along the way."

Does that justify torture and killing? I don't know. He was pure evil; I could sense that the minute I walked into that warehouse. Etienne seems to have an evil little flicker here and there too.

"You seemed very into the torture part when I first got there." I need to confront him on what I fear the most- that he may be evil at heart, even though I know that title doesn't feel like the right fit for him.

"There was a time when I liked that particular detail. I went through a very dark period a long time ago and have done things that I am not proud of. Now, it is just something that I am good at, given my abilities to sense and intensify emotions."

For some ungodly reason, in the midst of this heavy conversation, thoughts of being chained up like Erik's visitor flash through my mind, making my cheeks go hot.

Of course, I would take a discussion on this level and find a way to relate it back to sex somehow.

"Are you going to share what made your cheeks light up in such a lovely pink, once again?"

How about...no. "No, not appropriate. We are having a serious conversation." His eyes darken and fixate on me, causing that heat in my belly to spread.

"Stop it!"

He looks up and around innocently. "What? I did nothing."

Ugh. "What would you have done if I hadn't been there?" I need to get back to the important debriefing.

"Why do you ask?"

"Because, believe it or not, I worry about your safety!" I say angrily... that came out of nowhere. It could be because I don't like the fact that he doesn't think anyone worries about his well-being. He looks at me like I am crazy for raising my voice in public.

"You should not worry about such things; I am able to handle my business."

I am not convinced. "You sure about that? I heard the hinge start to give, which triggered me to pin his arm back before any of you had noticed."

He is starting to look pissed that I would question his ability to perform in his line of work. "True, and that is because your hearing is at a higher level than ours. If you had not been there, things might have gotten a bit more out of hand before we regained our hold. If that had been the case, I would have ordered Emile to kill him instead of trying to spare his life."

Emile wasn't even in the pit; how well would that have worked?

"Why didn't you have Emile do that sooner? How do you know that Emile could have killed him in time?"

"You are a nosy little thing, aren't you?"

"Yes, I am. And, I deserve answers."

He sighs and relents. "Emile never misses when he intends to kill."

"Emile? Laid-back Emile? Never?"

Etienne squints his eyes with complete seriousness and replies, "Wouldn't you be pretty laid-back if you knew that you had that kind of... gift?

Wouldn't you also want a gift like that instilled in someone who is level-headed and good-hearted? It would be bad in the wrong hands."

"Never?"

"Never."

"Wow, never. Hey, why no guns?" He grunts at my inquisitiveness.

"You will learn more in time. For now, just know that most bullets cannot penetrate our muscle fibers; it has to be a special bullet or blade with a serrated edge." No wonder there is a whole militia of vampires out there trying to keep things under control, super-powers is right!

"What you said about news getting back to 'headquarters' about me; what are the chances of all that business really happening?"

"Slim. Can we discuss something else?"

Tired of my Q&A already? "I guess… what do you want to talk about?" As soon as I ask that, I do a mental forehead slap.

"I want you to tell me what made you blush the second time."

"Even after the lecture in the car on how I am not 'betrothed' to you and I am free to do as I please, knife in your side, yada-yada-yada?"

"Was that a question?"

Is he serious? If I were to sum up in one question what I really want to know... what would I ask? Does he love me? "Honestly, I would rather you tell me the real reason why you want me to leave my husband for you." He almost spits the swallow of mocha he is taking back into his cup. He coughs and sits up straight, wiping his mouth.

"I will make you a deal; you tell me why you blushed, and I will give you an honest answer."

"An honest answer that does not involve the obvious 'human not compatible with vampire' chords?"

"Yes, I will tell you how I really feel and not project opinions to mask the truth."

Well, well, that just might be worth it. But, do I really want to know the answer? Yes, I do.

"I, uh... when I went to your house on Sunday, when I was feeling sick..."

"Oh, this must be good if you are fumbling your words."

"Do you want me to tell you or not?"

"Yes, please, do continue." Boy, he is having fun watching me squirm.

"I might have spied Erik and his... 'friend' having some fun. I went looking for someone as no one was answering the front door, and Erik's light was on. She was... restrained and enjoying it. Talking, just now, about shackles had me picturing... you and me. Of course, I am a dirty pervert who can easily switch from gore to sex."

Etienne sits stunned, just looking at me with those damn eyes that see right through me. I pick up my mocha and become very interested in it; his silence is torture. I hope that he doesn't think that I am a pervert.

"Are you saying that you fantasize about me restraining you and having my way?" I blush again. In truth, yes, and it isn't the first time either. I know that he would never hurt me. I also know that he has no real power over me, giving him control in that area could be liberating and so much fun- solace in the surrender. I have never fully let go of my control for anyone. He is the only one that I would trust with that. That would be a new level of intimacy for us. "Yes," I whisper.

He sucks in his breath hard and takes a minute to compose himself.

"Alright, I told you; now, it is your turn."

"After what you just verbalized, you must excuse me for a moment as I regroup."

"Did I offend you?" I hardly doubt that I did.

"Absolutely not. I, too, have shared such desires." It is my turn to take a deep breath. Holy shit. Now, I am the one who needs a minute.

"Sasha, I want you to leave your husband and come with me because I have spent my 110 years as a shell of a man compared to who I am when I am with you. I never knew it was possible to have someone lovingly hold up a mirror and show you all that you could be instead of what you are not. I want you in any way that you will allow. I want you in every possible way for myself." Damn it, why couldn't he reply with one of his asshole remarks that usually piss me off? I am speechless, which is rare lately. "Sasha, say something." So what he is saying is that he loves me? Why is this happening? I would rather be the thorn in his side that is irritating him.

"You love me?" I breathe.

"Yes, I love you beyond measure. I experienced the same transcendence you did that first night of training. I just didn't understand it. When I finally did, I didn't want to accept it."

"And now?"

"I can't escape it." Damn it.

"Tell me why you stay with him?" He looks at me openly, his eyes full of compassion.

"He is an innocent bystander in this collision. He deserves everything he desires and more. I promised long ago to fulfill the role of the wife he deserves. He is a good man."

"People grow, and their needs change. Are you able to fully give him what he desires or deserves when you are splitting yourself in two?"

Probably not. "There is also this tie I have to the time we all spend together as a family. Seeing the happiness in my children's eyes while we are all spending time together is priceless; I never want to hurt them by ripping our family apart."

"How do you know you are 'ripping' your family apart? Sure, it would be a traumatic change, but it doesn't necessarily have to be a painful process."

Obviously, he doesn't know first-hand how bad divorce can be on kids.

"Hypothetically speaking, if I leave him, allowing him to find happiness with someone else, he would never let me see my children again. He already treads lightly around me, and I am always having to prove that I am not a danger. I cannot live without my kids; they are my heart and soul. Might I ask, what if I did leave and it was a peaceful separation? One with my kids still in the picture; are you willing to play step-daddy?" He gives me another one of those surprised shitless looks. "Well?"

He is choking on his words. "I hadn't thought of that; I don't really care much for children."

"Then, let that be your second reason for my actions affect them as well, not just you and Stephan." Just then, a text from Stephan beeps across my phone.

"Where are you?" I completely forgot to give him a heads up.

"I met some friends last-minute for coffee; I am so sorry that I didn't call first. I will be home in a little while." I text back and look up to find Etienne staring at me, questioning my rude interruption.

"I was due home long ago and didn't tell him I was going out." He doesn't push it further.

"What if I told you that I am willing to try with your children? Would you leave him?" He is being honest; he is not telling me what he thinks that I might want to hear. If he is willing to accept and love all of me, which includes my children, then that would be worth considering. "I would tell you that I will think about it."

"So, you will consider the possibility?"

"Yes." I will consider the possibility, but I am not making my mind up right now. I feel like a horrible person to even consider tearing my family apart, and an even worse person for possibly robbing Stephan of precious time that he could be spending with someone who can give him more- who he can grow old with.

"Etienne?"

"Oui?"

"I don't know how long I will need, but you will have to give me time to make this decision."

"As I said, I will take you however I can have you. If it must remain a few hours a week for now, or however long, I will wait." I smile. The rushed, lustful energy is absent. It is simply the two of us having the most honest conversation we have ever had.

I really am going to sit down and finally grapple with the decisions I need to make. No more putting things away in the denial closet. Choosing not to be with Etienne is starting to become painful. It is like having someone rip you away from the one thing that sustains you- heart, mind, body, and soul, while being expected to act like it doesn't make a difference. Well, it does make a difference, and I have a feeling that is the real reason my feeding needs have increased, as well as my bad mood swings. We are destined to be together, whether we want it or not. The more we, or should I say, I, fight it, the more determined our essences become to draw us together. Every day that I choose to stay with my family is like trying to force together two magnets repelling each other. It just doesn't quite work. Etienne, Stephan, and my boys all deserve more than I am giving them.

~The end, for now. Stay tuned for part two. You can follow the series progress at: www.lunareclipseseries.com or follow us on facebook @ https://www.facebook.com/midnightbloompart1